DANGEROUS DAYS FOR THE HOME FRONT NURSES

RACHEL BRIMBLE

Boldwood

First published in Great Britain in 2025 by Boldwood Books Ltd.

Copyright © Rachel Brimble, 2025

Cover Design by Colin Thomas

Cover Images: Colin Thomas

The moral right of Rachel Brimble to be identified as the author of this work has been asserted in accordance with the Copyright, Designs and Patents Act 1988.

All rights reserved. No part of this book may be reproduced in any form or by any electronic or mechanical means, including information storage and retrieval systems, without written permission from the author, except for the use of brief quotations in a book review. This book is a work of fiction and, except in the case of historical fact, any resemblance to actual persons, living or dead, is purely coincidental.

Every effort has been made to obtain the necessary permissions with reference to copyright material, both illustrative and quoted. We apologise for any omissions in this respect and will be pleased to make the appropriate acknowledgements in any future edition.

A CIP catalogue record for this book is available from the British Library.

Paperback ISBN 978-1-83561-783-0

Large Print ISBN 978-1-83561-784-7

Hardback ISBN 978-1-83561-782-3

Ebook ISBN 978-1-83561-785-4

Kindle ISBN 978-1-83561-786-1

Audio CD ISBN 978-1-83561-777-9

MP3 CD ISBN 978-1-83561-778-6

Digital audio download ISBN 978-1-83561-780-9

This book is printed on certified sustainable paper. Boldwood Books is dedicated to putting sustainability at the heart of our business. For more information please visit https://www.boldwoodbooks.com/about-us/sustainability/

Boldwood Books Ltd, 23 Bowerdean Street, London, SW6 3TN

www.boldwoodbooks.com

For my girls, Jessica & Hannah – love you, always xx

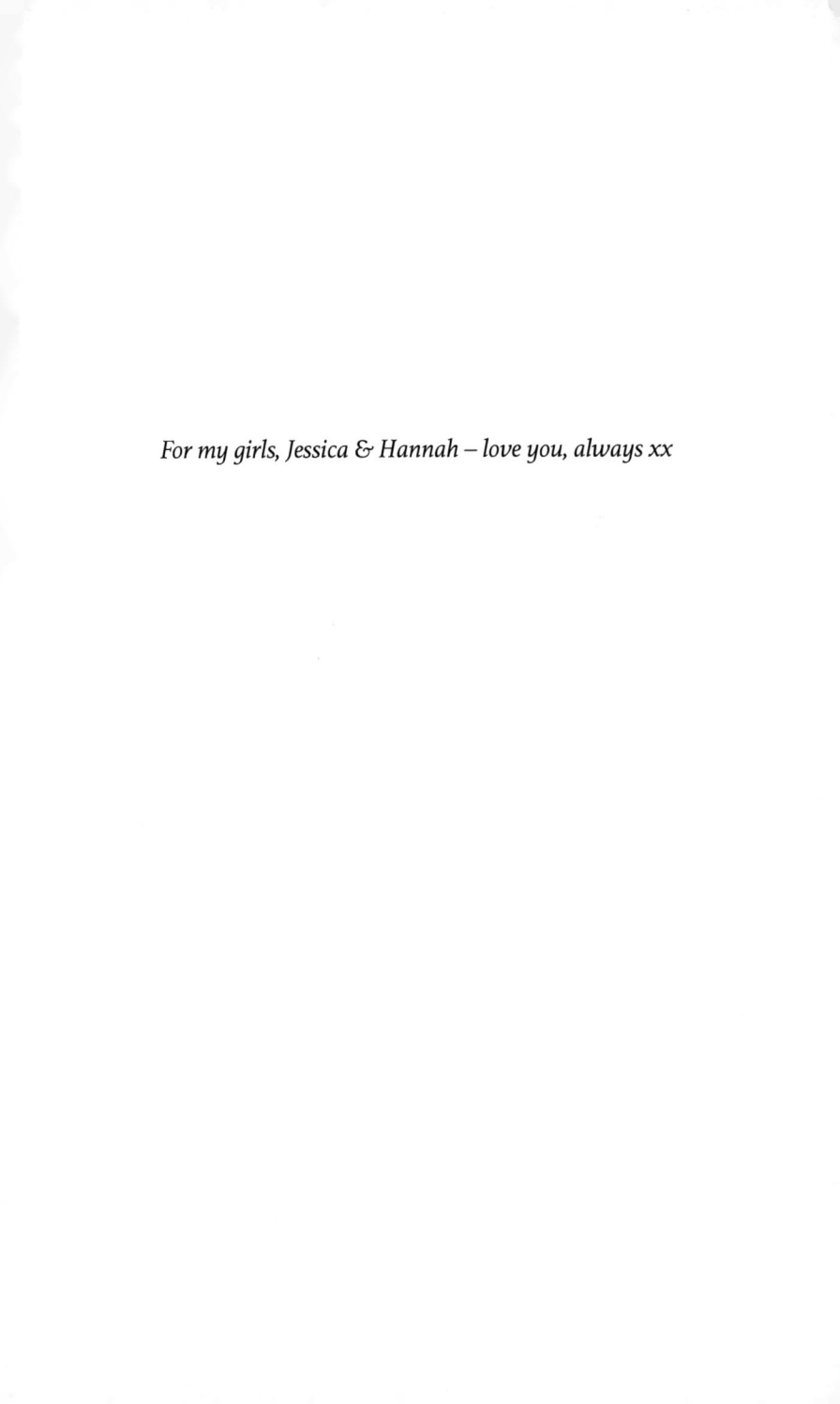

1

FREDA

Bath, April 1942

Freda Parkes squeezed her eyes shut and tried to hear past the ringing in her ears, the screaming and crashing, the rapid thump-thump-thump of her heart. The fact she could hear these things at least confirmed she wasn't dead.

She prised her eyes open, terrified to see the damage the bomb blast had wreaked.

Chaos reigned the length and breadth of the hospital ward, patients buried beneath medical equipment and shattered glass, or else crouched on the floor and underneath beds, their arms over their heads as they took cover. She winced and moved her hand to her painful hip that would almost certainly be bruised, but as far as her nursing training had taught her, she seemed to have escaped any broken bones, which was something to be grateful for considering all the injuries around her. Where were Sylvia and Veronica, her fellow nurses and dearest friends? Were they all right? Alive? Sickness coated her throat as Freda struggled to her feet and tried to steady her shaking legs, get herself under control and focused. Her patients would need her to be strong, brave and ready to help them. And what of her mum and dad? Her sister, Dorothy? Was the entire city under attack?

She wobbled on her feet and gripped the edge of the toppled cabinet beside her. The room swam in front of her eyes for a moment, the screams and cries all around floating in and out of her consciousness. Wiping her forehead with the back of her shaking hand, Freda battled to work out who to go to first. Since the start of the war, just over two and half years before, Bath's Upper Borough Hospital where she worked had grown into the main transfer hub for injured patients coming from Bristol. All this time Bath had remained unbombed, Hitler bypassing the historical city – until now...

Now it seemed they were under fire the same as so many other cities throughout Europe.

The distant boom of bombs and the scream of sirens continued outside as Freda stumbled to the closest bed where Mrs Cowley, who had been suffering with her fractured nerves before the blast, was visibly trembling where she sat on the floor, blood seeping down her temple. Freda swallowed as a horrible culpability enveloped her. Time and again, she'd almost wished for this bombing... yearned to be part of the *real* war, rather than continuing to play a smaller part on the home front.

And so your wish has been granted. Happy now, young lady?

Shame writhed inside her as she forced her mother's disparaging voice from her conscience.

'It's all right, Mrs Cowley,' she said, gritting her teeth as she struggled to crouch beside the frightened woman. She gently took Mrs Cowley's chin between her thumb and forefinger and turned her head side to side. 'You've got a small cut on the side of your head, but nothing that can't be cleaned up. Do you think you can stand for me?' Freda looked over her shoulder and saw Sylvia, her face streaked with dust and dirt, tendrils of her bright auburn hair fallen in disarray from beneath her cap. Recently promoted to senior ward nurse, Sylvia pointed left and right, issuing orders. Drawing strength from her friend's steadfast conduct, Freda faced Mrs Cowley with renewed fortitude. 'The Germans won't keep us down. It looks as though—'

'Nurse! Nurse! Please, can someone help me?'

'I'll be right back,' Freda said as she patted Mrs Cowley's leg and pushed up from the dust-covered tiles.

Boom!

Freda's heart leapt into her throat as another explosion reverberated through the ward, the floor juddering beneath her feet, bloodcurdling screams puncturing the air. Ducking her head, she rushed towards Mr Jackson's pleas for help. He lay in an awkward position, half-on and half-off his bed, his previously broken arm and leg thankfully still on it, although goodness only knew the pain he would be in once the shock of the blast wore off.

'It's all right, Mr Jackson,' she shouted as she came closer, barely missing another patient being sick on the floor beside her. 'Let's get you back onto the bed and be thankful nothing landed on top of you, eh?'

Ignoring the pain that shot through her leg and hip, Freda shoved her hands firmly beneath his armpits, took a deep breath and hefted him fully back onto the bed. The once white sheets were now coated in pieces of plaster that had fallen from the ceiling, and an empty tumbler and jug had toppled from the upended side table onto the floor. Blood seeped from his bottom lip and a nasty gash showed above the collar of his pyjamas, but

Mr Jackson looked well enough under the circumstances. She glanced around the ward. The screen of smoke that had made it difficult to see anything after the first blast had begun to clear even though bombs continued to explode far too close for comfort. Her mind once again drifted to her parents and sister – to Richard, a man she refused to fall in love with – and Freda lifted her chin against the dread that clutched her heart. No, she would not think of her loved ones. Not yet. Her priority right now had to be her patients.

She squeezed Mr Jackson's hand. 'I'm going to leave you for just a few minutes and see who else needs help. I can see Nurse Roberts and Sister Dyer issuing instructions. We'll soon have you somewhere safe, I'm sure.'

'Do what you have to do, my lovely.' Mr Jackson scowled, blood from his lip sliding to his chin, his eyes bright with fury. 'Those German animals can keep dropping whatever they bloody well want. They'll never scare me and don't you dare let them scare you. Do you hear me?'

'I do,' she said. The poor man had come to them from Bristol two weeks before and was now well on his way to recovery, but the bitter anger in his eyes spoke of so much more than physical injury. 'Bath will get through this war, same as the rest of the country.'

His livid gaze lingered on hers before he gave a curt nod. 'Too right. Now go. There are people who need seeing to.'

Freda flashed him a smile before turning away to see who else she could comfort, even if she couldn't do anything practical until she'd managed to determine what equipment and supplies were available. She looked across the ward and locked eyes with Veronica, having no doubt the panic and shock in her friend's eyes was reflected in her own. They stared at each other a moment longer before each of them rushed to attend to whichever patient was closest to them.

Approaching Mrs King, Freda flinched as another explosion came from what sounded like the north side of the hospital. 'How are you doing there, Mrs King? Still in one piece?'

The other woman, mother to four children under seven who had all been evacuated to a small Wiltshire village, nodded, her grey eyes wide with fear. 'I think something's wrong with my leg, but I don't want to look.'

Freda slid her gaze to Mrs King's leg and visually assessed the injury that made her stomach turn over. Fighting to keep her face impassive, she met Mrs King's worried eyes. 'You've got a large piece of glass lodged just above your knee, but it's nothing to worry about.' Freda straightened and opened the metal cupboard beside her that had somehow managed to stay upright. She pulled out a cloth, saline, gauze and a rolled bandage. 'I'm going to put a dressing as tightly as I can around the glass. It's important we stem the blood flow. Then I'll see about giving you a precautionary tetanus shot and something for the pain before we see what we can do about moving you to surgery.'

'Surgery?' The other woman's eyes widened. 'But—'

'Now, no fretting,' Freda said firmly as she quickly and expertly cleaned and bound the wound around the glass. 'I daren't remove the glass without a surgeon's say-so. I'm sure one of them will see to it quick smart and you'll be stitched up in no time.' She smiled and tipped Mrs King a wink. 'Let's hope it's one of the dishy surgeons, eh?'

A whisper of a smile lifted Mrs King's lips before she dropped her head back against the wall behind her and shut her eyes. Uncertainty and the question of how long this raid would last swirled in Freda's mind as she looked around. The ward was in such disarray, such confusion and turmoil, it was impossible to differentiate where she was needed most.

Boom!

She flinched. Why in heaven's name did she think herself capable of leaving nursing to become a journalist, one day reporting from the field for the *Chronicle* or even a national paper, when she wasn't even sure where to start when she was in familiar surroundings and armed with her nursing skills? A horrible sense of inadequacy twisted inside her before she spotted Veronica struggling to manoeuvre a patient into a wheelchair.

'I'll be right back, Mrs King,' she said, before heading over to help her friend, noticing how many patients were cradling their arms and wrists, or hobbling on injured legs and feet. No doubt there were going to be innumerable breaks and sprains to deal with.

'V? Are you all right?' she asked, flitting her gaze over her friend, checking for injury. 'Your head is bleeding.'

Veronica touched her fingers to the blood trickling over her forehead, glanced at her fingers. 'It's fine. Something gave me a whack in the first explosion, but I've no idea what. Here, can you help me get Mr Green into this chair? He's passed out, but the pain will be excruciating when he comes around. It's better if we can move him before he wakes.'

They worked in tandem, neither needing to ask the other which way to move or lift. She had worked with Sylvia and Veronica on the same ward since they left nursing training nearly eight months before. The war had meant their experience had been accelerated by having to cope with the influx of injured men and women from Bristol. The burns and missing limbs, the loss of sight and hearing, and patients hankering for missing or lost loved ones had meant scenarios that would have once been rare for a newly qualified nurse to deal with had become the norm.

Freda drew in a strengthening breath. Now it seemed Bath was in Hitler's crosshairs. Well, helping Bristol's injured had set her and the other nurses in good stead and they would not waver under this attack or any other that might or might not follow.

Bracing herself, she met Veronica's gaze and they lifted Mr Green into the chair.

Veronica blew out a breath and gripped the chair's handles. 'I'll get him off the ward. We need to give the patients the impression we're doing something. I haven't seen Sylvia or Sister, have you?'

Freda scanned the ward, catching sight of Kathy Scott, another nurse who had started work at the same time as them and who – more often than not – tested Sylvia's patience to the limit, but she and Veronica tolerated Kathy easily enough.

'Sylvia's around somewhere.' Freda squinted through the debris as a shower of plaster came loose from the ceiling a few feet away from her. 'Sister Dyer's over there. Goodness, she looks more than a little shaken. Something I thought I'd never see.'

'Me neither, but it seems even Sister can't keep up her sternness under fire. Not that I blame her. I wouldn't want to be responsible for the nurses as well as the patients under these circumstances, would you?' Veronica turned away. 'I'll see you in a bit.'

As Veronica headed for the ward's double doors, Freda hobbled back towards Mrs King, sending up a silent prayer of gratitude. It could be her imagination, but the distant bombing appeared to be becoming more sporadic. Was it too soon to hope the attack was coming to an end?

As she reached Mrs King's bed, she tried to ignore the faces of her parents, sister and Richard as they rose in her mind's eye.

Should she even be thinking about Richard with the same level of concern that she felt for her family? He was little more than a colleague at the *Bath Chronicle*. Yes, they'd been out to dinner and dancing a couple of times, but that didn't make him her beau.

She shook off her nonsensical thoughts and focused on the here and now.

2

SYLVIA

Sylvia Roberts cradled her sprained wrist with her other hand and squinted through the dust and debris at the pandemonium around her. Even though she was a damn sight more shaken than she would ever admit, it was clear the staff needed to be pulled into some sort of working order if they were going to do their best for the thirty patients she and her team were currently caring for. Almost every nurse, including her beloved friends, Freda and Veronica, had glanced her way countless times, clearly waiting for her to take charge.

She spotted Sister Dyer helping patients up from the tiled floor and into chairs or onto beds. Having worked more closely with the sister recently, it was clear to Sylvia that the bombing had well and truly – even if temporarily – knocked Sister Dyer off her bullying perch, and by some margin.

'Which is just as well,' Sylvia mumbled. 'Otherwise, I'd have knocked her off it myself.'

The bombing appeared to be lessening, but that wasn't reason to rest easy when she had seen first-hand the terrible condition, both physically and mentally, of the people who had come into the hospital from Bristol over the last few months. Being caught up in the effects of a single blast could irrevocably change lives, but if anyone could teach her and the other nursing staff what to do under fire, it was the Bristolians.

Her mind drifted to her mother, and Sylvia's heart constricted with the depth of her worry. No, she had nothing to fear. Eileen Roberts was as tough as old boots and likely enough to deal with Hitler, his cronies too, as though they were little more than bothersome insects. Sylvia pulled back her shoulders. Her mother would be just fine. And so would she.

Noticing Mrs Perry looking terrified as she lay beneath a storage cupboard that had fallen at an angle against the tall metal headboard of her bed, and thankfully – inexplicably – stuck there, Sylvia rushed forward, praying the cupboard stayed put until she could move poor Mrs Perry out of its path.

'Well, what a position to get yourself in, Mrs Perry!' She laughed, using her good hand to gently draw Mrs Perry forward and then lift her arm over her shoulders. Sylvia carefully but firmly eased her patient from the bed. 'I think someone upstairs was looking out for you,' she panted once Mrs Perry was a safe distance from the bed. 'You would have been pushed through your mattress had that cupboard fallen on you.'

'I would indeed, m'dear.' Mrs Perry flashed a grin, her sparse teeth glinting in her dusty face. 'But Hitler's cronies just keep on missing me, don't they?'

Sylvia grinned back, buoyed by the determination shining in Mrs Perry's eyes. 'Come on, let's find you somewhere a bit more comfortable to sit. As far as I can tell, I think they've only managed to cause damage on one side of the hospital, thank God.'

'Hmm, for now.'

Sylvia led Mrs Perry forward, hazarding a guess that bombs

exploding in a city the majority of the patients had come to consider their refuge would set some of them back weeks in their recovery. The initial blast had blown three windows on only one side of the ward, which meant that the crux of the blast must have been a distance from the hospital. Therefore, there was still hope they'd avoided a direct hit. With the blackout curtains torn to shreds, the outside world was exposed to all in the ward, the night sky eerily lit in orange and yellow from the fires that raged all around the hospital, the noise deafening as aeroplane after aeroplane flew over, firing red tracer bullets or dropping incendiary bombs.

Sylvia clenched her jaw, silently cursing the Germans to high heaven. Moving patients somewhere safer than the fourth floor had to be the priority. She'd talk to her friends first and go from there. At least she could rely on Freda and Veronica's cooperation rather than the potential shock-induced resistance she might experience with some of the other less courageous nurses.

'Right, here you go,' she said as she slowly lowered Mrs Perry onto a visitor's chair. 'Will you be all right there for a few moments while I find out what's to be done next?'

''Course, you get on with your work, Nurse. You're a diamond, you are.'

Tipping her a wink, Sylvia left Mrs Perry and approached Veronica while gesturing Freda over from one of the beds. Once she was with her friends, Sylvia's tension eased a little. 'I want to put a suggestion to you two before I go ahead with it.'

Freda frowned. 'About what? Is your wrist all right?' she asked, nodding at Sylvia's arm. 'It's not broken, is it?'

'No, it's just a sprain. Listen—'

'Here.' Freda grabbed a pillow from the bed alongside them and took off the pillowcase. 'Keep talking while I put together a sling for you.'

Veronica dabbed the back of her hand to her forehead, her eyes frantically scanning the ward. 'We need to get on, girls.'

Doing her best not to upset Freda and her ministrations, Sylvia let her friend help her. 'Sister Dyer seems to have been knocked sideways by this raid and isn't taking charge as she should be,' she said. 'The whole bloody ward is in chaos so I have no choice but to step into the breach.'

Veronica shot a look at the sister's turned back. 'Do you think you should?'

'Yes, I do,' Sylvia said with an authority she did not entirely feel. 'She promoted me to senior nurse, didn't she? Surely that means she trusts me enough to start making some decisions around here. So we're going to move all the patients off the ward and downstairs. Preferably to the basement wards.'

'Good idea,' Freda said, knotting Sylvia's rudimentary sling with a flourish and a satisfied smile. 'There you go. That will do you for now.' She met Sylvia's gaze. 'Do you want us to give the other nurses the heads up? That way everyone will be ready to go once you've spoken to Sister.'

'Would you?' Sylvia smiled at her friend, appreciating Freda's habitual steadiness more than ever. 'There is a certain nurse I cannot cope with right now, so if you could speak to Kathy—'

'Oh, my God! What are we going to do?'

Right on cue, Nurse Kathy Scott burst between them, her face stricken with panic, capless, her dust-covered hair closer to grey than its usual blonde. 'How can you three stand around chatting in your silly little circle when the world is falling in on us!'

For the love of God...

Sylvia glared. 'For your information, Nurse Scott, I was just—'

'Don't *Nurse Scott* me, Sylvia Roberts. You might be senior ward nurse, but that counts for nothing under the circumstances. Any minute now we could die, be bombed to smither—'

'Just shut it, will you?' Sylvia hissed from between clenched teeth, gripping Kathy's elbow with her good hand. 'Look, I can see you're scared, we all are, but you need to get a hold of yourself. I've told you before, our work and everything we do is never about us, it's about the patients, and right now, they need to believe us capable of looking after them.' She pinned Kathy with a stare. 'No matter what.'

Freda stepped closer and eased Sylvia's hand from Kathy's elbow. 'Sylv...'

Shaking with her own fear and deep irritation towards Kathy, Sylvia released her and took a long, calming breath. 'Are you hurt?'

'No,' Kathy said with a petulant pout. 'I'm fine.'

'Good, then please go to the other wards on this floor and the one below and see the lay of the land. It might be that some are better off than us, some worse, but we need to know either way.'

But Kathy didn't move. Instead, she continued to stare at Sylvia, her eyes glazed.

'I'll go with her,' said Veronica, taking a firm hold of Kathy's arm.

Sylvia nodded, knowing it was for the best that Kathy was removed from her vicinity.

'Could one of you just do me a huge favour while I'm gone?' Veronica asked, her green eyes wide with worry. 'Could you check on Officer Matthews? Time and time again I've tried to get to him but have been waylaid helping others.'

Freda nodded. 'I'll go and see him right now.'

Veronica flashed a grateful smile and then steered Kathy away.

Sylvia scowled after them. 'Bloody woman.'

Another explosion boomed nearby and the fragile calmness that had begun to emerge on the ward was immediately splintered with terrified screams and panic. Sylvia instinctively grabbed Freda and pulled her to the tiled floor.

Sylvia's heart raced and her ears rang. 'Are you all right?'

Freda nodded. 'Yes. You?'

'Yes.'

They exchanged a weak smile.

'Let's go,' Sylvia said.

They quickly stood.

'Stay safe, Sylv.'

Freda's arms came around Sylvia in a quick hug before she strode purposefully towards the far end of the ward, clearly determined to deliver on her promise to Veronica that she would check on Officer Matthews.

Spotting Sister Dyer alone, Sylvia marched towards her, battling to hide her shock at the sister's paleness and unexpected anguish in her eyes. The woman was as strict as they came and twice as nasty when she put her mind to it, but in that moment, Sylvia saw a fellow colleague, her senior no less, stripped bare and entirely vulnerable.

Swallowing hard, she stood tall and looked Sister Dyer in the eye. 'I have sent Nurses Campbell and Scott to check on the condition of the other wards and report back to me,' she said. 'I think we should concentrate on moving all the patients as quickly as we can to the basement wards. That way, if we do take a direct hit, we'll have a better chance of being unaffected.'

The sister stared at her, said nothing.

'Sister!' Sylvia said sharply. 'Do I have your authority to carry out my suggested course of action?'

Sister Dyer blinked and when she looked at Sylvia this time, her eyes cleared. 'What?'

'The patients,' Sylvia said. 'Do I have your permission to move them to the basement?'

Another couple of seconds passed and then – thankfully – determination seeped into the sister's gaze, colour staining her cheeks as she looked at Sylvia's sling. 'What happened?'

'It's just a sprain. I'm fine. The patients, Sister? Do I have your permission to get them all moved downstairs?'

'Yes. Move the patients. Good idea. Excellent work, Nurse Roberts.' Sister Dyer beamed, her gaze clear. 'You direct the nurses to move patients on one side and I'll do the same on the other.'

Half expecting the sister to rap her heels together and salute her, Sylvia took a step back, but Sister Dyer merely nodded and, with a sharp about-turn, strode into the fray, arms moving like pistons at her sides.

'Well, I'll be...' Sylvia smiled before walking across the ward. Grabbing a chair, she stood on it, cleared her throat and clapped. 'Right, can I have all the nurses' attention, please. Everyone, quiet!'

3

FREDA

Once Sylvia had given instructions that the nurses were to move all the patients down to the lower floors – ideally the basement – Freda wanted to make sure she spoke to Officer Matthews before anyone else commandeered her attention and she ended up disappointing Veronica by not doing what her friend couldn't right then. The poor man had suffered such severe injuries. Having been brought into the hospital more or less covered head to toe in bandages, his face still being dressed and re-dressed almost daily, his pain made him more than a little volatile, and Officer Matthews did not suffer fools lightly.

Taking a deep breath, Freda mentally prepared herself for the sharp end of his tongue, but as she drew closer to his bed, apprehension inched over her shoulders, and Freda slowed her steps.

The bed was empty.

Empty of Officer Matthews *and* debris, which was extremely fortunate, considering how close his bed was to the window. It was just as well the first bomb, and the biggest blast, had permeated the ward on the other side, otherwise he would've likely been showered in potentially lethal shards of glass like at least six other patients had been.

Where was he?

Freda looked over the heads of patients as they moved to and fro about the ward, some walking alone, dazed and confused, others on the arms of the skeleton nursing staff.

'God damn it,' Freda muttered. 'Where are you?'

As much as she and Sylvia had advised Veronica to lessen her personal involvement with regards to Officer Matthews's well-being, their best intentions had fallen on deaf ears and so the young officer had come to take up a big part of Veronica's time and care. So much so, she'd be absolutely distraught if anything had happened to him.

A deep, chest-wracking cough sounded from the floor on the other side of the bed and Freda raced around its foot.

'Oh, Officer Matthews,' she cried, distressed to see him lying awkwardly, one arm trapped beneath his heavily bandaged torso, some of the bandages that covered the entirety of his face askew. 'Let me help you.'

'I just need you to move my bloody legs,' he growled, beads of perspiration glistening on his neck, his entire body trembling. 'Don't fuss, for God's sake.'

Ignoring his snappishness, Freda leaned down and, grimacing from the screaming pain in her hip, firmly planted her feet and purposefully slid her arms under his armpits. 'Ready? One, two, three.'

With her skill and the officer's added strength, she managed to manoeuvre him onto the bed where he collapsed onto his back, his position not much better than when he'd been on the floor.

'How's that?' Freda asked. 'Is that any—'

'Where's Nurse Campbell?' he demanded gruffly, his startling blue eyes blazing with anger. 'Is she all right?'

Freda met his intense gaze, her patience thinning when fear and terror hovered all around them, bombs exploding now and then, patients wailing and screaming. Did the man have no care? How Veronica so effortlessly tolerated his more-often-than-not stinking attitude, she had no idea.

'Well, Nurse? Where is she?'

She pinned him with an unwavering stare. 'She's checking over the lower wards at the moment, in the hope they're in a better state than ours. That way, we can move everyone somewhere safer. The bombing seems to be lessening too, so—'

'Lessening?' He sniffed derisively and grunted as he struggled into a seating position. 'You don't know anything. They'll be back soon enough.'

Freda bristled, her defences rising.

It was a constant frustration to her that she didn't know enough about the brutalities of this war and what it was really like for those who had been bombed for weeks, months, some even years. Yet now it seemed Bath was under attack, and if her misplaced yearning to experience the war first-hand had been answered, she didn't need to be reminded how little she knew of what that might mean for the city's people.

'They've gone to refuel and rearm.'

She blinked from her concern. 'What?'

'The Germans.' Officer Matthews glared across the ward. 'They'll be back and I have no doubt the second attack will be worse than the first.'

'Worse?'

'Don't you understand?' He nodded at the shattered windows on the opposite side of the ward. 'They've lit the bloody city on fire. When they come back, they'll be able to see, identify, and drop their bombs and fire their machine guns with precision. What they intend to destroy by attacking Bath will be easy pickings this time around.'

Sickness rose in Freda's throat. If what Officer Matthews predicted was correct, it was likely the resulting fatalities would be in the hundreds, maybe more if the Germans were intent on a prolonged raid like those they'd inflicted on Bristol.

'This is a revenge attack,' Officer Matthews continued. 'Nothing more, nothing less.'

'Revenge?' Freda snapped her gaze to his, her instinct for a story piqued. 'For what?'

'I might be wrong, of course. How can anyone know what that bastard Hitler is thinking? But I can't see what we have in Bath to bother him. There's the gasworks, I suppose. The railway line to London. But to me, attacking Bath is a waste of German ammunition and manpower. If I had to hazard a guess, this is retribution for the RAF bombing their historical towns a few weeks back.'

'We bombed historical towns in Germany?' Another explosion shook the ward and Freda gripped the bed's headboard. 'I didn't know that.'

'Why would you? As an officer in the RAF, I think I need to know more than a civilian, don't you?'

Freda pursed her lips and crossed her arms. Better to let him continue uninterrupted if she wanted to learn more.

'The RAF dropped bombs on Lubeck, Rostock, more if I remember rightly. Mark my words, that's what tonight is all about.' He clenched his jaw before heaving his legs over the side of the bed, the perspiration on his neck now running in rivulets and pooling in the hollow between his clavicles. 'Is she hurt?'

'What are you doing?' Freda exclaimed, grasping his upper arm to steady him, half her mind still on what he'd told her about the possible cause for the attacks. Did Richard know about the RAF's attacks on Germany's towns? Did anyone at the *Chronicle* know? 'Is who hurt?'

He cursed as he rather tremulously lowered his feet onto the floor tiles. 'Nurse Campbell, of course!'

Freda braced against his weight. The man was quaking from head to foot and was clearly in severe pain, blood seeping through his bandages in several places, meaning his healing wounds had been split open again.

'Officer Matthews, please.' She gritted her teeth as he began to walk. 'Where do you think you're going?'

'Where is she? Is she hurt?'

'Nurse Campbell has taken a knock to her head by the look of it, but she seems—'

He stopped and pinned her with a glare. 'By the look of it? What does that mean?'

'She has a cut on the side of her head, but she's well enough.' Freda tightened her grip on his arm as he began to hobble forwards again. 'Clearly you're determined to move, so I advise you to stop fretting about Nurse Campbell for the time being and let me help you off the ward and downstairs.' She blew out a breath. 'I promise you are in a much worse way than Nurse Campbell is right now.'

Despite her firm words and even firmer hold on the officer, Freda's heart kicked with sympathy as her sensible mind whispered its warning. He looked towards the ward's doors, his gaze dark with distress and obvious concern for Veronica. She had no doubt he would have run through the doors to look for her if he could. But whatever brewed between him and her friend only spelled bad news... especially if Sister Dyer got wind of anything untoward going on.

'Come on, let's be having you,' she said, trying to inject some joviality into the situation. 'No more dilly-dallying.'

'If this is a revenge attack, you know Hitler will just wreak unnecessary havoc, don't you?' Officer Matthews said as they made slow progress along the long length of the ward, people moaning and crying all around them. 'He will have no qualms how many civilians he murders, how many men, women and children.'

Freda shook her head, her heart heavy. 'My father thought an attack on Bath inevitable months ago, so I shouldn't be entirely surprised.'

'Your father?' He gave a dismissive snort. 'And what does he think he knows then?'

Her annoyance rose once again and Freda fought to keep hold of her professionalism. Veronica had mentioned more than once that Officer Matthews's brusqueness needed firm handling.

'He's a police officer, serving on the home front and doing a fine job of it,' Freda said, holding his sceptical gaze and jutting her chin. 'My father is a good, kind, upstanding man, Officer Matthews, and I'd appreciate it if you controlled your tone when you speak about him.'

Silence fell and he stopped, looked hard into her eyes until she took a small step back. His eyes were the brightest blue and disconcertingly intense.

'I apologise, Nurse Parkes,' he said quietly. 'Truly. I shouldn't have assumed...'

'Apology accepted,' Freda said, suddenly understanding a little of how Officer Matthews had managed to capture Veronica's attention. His eyes were the only part of his face visible, which seemed to make them somewhat captivating. Plus, Veronica certainly didn't shy away from a challenge and would have immediately seen the tetchy, horrifically injured officer as her problem to conquer. The fact Veronica had survived more personal harm and life-changing trauma than her and Sylvia put together had proven beyond doubt she was the strongest out of the three of them. What Officer Matthews would never realise was that his moodiness would be like water off a duck's back to Veronica after what had happened to her at the hands of a man far more threatening.

'There you are!'

Freda started as Veronica practically screeched to a stop in front of them, her cheeks red and her green eyes bright with relief as she stared at Officer Matthews without as much as glancing at Freda.

'Oh, you're bleeding,' she said, her gaze resolute as she appraised him from head to toe before finally looking at Freda. 'I'll take over from here. Can you tell Sylvia the lower floors on the south side are practically untouched, the basement too? We should definitely follow her plan and move everyone downstairs as quickly as possible.'

Freda released her hold on Officer Matthews as Veronica slipped one hand around his back and the other around his elbow. Burying her heightening concern about what was happening between a nurse and patient right in front of her eyes, she looked away. 'Yes, Officer Matthews thinks the planes have disappeared to refuel, but they'll almost certainly be back. So we should get a move on.'

Veronica absently nodded, her concern entirely focused on Officer Matthews as she led him towards the ward entrance.

Exhaling a shaky breath, Freda watched them go. What good would it do to raise her concerns now? She just hoped Veronica knew what she was doing.

Looking around the mass of moving patients and nurses, Freda spotted Sylvia farther along the ward working with Kathy

Scott as they moved a bed with three patients sitting on top of it, each bloodied and cradling arms or wrists that appeared sprained or even broken. Freda hurried over to help, her gaze drawn again and again to the windows, the night sky flickering orange and pink as the city burned.

A shameful longing to go outside and see what was happening stirred inside of her and she purposefully snatched her gaze from the windows. What was the matter with her? The last thing she should be thinking about was her reporting, but she couldn't help wondering if Richard was out there amid the terror, screams and chaos, his notepad and pencil in hand. Was he putting himself in danger in pursuit of people's stories, their bravery and losses? Her heart stumbled. Was he even alive? She inhaled sharply and an unexpected sob caught in her throat. No, Richard would be fine. So would her parents, and so would her sister. They had to be.

4

SYLVIA

'Excellent thinking and foresight, Nurse Roberts. Truly excellent.'

'Thank you, Sister.'

Sylvia forced a smile. The last thing she felt was excellent. About anything. Including her role as senior ward nurse. All she really wanted was to hightail it out of the hospital and into the closest pub. If any of the local pubs were still standing, of course.

Sister Dyer continued to talk, her eyes narrowed as she surveyed the frantic hustle and bustle of the ward, seemingly oblivious to Sylvia's tension.

'I suggest we reconvene every half an hour or so,' she mused. 'We need to ensure we are on the same page at all times to avoid giving the nurses differing instructions.' The sister faced her, and Sylvia was discomfited by the whisper of uncertainty behind the habitual steeliness in her grey eyes. 'I am woman enough to admit that the first blast shocked me to my core, Nurse Roberts, and I was glad to have you beside me to take over until I managed to pull myself together.' She briefly touched Sylvia's arm before lifting her chin. 'It won't happen again.'

Sylvia was momentarily at a loss what to say. Was the battle-axe actually admitting weakness? Instead of making her feel gleeful in what Sylvia would have once accepted as a triumph, Sister Dyer's humbleness only proved to heighten the pressure Sylvia felt she was under. Yet, knowing she hadn't been alone in her shock and that maybe she was up to her new role after all, Sylvia drew in a strengthening breath and looked across the ward.

'Well, I'm pretty sure we haven't seen the last of the bombing, so we should keep moving the nurses and patients along. If the hospital is hit again, it could be worse than before. Judging by the noise and screams on the streets during the raid, I think the hospital got off lightly.' Sylvia paused as her mum's mischievous eyes and smile, permanent cigarette in hand, flashed in her mind. 'God only knows what's happening out there.'

'Indeed, but it's up to us to find out. Sooner or later, someone from the ward will need to go outside to liaise with ambulance drivers and ARP wardens in the hope we can keep ahead of the increased casualties that will inevitably come into the hospital.'

'Yes, I'm sure surgery will want to prioritise who is seen and in what order. It will be up to the nurses to duly follow their instructions and support them as best we can.'

'Possibly.' The sister sighed heavily. 'Then again, it might well be a case of more fatalities than casualties. Bath is entirely exposed and vulnerable to whatever the Germans have planned for us next.'

Sylvia frowned. 'Isn't every city vulnerable when it comes to Hitler? The man is clearly insane, and how in God's name do you protect people from insanity?'

'But other cities have adequate night-cover, strategically placed anti-aircraft guns and so forth. Bath has nothing, as the powers that be decided we wouldn't be a target. How wrong they were.'

Sylvia shivered, her need for a drink gathering strength. She suddenly had a faint memory of Freda saying Richard Sinclair, the journalist she worked with at the newspaper, had been concerned about the lack of protection over Bath should it ever come under attack. Now it seemed his fears had been well and truly realised.

'So,' Sister Dyer said, interrupting Sylvia's thoughts. 'If the Germans do come back – which I believe they will – their second assault will be worse than the first. From what I heard when I went to the ambulance bay earlier, they machine-gunned the streets so goodness knows what they will do next.'

Shocked, Sylvia stepped back and stared wide-eyed at the sister. 'They're machine-gunning civilians?'

Sadness and anger shadowed the sister's eyes. 'Yes.'

'Right.' Sylvia pulled back her shoulders and shook off the anxiety pulsing through her. 'Then Hitler needs to know Bath won't be beaten. How can we falter when we've treated so many Bristolians who've gone through weeks and weeks of this? This is Bath's first and hopefully only raid. We get to work and stand united. No more worrying, no more fear.'

Sister Dyer smiled. 'I knew I was right to promote you, Nurse Roberts.'

'We'll encourage any patients who can walk unaided to make their way downstairs and then staff can assist those in wheelchairs and beds to relocate as efficiently as possible.'

The sister cast her steely gaze over the hubbub of her ward and nodded curtly. 'You oversee the transfers from the ward, and I'll go to the surgery floor and do my best to speak with Mr Martin. It would be helpful to know what surgery he can and cannot deal with at the moment. The poor man and his fellow surgeons will all-too-soon be overrun with the injured.'

The sister walked away and Sylvia stared after her, pressing her hand to the swarm of nerves that took flight in her stomach. With Sister Dyer off the ward, she was in charge. This was not the time to weaken, think about her mother, her friends... Or even Jesse, the love of her life – the man she'd rejected – who was serving God only knew where. Striding forward, she glanced at Kathy Scott helping Mr Allington, whom Sylvia knew was more than capable of walking when he was due to be released from the hospital in a day or two. Whether that would happen now was another matter altogether, of course.

'Nurse Scott,' she snapped. 'What are you doing?'

Kathy turned and immediate dislike clouded her eyes. 'I'm taking Mr Allington to the basement.' She raised her eyebrows. 'As per your instructions, *Senior* Nurse Roberts.'

Sylvia smiled wryly, her patience with Kathy already stretched to breaking again despite being in her company for less than ten seconds. She slid her gaze to Mr Allington, who seemed more amused than afraid as he flitted his attention back and forth between her and Kathy.

'Do you think you could make your way down the stairs without help, Mr Allington?' she asked. 'Only we're a bit thin on the ground and we need nurses to assist patients unable to walk.'

He immediately stood straighter, chin jutted and pride clear in the firm set of his jaw. 'I am more than capable of sorting myself out, Nurse Roberts,' he said. 'Didn't I help four kiddies out of a burning house in Bristol? Even went in and got their dog out afterwards.'

Sylvia lowered her tense shoulders, touched her fingers to his arm. 'I know you did, and haven't I told you umpteen times how you're my own personal hero?' She winked. 'Now, go on.

Make your way down to the basement wards and there will be someone to help you. I'll see you soon, all right?'

''Course. See you in a bit, Nurse.'

He grinned, showing more gum than teeth before tottering away, waving his hand to anyone he passed as though he was walking through the local park rather than a hospital ward in terrified chaos.

'Right.' Sylvia rounded on Kathy. 'You and I are not doing this tonight, tomorrow or the next day. Do you understand?'

Kathy glared. 'Doing what?'

'You know damn well what. Bickering. Giving one another a hard time. We call a truce. Bath is under attack, and we are its backbone right now. No more messing about between us. Our patients need us.' Her next words caught like barbed wire in her throat, but she swallowed past them. 'And I need you right now, Kathy. Just as much as I need Freda and Veronica.'

It was a lie, of course. She knew it, and so did Kathy. Still, if it meant the woman cooperated for the time being…

Kathy's smile was slow and wolf-like, her hazel eyes glittering with satisfaction. 'There now, that wasn't so bad to admit, was it? What is it you'd like me to do next? Your wish is my command.'

Ignoring how much it rankled to have to behave herself in that moment, Sylvia sighed. 'I want you to come with me. We're going to work together like we never have before. Once this raid is over, and if we've managed to successfully work side by side, you owe me a promise and then we'll see where things go between us after that.'

Kathy narrowed her eyes. 'A promise about what?'

'You know exactly what.'

Kathy's eyes glazed with thought for a second before they widened. 'Are you talking about the secret I've been keeping from Sister about you and your precious friends? You're bringing that up now?'

'Haven't you threatened on more than one occasion you would tell her?'

'Oh, Nurse Roberts, don't you fret. What we're going through now is enough for me to forget about you and your friends stealing a patient away into the night, taking her off the premises without permission and basically breaking every hospital rule under the sun.' Kathy flashed an exaggerated, sickly-sweet smile. 'Although, it's highly amusing that all this time you've thought me the type of person to snitch on my colleagues. I'm not who you think I am at all. Then again, you and your little friends haven't got to know me in the slightest, have you?'

'No, we haven't, and do you know why?' Sylvia leaned in closer, relishing the fact her nemesis stepped back. 'Because you've been nitpicking and bothering me during and ever since training. You never seem to let up, Kathy.'

The other nurse shrugged. 'It's a bit of fun, that's all.'

'Well, this is the first time I've asked for your help since we started working together months ago. So, you do well by me now, and then – and only then – will I start thinking about you coming out with me, Freda and Veronica after work.'

Kathy studied her before she slowly smiled. 'You've got a deal, Nurse Roberts. I'm glad you are finally seeing how much easier things could be between us.'

Kathy sauntered past her, and Sylvia fought the urge to stick out her foot and trip Kathy over. Sending up a silent prayer that God gave her due patience to cope with the time she was being forced to spend with Kathy, Sylvia breathed deep. When all was said and done, even with worry for her mother's welfare taking up so much of her thoughts, there was nothing more important than the safety of those under her care right then. Kathy Scott or no Kathy Scott.

5

VERONICA

Veronica stole glances at Eric – Officer Matthews – as he lay on a gurney, staring ahead and thinking goodness only knew what.

Their progress to the basement wards had been slow and arduous. The continuous shouting and crying, banging and clanging, scraping of furniture and equipment had echoed all around them, bouncing off the floors and windows. She had no doubt whatsoever that this raid would be re-igniting Eric's worst memories of his time serving overseas. The bombs had been so loud, shaking the hospital walls and windows and sending equipment hurtling here, there and everywhere.

Yet neither of them had exchanged more than mutual concern for one another and platitudes since they'd been alone together, and she could not bear the ridiculousness of it any longer, when it felt as though Bath was imploding all around them. But what could she say to him? What words would help him? From the moment their eyes met, when she had collected him from the ambulance bay seven or eight weeks before, she had felt a powerful, almost overwhelming comfort and familiarity whenever she was with him. As though he was someone she could trust. And that feeling had not vanished, or even diminished, in the entirety of his time at the hospital. If her instant trust in a man – any man – wasn't ludicrous enough after what she'd been through at the hands of another, it was made even more ludicrous by the fact she didn't know Eric at all. Had never met him before he came so abruptly into her life.

Veronica battled against her deeply embedded fear and trauma that the vile events of one afternoon almost five years ago always instilled in her. Fear and trauma that meant the only people she had miraculously grown to trust were her new best friends, Freda and Sylvia. The fact she trusted them was so precious to her, but the instinct she had towards Eric Matthews was different. Something she couldn't name. It wasn't attraction or romance. It was… She didn't know what it was.

'Good God.' He blew out a breath. 'This must be what the underground Tube stations look like during London's raids. How many people are you hoping to ram onto this basement floor, for Christ's sake? It's bloody ridiculous.'

Heat rose in Veronica's cheeks. It was true enough. People were lying side by side like packed sardines on the floor, or else slumped on chairs or lying on beds, every available space occupied. What else could they do? There were four floors, including the basement, in the hospital, and the first floor was taken by surgery, both operating theatres and recovery wards. The other two floors were normal wards and higher up, thus more susceptible to bomb damage. Sylvia had been absolutely right to order the patients be brought to the basement for safety.

She glared at him. 'Now you listen to me. I might be used to your brusqueness and distance, but the last thing I want is you subjecting others to it when every single patient is going to be traumatised by this raid, regardless of whether or not they are hurt physically.'

'Is that so?'

'Yes, and you know it, too. How can you not after serving and seeing what you've seen? People need to be down here to give them the best chance of safety and I don't need you upsetting anyone. Promise me.' She held his disgruntled gaze. 'The last thing patients need is you adding to their tension and fears.'

Their eyes locked and Veronica's heart beat an uneasy rhythm. He could glare and snarl all he liked; she'd learned every one of his moods was founded in frustration and fear rather than anger or judgement.

'I won't say anything to anyone,' he muttered. 'You know that.'

She did know. In fact, Veronica swore if Eric Matthews could get away with speaking to no one but her on the ward, he'd be a darn sight happier, which was why she counted herself as the person who knew him best – even if, at times, she felt she didn't know him at all. Yet, since the day he'd arrived at the hospital, there had been instances that made her certain he knew her too. She'd wasted so much time wrangling over the quandary of how or what the connection was between them, but she was too afraid to ask him and hear the answer. The way his eyes glazed over or turned icy-cold when he looked at her sometimes told her that, if they had been associated in the past, that association would have come with unresolved issues. Yet, other times he looked at her with such care in his lovely blue eyes, she felt entirely comforted.

She cleared her throat, dragged herself into the here and now. 'Now that you're settled, I want to have a look at what's going on under those bandages,' she said, studying him. 'I'm not happy with the amount of blood that has come through on your chest and back.' She glanced at the metal cabinets intermittently lining the walls between the sparse number of beds, chairs and side tables. 'I'm pretty sure there will be plenty of dressing materials and antiseptic intact down here. Everything appears to have escaped any disturbance, so we'll be grateful for small mercies. How's your pain? I can find you some—'

'I'm fine. Don't fuss. You've got more than me to worry about.'

'But I do worry about you.' She raised her eyebrows. 'More than you deserve half the time.'

'You'll get no argument from me there.'

Veronica stared at him as he continued to look ahead. Sometimes she longed to remove the bandages covering his face so she could see his facial expressions, better gauge what he was feeling or thinking. He had come to mean something to her – more than something according to Freda and Sylvia – and it was time that they dealt with the big fat elephant in the room that sat like a boulder between them.

She opened the cabinet adjacent to the bed, relieved to find it full of supplies. She extracted antiseptic, cotton wool, gauze and bandages.

'Now,' she said, bracing herself for the task ahead. 'It usually takes two nurses to change the bandages around your torso, but we'll have to manage as best we can.'

'Why don't you leave me be and give your time and energy to one of the other poor sods down here? It doesn't look as though you'll be stuck for choice.'

Veronica narrowed her eyes, knowing he was purposely putting her off from nursing him. Unless she was off shift or working with Mr Martin in surgery, it was always her and another nurse who saw to Officer Matthews. The only bandages she'd never removed – under his specific, unchanging request that she never did – were the ones on his face. He allowed any of the other nurses, but not her, and the vehemence with which he had insisted on it being that way had annoyed Sister Dyer no end, but to save Officer Matthews's sharp tongue from slashing her, she agreed to his request every time he demanded it.

'Well,' he said, facing her and quirking an eyebrow. 'Off you go.'

'I'm not going anywhere,' she retorted, pulling out a length of bandage from the roll and picking up a pair of scissors. '*I'm* looking after you for the time being and I would be grateful for your undivided corporation.'

Despite his glare burning holes in her bowed head, Veronica cut a length of bandage and completely ignored him. He could sulk all he wanted, he wasn't getting rid of her. Not this time. Sylvia and Freda had told her what they could about Eric's facial features beyond his horrific burns, but nothing they said had provoked the slightest recognition for her. She had to know who Eric was and what he meant to her.

She poured an inch of antiseptic into a bowl, making sure nothing went to waste when no one had any idea what the Germans had planned next. Supplies could soon be like gold dust. Once she'd cleaned her hands, she finally met Eric's irritated gaze, smiled and set about undoing the pins holding the bandages wrapped around his torso.

'Let's see what's going on along your chest first, shall we? The bleeding doesn't look too bad so I'm sure I can get you cleaned up soon enough.' She grimaced. 'But as I said, the unwrapping and rewrapping is going to be a challenge – and painful, I'm afraid – with me doing this alone, but we'll manage well enough between us, I'm sure. Just move as far onto your side as you can. That's the ticket.'

For the next half an hour, Veronica worked efficiently and methodically until the two burns that had split open on his chest had been cleaned and treated, as well as the one on his stomach.

She applied fresh bandages but her work was certainly below par, working solo on a two-nurse job.

'Nurse!'

Veronica looked farther along the ward at Sister Dyer. 'Yes, Sister?'

'Once you've finished with Officer Matthews, I'd like you back upstairs. Moving patients takes priority for the time being.'

'Yes, Sister.'

Veronica turned to Eric. 'Right, you're done for now,' she said, blowing out an exhausted breath, her arms and shoulders aching with fatigue. 'You can take a well needed rest for a while. All right?'

'Of course it's all right. I'm alive and it's pretty much guaranteed hundreds of others in Bath are in a far worse state than me.' The anger was back in his eyes, the glint of unshed tears, too. 'Just go where you're needed. I'm not going anywhere.'

Their weeks together had taught Veronica when to adhere to his gruff demands and when to argue against them. This was one she would adhere to… once she'd taken the leap she should have taken weeks ago. Maybe it was the bombing, the risk of death coming so much sooner than they'd all assumed having spent the war living in a place that had bypassed attack for almost three years, but now was the time to challenge Eric Matthews like she'd never had the courage to do before.

'Fine, I'll go,' she said, her heart racing as she gathered the dressing paraphernalia with slightly trembling hands. 'And when I come back, I'll deal with your other bandages.' She swallowed and met his unwavering gaze. 'The ones on your face.'

Silence stretched between them even as shouting and crying reigned throughout the ward.

'No.'

'Eric—'

'No!'

She flinched, guilt and frustration writhing inside her even as she planted her hands on her hips and pinned him with a glare. 'Why not? I've seen a million burns and scars since the start of this war. There is nothing I haven't seen.'

'Do you think that's why I won't let you see my face? Because I think you won't be able to handle my injuries?' His bright eyes burned into hers. 'It's got nothing to do with that. Nothing.'

'Then what…' Her frustration gathered strength and turned into indignation. 'I know you, don't I? That's why you don't want me to see your face. But why? If we know each other, it's a good thing we've been thrown into each other's paths again, isn't it? Unless…' She swallowed, trepidation whispering through her. 'Unless it's a bad thing that I know you.'

'Nurse Campbell!'

Veronica jumped and turned.

Sister Dyer bored down on her, arms swinging. 'Forget moving the patients for now, you're needed in theatre. I'll take over seeing to Officer Matthews. Off you go and make sure you come straight back as soon as Mr Martin has passed on whatever it is he wishes to tell you.'

'But—'

'Now, Nurse Campbell!'

Veronica snapped her gaze to Eric, but he'd turned his bandaged face against the pillow, his gaze directed to the bed beside him. Knowing she had little chance of winning a fight against him *and* the sister, she lifted her chin and made for the ward exit. Now she'd found the gumption to ask Eric who he was, the worst was over and, one way or another, she'd get some answers from him.

6

FREDA

Freda carefully lowered a male patient she didn't know very well onto a wheelchair and gave him an encouraging smile. 'There you go. I've checked you over and you'll be just fine.'

'Thank you, Nurse.'

'You're welcome.' Freda nodded at Carole Taylor, another nurse who had graduated from nursing training at the same time as her and had ended up working on the same ward. 'You go along with Nurse Taylor now and she'll get you settled.'

Carole wheeled him away, chatting all the while in her usual friendly way. Freda smiled and absently rubbed her bruised hip, the pain already beginning to fade. Bold in figure and personality, Carole had budded up with another graduating nurse, Martha Carr, when she started working on the ward, and slowly all six of them including Kathy, Sylvia, Veronica and herself were getting to know each other and their individual ways of working as the weeks and months passed. It felt reassuring. Especially now, with the Germans' rampage wreaking carnage through Bath's streets.

Blowing out an exhausted breath, Freda lifted the watch

pinned to her chest. Three-eighteen. She couldn't even begin to work out how many hours she had been working without a break. It had been about three and half hours since the bombing stopped and the all-clear sounded. Nowhere near long enough to hope that Hitler wouldn't stage a second attack.

She headed to the exit and started up the stairs. There were still at least another half a dozen patients to bring down to the basement. Freda paused at a stairway window and pulled aside the blackout curtain. She could not see what damage lay past the hospital entrance and the narrow cobbled street that ran adjacent to it. How she longed to know what was happening outside! Were people lying dead in the street? Suffering from horrendous injuries with no one helping them? Tears pricked her eyes and she dropped the curtain, fighting not to cry, fighting not to race outside to help.

She had to concentrate on her work here. What she did inside the hospital mattered too. Freda repeated the sentiment over and over in her head as she continued up the stairs. All too often she felt the exact opposite about her work at the hospital, instead believing her writing would make a bigger difference to Bath's people in the long term. She'd been persuaded into nursing by her mother who considered the vocation as suitable for 'a good girl', which had only resulted in Freda frequently, and strongly, resenting her acquiescence all the more as time wore on.

But working on a ward that treated the incoming from Bristol's overflow meant she and her friends had seen more pain and anguish than most in Bath, and the fact they were somewhat forearmed did not make the prospect of what lay ahead any easier to face. Freda's stomach knotted with anxiety and she forcefully buried her dread of what awaited her once she got news of her family and colleagues, both at home and the *Chronicle*.

When she entered the upstairs ward, firm fingers gripped her elbow. 'Hey, you. How are you getting on?'

She turned, the sight of Sylvia's face easing a little of her tension. 'Good as I can be. How about you?'

'Well enough.' Sylvia sighed. 'But I'd be a lot better if I could stop thinking about my mother for five minutes.'

Freda blew out a heavy breath. 'I can't stop worrying about my parents and Dorothy either. All we can do is hope and pray they have found shelter somewhere. Thinking anything else won't do either of us any good.'

'I know, I've already told myself that what we are doing here is the best we can do for now. Everything else will come to pass soon enough.'

They lapsed into silence before Sylvia spoke again, her voice decidedly more stalwart. 'Right, well, V's just been called to surgery and I can't imagine she'll be back for a while.'

'Because?'

'Sister thinks twenty or thirty injured people have been brought in by the fire wardens and ambulances. Some with limbs hanging off and God knows what else.'

'My God. How are the other wards doing? Have you spoken to V's mum?'

'Sister Campbell?' Sylvia frowned. 'Haven't seen her. Is she even on shift? Veronica would've said, surely.'

'Well, let's hope she is then if V hasn't said anything. The way things are outside, it will be better for V if her mother is in the hospital. Especially when they haven't been getting along lately as they used to.'

'Well, that's what comes with a daughter longing to leave home and a mother desperate to have her stay.' Sylvia shook her head. 'Come on, we'd better get on with it. It might be wall to wall patients downstairs, but all the supply cabinets are intact, so that's something.'

'It certainly is.'

'And as you're here, I might as well tell you and the other nurses the latest.'

'What latest?'

'The surgeons and theatre staff are in charge of prioritising patient care on a case-by-case basis and from here on in, we have to wait for instructions from them.'

'Well, I don't envy them having to pick and choose who gets what treatment and when, but needs must I suppose.'

'Exactly, but in the meantime, we'll do what we can to treat any minor injuries on the spot, give tetanus injections and as much TLC as we can spare.' Sylvia's jaw tightened as she stared around the ward, her tiredness and tension showing in her pallor and the grey smudges under her eyes. 'None of us have a clue what it's like outside and until we do...'

Freda's desire to get outside niggled once again, quickly followed by a horrible frustration that she'd forever feel she wasn't doing enough, whether that be at the hospital, the paper... even at home. The thought that little more than marriage and children lay ahead of her made her shiver with dread. Right now, she had absolutely no desire to get married and become beholden to someone else for the rest of her life. Who knew if that would change in time, but for now, no thank you.

'Earth to Freda.' Sylvia waved her hand in front of her face. 'Come on, let's get the rest of these patients downstairs. I'll let the other nurses know the way of things as we go.'

For the next half an hour or so, she and Sylvia worked side by side like a well-oiled machine. Even though, in the past,

Kathy Scott had managed to orchestrate moments where she successfully ensured Freda, Sylvia and Veronica were separated in their work, it never lasted long. Sister Dyer knew a good thing when she saw it and the three of them worked best when they worked together... which only served to irritate Kathy – and what Freda assumed was her misplaced jealousy – all the more.

'Where's Kathy?' Freda asked as they entered one of the basement wards with Mrs Bower and Mr Cannon. 'Isn't she supposed to be working with Nurse Carr?'

'I've got no idea where she is,' Sylvia said, scowling as they carefully eased their patients onto two empty chairs. 'Right, Nurse Parkes and I will have to love you and leave you, but I'll make sure one of the other nurses brings you both a cup of tea, all right?'

Freda smiled at the two patients and walked with Sylvia back up the stairs. The next job was to gather as many supplies as possible and bring them downstairs. Now that the bombing had stopped, the crashing and splintering, bloodcurdling screams and shouts had quieted and the ringing in Freda's ears was gradually subsiding, her heartbeat resuming a more normal pace, even if the adrenaline flowing through her veins hadn't lessened. Then again, she wasn't entirely sure she wanted that to happen. After all, what could any of the nurses rely on but adrenaline to keep their spirits determined and their energy high?

'God, I'm absolutely worn out,' Sylvia said as she gripped the banister. 'What do you think it's like out there?'

'Terrifying. Desperate. Helpless.' Freda briefly closed her eyes. 'The only thing that's guaranteed is that it will be awful.'

When her friend didn't respond, Freda turned.

Sylvia's face was ashen, her eyes wide. 'I'm scared, Freda.'

Freda's stomach knotted. She had thought her friend incapable of being afraid of anything. Sylvia was wise beyond her years, tough and street savvy.

Fear tiptoed along Freda's spine as she forced a smile. 'So am I, but we'll be all right.'

'But what if we aren't?' Tears shone in Sylvia's big brown eyes as she tucked an auburn curl behind her ear with shaking fingers. 'What if Jesse is dead? What if my mum, your mum—'

'Hey, stop it.' Freda's mouth drained dry. Sylvia was the happy-go-lucky one, the one with enough sass to take on anything and anyone. Yet nothing but deep panic showed in her eyes. 'We're going to get through this. So are our families and Jesse. All of us. V, too. Do you hear me? Don't you falter on me now, Sylv. I need you.'

Sylvia squeezed her eyes shut, drew in some long, slow breaths before opening them again. 'What the hell is wrong with me?'

Freda gripped her friend's arm. 'Nothing's wrong with you. Now come on, we can do this.'

Sylvia stared at her for a long moment before the fear slowly seeped from her eyes and was replaced with bright and familiar determination. 'You're right. We can. We have to.'

'Exactly.' Freda gave Sylvia a firm hug and stepped back, her stomach knotting with trepidation. 'Some of the patients are saying a second attack is imminent. We have to put on a brave face, no matter what we might be feeling inside.'

'I wouldn't be surprised if they come back. Hitler does nothing by halves, does he?'

'If there is a second attack, it will be worse than the first. The whole city is alight. The burning buildings will act as beacons for the German pilots. Officer Matthews said something about that being Hitler's plan all along.'

'Will you write about this? About how it is in the hospital?'

'I can't think about that right now, but I'm sure I will eventually.' Freda sighed. 'But I doubt the paper will want anything from me for a while. They've got Richard and the other staff writers to do the serious, more important articles. What I write, women's issues and so forth, will be put on the back burner. Which I think is absolutely right, by the way.'

'Well, all I know for sure is that Hitler is a murdering...' Sylvia shook her head, her cheeks reddening. 'Let's just hope our families are all right. Everything else we'll deal with.'

At the mention of family, Freda felt an overwhelming need to share her concerns about her sister, Dorothy, with her dearest friend.

'Sylv?'

'Uh-huh.'

'If anything happens to me—'

'Nothing is going to happen to you,' Sylvia said firmly. 'Or to any of us for that matter.'

Freda swallowed. 'I know, but... there's something going on with Dorothy and if something does happen to me then I need you to look out for her.'

Sylvia frowned. 'What do you mean, something's going on with her? Like what?'

'I don't know.' Freda worried her bottom lip. 'She's young, beautiful, has a fiancé she loves and he loves her...'

Sylvia arched an eyebrow. 'Sounds to me like she's pretty much got it made.'

'I know, but—'

'Look...' Sylvia put her hand on Freda's shoulder. 'Whatever might or might not be wrong with Dorothy, I'm sure tonight has put it into perspective for her, the same as it has for all of us. Let's just concentrate on getting through whatever the Germans have planned.'

Freda nodded and held on to the hope Sylvia was right and her often self-centred sister would finally get her first real grip on reality and make a few changes for the better. After all, with Bath under attack, alongside major cities up and down the country, it was time for Dorothy and all of them to accept that the problems they'd thought bad before were nothing compared to what their futures might hold.

7

VERONICA

'So to that end,' Mr Martin said, 'I have cleared patients from both surgical theatres. They have now left us and are on their way to the Royal United.' The senior surgeon's face was etched with tension, his jaw tight. 'The raid was a shock and we were unprepared for it, but I managed to stabilise a lot of incoming patients in situ in the receiving room that I set up by the ambulance bay. Most have been directed to the public shelters.' He pushed his hand into his grey hair and held it there. 'God willing they will get to safety, but if the Germans return for a second raid, we will be inundated. Ambulance drivers and volunteers will be doing their best to cope with the carnage from the first raid. Therefore, we must prepare for what happens next. None of us can predict what will come through these surgery doors.'

Veronica held Mr Martin's gaze, trying to gauge what his real feelings were about the terrifying ordeal currently unfolding in Bath – and in their small hospital, situated right in the very centre of the city.

'The ambulance drivers and volunteers know the bigger hospitals are on the outskirts of the city and that they have more equipment and beds,' she said. 'I'm sure they'll head straight to them, wherever possible.'

'Hmm, I'm not so sure they will, but we can hope.' He faced Betty Wilson, the hospital's only female anaesthetist, who had been trained on Mr Martin's insistence almost two years before. 'I want you working with me, Nurse Wilson, and I have two other anaesthetists on standby for possible emergency surgeries in the other theatres. We will stay here. You and I will begin by...'

Betty shot a glance at Veronica before snapping her gaze back to Mr Martin. Veronica's skin tingled with awareness as it always did whenever Betty looked at her, her concentration on what Mr Martin was explaining drifting. She bit back a shamingly inappropriate smile and fought the pleasure whispering inside her. What was wrong with her? It was almost as though she had a silly schoolgirl crush on the woman. Yes, Betty was pretty, full of life and wonderfully forward thinking, but still.

'Nurse Campbell?'

She jumped and blinked.

Mr Martin's eyebrows were raised expectantly as he looked at her. 'Do you have any questions?'

'Um, no. I...' Veronica scrambled to think of something – anything – to say, at the same time cursing the heat warming her cheeks as Betty's study burned into her. 'Actually, I wanted to ask if you want me to go to the ambulance bay and ask the workers there to bring all incoming patients to the receiving room for you to assess.'

'Good idea. I want to look over all patients for as long as I can cope with the number. It is my intention to give decisive instruction of where to take them in the hope most can be duly cared for by the nursing staff.'

Veronica nodded, her thoughts immediately turning to Freda and Sylvia and how they were getting on in the basement wards.

'Two surgeons have already arrived from Bristol to help.' Mr Martin blew out a tired breath. 'So that's something.'

'And I'm sure more will follow, sir,' Betty said, her hazel gaze confident on his. 'They've experienced what we're going through over and over again. If people can be spared to help us, I'm sure they will be.'

The lines on the surgeon's forehead deepened as he looked between Betty and Veronica. 'Heaven knows how any medical staff can be spared from Bristol, but I certainly won't be asking the question and risk them disappearing again. Right.' His steel-grey eyes were sombre as he focused on Veronica. 'Before you go to the ambulance bay, could you go to the basement and inform Sister Dyer I need you permanently in surgery until such time as I say otherwise? I'm sure she will have something to say about that, but that's too bad.' He scowled as he looked at the theatre door. 'We're going to be busy. Sister Dyer will know that as well as I do.'

'I'll go straight away, sir,' Veronica said. 'The nurses are in the process of getting all the patients downstairs. They are likely to be done now so I'm sure Sister Dyer will be fine with me being where I'm needed most.'

He gave a firm nod and turned to Betty. 'Go with Nurse Campbell. I want you both to get hold of as much dressing, gauze, suture kits and anything else you can. Everything will be in short supply soon enough but ask the sisters for whatever they can spare.'

Veronica began to walk towards the door. 'My mother is a sister on one of the wards, sir, and I'm pretty sure her ward was not affected by the raid as much as Sister Dyer's.'

'Very good. Off you both go. I want you back here as soon as possible.'

Following Betty from the theatre, Veronica exhaled a shaky

breath and shouted over the noise, screams and crying filtering through the shattered hospital windows, 'Are you all right?'

Betty stopped, her beautiful hazel gaze intense. 'Not really, but over my dead body will Hitler make me falter. I have too many plans for myself and this world to let that maniac take it all away before I've even started.'

Veronica frowned. 'Take all what away? Right now, I'm scared to think past today.'

Betty abruptly gripped Veronica's hand and she swallowed against the sensation the skin-to-skin contact with the anaesthetist evoked.

'Plans for *women*, V,' Betty said urgently. 'Plans for us to really live as we choose, to work in the jobs we choose. We can't let the good work of the women who came before us go to waste. There is still so much to do.'

The excitement she always felt around Betty surfaced again and despite the anarchy going on all around them, Veronica smiled. 'You never stop, do you?'

'Of course not.' Betty flashed a smile, making Veronica's stomach loop the loop. 'War or no war, we have to fight for the right to live as we choose. It's barely been fourteen years since we got the Vote. Everything takes a long time and God knows this war will put things back for a while, and that's only right.' Her eyes glittered with hardened determination. 'But once the dust settles and Hitler is six feet under, we have to resume fighting for whatever we want to happen next.'

'Hear, hear,' Veronica said, before purposefully dragging her gaze from Betty's. 'But right now, we should get a move on.'

Confused by her attraction to Betty as she had been a hundred times before, Veronica led the way to her mother's ward, which was situated just along the corridor from the ward where Veronica usually worked with Freda and Sylvia. The doors stood wide open, and bloodied and bandaged patients – many staring blindly ahead in dazed shock – sat on beds and in wheelchairs while others hobbled, with the aid of crutches and nurses, towards the stairwell. Veronica inhaled a strengthening breath and entered the ward, Betty close behind her.

'Mum?'

Her mother turned, her usually pristine uniform dirty and streaked with blood, her cap gone and her face pale. 'Oh, Veronica. Thank God you're all right.'

They briefly hugged, her mother's green eyes glistening with unshed tears before she flashed a weak smile. 'Are you here to help? We have so many more patients to move downstairs. Has Sister Dyer managed to empty your ward already?'

'I have no idea, and I'm not here to help you, unfortunately. I've been sent by Mr Martin for as many medical supplies as you can spare.'

'Spare medical supplies?' Her mother huffed a laugh and stood a little taller, her previous worry vanishing. 'You can take what you can find in the cabinet over there,' she said, pointing to a corner of the ward. 'But nothing more. I understand surgery will soon be under insurmountable pressure, Veronica, but so will the nurses.'

Veronica turned to Betty and tilted her head in the direction of the cabinet. Betty nodded and hurried away, leaving Veronica alone with her mother. 'I'm going to be assisting Mr Martin for the duration, Mum, but I'll come and see you again soon.' She squeezed her mother's hand. 'In the meantime, let's try not to worry about each other when we have so many patients relying on us, all right?'

Fresh tears flickered on her mother's lashes before she wiped them away with slightly trembling fingers. 'I love you, Veronica.

With all my heart. I don't know where I'd be without you. I really don't.'

A lump rose in Veronica's throat as habitual guilt loomed large once again. Her mother had no idea that she was saving every spare penny she had so she could move out of the home they shared together; no idea that all she wanted was to find a place of her own, far away from the street where they lived. That desire had not been provoked in any part by the need to escape her mother, but all because of the evil animal living a few doors down their street with his wife and three daughters. Mark Riley, the middle-aged neighbour who had raped her – in her own home – almost five years before. An evil, vile man who remained on their street without a care in the world.

'Veronica?'

She started and turned.

Her mother frowned. 'What is it?'

Veronica forced a smile. 'Nothing. I love you, too.'

'Are you sure you're all right? Only—'

'I'll see you later, Mum.'

Betty came up beside her, her hands full of boxes and bags of medical supplies. 'Ready?'

Veronica nodded and they left the ward, Betty heading back to surgery as Veronica strode along the corridor to speak to Sister Dyer. Her mother could never know that Mark Riley had raped her. Not ever. It would kill her.

8

FREDA

Freda gently eased a cushion between the shoulder and cheek of a sleeping patient as he dozed awkwardly on a chair in one of the basement wards, and then she looked towards one of the intact windows. Every time she walked past one of the hospital's shattered windows on the upper floors, the groans, screams and panic of men, women and children filtered through from Bath's devastated streets. Was Officer Matthews right and the enemy would return, refuelled and ready to finish what they'd started?

As thoughts of her family and Richard rose in her heart and mind, Freda battled to push them away and looked around to see who she could attend to next.

'Nurse Parkes,' Sister Dyer said as she marched towards her, her face set. 'A word, please.'

Freda pulled back her shoulders. The last thing she needed was to give the sister reason to start nitpicking at her, as she was often prone to do with Freda and the other nurses when the mood struck her.

'Yes, Sister?'

Sister Dyer looked about her, her usually ruddy cheeks pale.

'I have something to ask of you,' she said. 'Something you have every right to refuse to do and I will think none the less of you if you do.'

Intrigued, Freda frowned. 'What is it?'

The sister inhaled a long breath and as she faced Freda, slowly released it as though struggling with what she was about to say. 'Would you be willing to go outside of the hospital, Nurse Parkes? Onto the streets?'

'Outside?' Freda's heart picked up speed as what was almost certainly misplaced excitement simmered deep inside her. 'Well, yes. Of course. But why—'

'Nurse Campbell came to me earlier and asked for as many supplies as the nursing wards can spare for use in surgery. I think it would be beneficial to get some idea of just how bad things are out there.' Her grey eyes shadowed with worry. 'So many of the servicemen on the ward are adamant we've not seen the last of the Germans. They predict another attack is imminent, that they have merely disappeared to refuel and' – the skin at her neck shifted as she swallowed, her gaze wandering to the window – 'reload.'

Freda glanced across the ward at Officer Matthews where he lay on a bed in the far corner, his face turned towards the wall. 'Yes, Officer Matthews said much the same to me a while ago.'

'So it will be good for us to have an idea of what we could be dealing with over the next few hours. I have every confidence in the workers at the first aid posts, not to mention the women volunteers doing what they can, but it's up to us to do everything in between what they can do and what the surgeons can do.'

'All we can do is hope that some of the ambulance drivers will take into account the size of this hospital compared with the Royal United and take most of the severely injured there rather than here.'

'Indeed, and if you can tell as many first aiders and volunteers exactly that, all the better. What do you say, Nurse Parkes? Are you willing to go outside and find out what you can?'

Adrenaline seeped into Freda's veins and she stood a little taller, feeling as though she was about to step into battle, her heart swelling with pride – with daring. 'Absolutely.'

'Good.' Relief lowered the sister's shoulders as she touched Freda's arm. 'Come and find me upon your return, but no heroics while you're out there. Do you understand? This is purely information gathering. I want you safely back here as soon as possible.'

'Yes, Sister.'

Nurse Dyer's concerned gaze lingered on Freda's before she gave a firm nod. 'Then off you go.'

Freda turned and made for the ward exit, the cries and screams outside no longer shrouding her in shame and guilt that she was in the hospital relatively safe and uninjured, but instead igniting her courage and providing a powerful incentive to stand alongside them. She made her way upstairs, nodding at nurses she knew and silently praying she didn't bump into Sylvia. She might be the protector in their friendship trio, but the raid had shaken her, and shaken her badly. That had been plain to see on every inch of her friend's face and in her demeanour, and Sylvia would not be happy about her leaving the safety of the hospital.

Freda entered the staffroom and shock brought her to a standstill. 'My God...'

The single window in the staffroom had been blown inwards and glass strewed the dark brown carpet, the curtains either side shredded and hanging in limp strips. Half a dozen of the lockers either side of the window lay on their sides or face down, bent and misshapen. Thick dust covered the upturned tables and chairs, and nurses' personal belongings were scattered everywhere, amongst the crockery and cutlery that had evidently spilled from the open cupboards and drawers in the small tea-making area.

Freda stepped over the debris towards her own locker that, by some miracle, had escaped undamaged. She grabbed her coat and quickly buttoned it, slung her gas mask over her shoulder and slid a torch from the top shelf. Fear dared to skitter along her spine, and Freda muttered a curse as she tightly gripped the torch, Prime Minister Churchill's speech of almost two years before echoing in her mind...

We shall go on to the end... We shall defend our Island, whatever the cost may be...

'Do your worst, Hitler,' she whispered. 'Britain will still be standing come the end.'

Battling the treacherous tears that pricked her eyes, Freda hurried from the staffroom, down the stairs and along one corridor after another, thankful they still had power. Eventually, she reached the main entrance doors.

The scope of fire throughout the city meant the sky was lit close to daylight. Shades of bright orange and yellow flickered and glowed, interspersed with wisps of grey-black cloud. Upper Borough Walls, the street where the hospital was situated, was narrow and cobbled, the buildings either side three or four storeys high, flames dancing ominously from the roofs of some, others seemingly untouched. People with faces blackened and streaked with smoke and dust ran back and forth along the street, some hobbling and bleeding, their arms around each other, their heads bowed, their clothes filthy with grit and grime. Unsure where to head first, Freda forced her shock and fear into submission and strode into the fray.

Surely the Germans would have focused on the industrial area near the river? But that was quite a distance from the hospital. The sister would want to know what was happening in the surrounding streets close by. The people likely to want their medical help. Once again, her family and Richard flitted into Freda's mind. Were they all right? Had they made it to a shelter? Was her street intact? Her house? The newspaper office? She was quite sure it had been gone eleven o'clock when the raid struck hours before so it was unlikely Richard would have been there when the attack started, but…

Fighting against the panic building inside her, Freda firmly put one foot in front of the other, taking in as much as she could. She would go towards Gay Street and the Circus beyond. Speak to the public and workers along the way to gauge the depth of injuries – both physical and mental – and try to ascertain what the servicemen and women thought would happen next. There was little else she could do but follow the sister's instructions and gather information. But when she reached the bottom of Gay Street, she was deflected around Queen Square where several houses were in flames, people crying and wailing. Fire hoses ran like tangled snakes along the pavement, people operating static pumps and doing what they could to douse the flames.

Freda stopped the first WVS volunteer she came across, a woman in her mid-twenties, the whites of her eyes bright against her dirty face.

'Do you know which areas are the worst hit?' Freda asked. 'Are you and the other volunteers managing?'

'I wouldn't say we're managing.' The woman continued to scan the anarchy around them rather than look at Freda. 'But we're doing our best. The ambulance drivers are trying to take as many injured as possible out of the city to the Royal United, and the Women's Voluntary Service are opening their homes and other buildings where we can offer support and care for shock even if we can't do a lot medically.'

'Well, that's amazing to hear. I'm a nurse working at Upper Borough Hospital and have been sent out in the hope of gaining some idea of what is on the way to us. You have given me hope that we will cope with whatever comes our way.'

The woman didn't offer as much as a smile, her gaze far from impressed or reassured. 'Well, good for you, Nurse. I hope you're right.'

Freda opened her mouth to apologise for how nonchalant she must sound, but the woman had already jogged away. 'Damnation.'

Stepping up her pace, Freda shouldered her way through the throng of people that flowed past her. Why were so many on the streets and not at the shelters? Were the public really that confident that Bath wouldn't be hit again?

'Freda! Freda!'

She spun around and was whipped into the circle of two strong arms. She gasped as the breath was stolen from her lungs. 'Richard! Oh, thank God.' Tears leapt into her eyes as she stared into his smiling face. 'Are you all right?'

'I'm fine.' He grinned, his beautiful blue gaze darting over her face. 'You?'

'I'm as well as I can be.'

'What are you doing out here?' He looked at her uniform through the gap in her open coat. 'Why aren't you at the hospital?'

'Sister sent me outside to see what was happening.'

'I see.' His smile faltered and he frowned. 'I suppose that makes sense, but is it wrong of me to wish she'd chosen someone else?'

Freda smiled. 'No, it's sweet of you, but I'm glad she chose me.'

He laughed. 'Yes, I imagine you are considering your contributions to the paper.'

'I'm never one to shy away from trouble, you know that.'

'Indeed, I do.'

They stepped back as a couple each carrying boxes of belongings barged past them and Richard clasped her elbow. 'It's fortuitous I came across you.'

'Oh?'

They both flinched and ducked as an explosion sounded not too far away, followed by screams and cries that chilled Freda's blood.

'We should get moving,' Richard said, staring along the street before meeting her eyes. 'But before we do, I should tell you that William, the *Chronicle*'s intrepid editor' – he winked – 'is already assigning the staff writers pieces he wants written about the raids and he hoped you might consider writing an article from the point of view of a nurse at the hospital.'

'No, Richard.' Freda shook her head. 'The last thing I can think about is submitting an article to the paper right now. The suffering is too much. I'm sorry.'

'Of course.' He blew out a breath. 'I shouldn't have asked.'

A moment's awkward silence hovered between them before Richard spoke again.

'William and I were working late tonight, and we strode straight into the thick of things as soon as the first incendiary bombs were dropped, but God only knows where he is now.'

'But that was so late,' Freda said. 'I assumed you were at home.'

'Not tonight. Both of us were convinced something would happen in the city either tonight or tomorrow.'

Humbled and in complete admiration of his journalistic instinct that she knew had been proven accurate time and time again, Freda almost wished she hadn't come to care for him as she had. She didn't want to think about love, men or relationships. In her experience, romance too often led to subservience for women and little else. She had not given Richard any indication of how she viewed their relationship, never clarified the depth of her decidedly changeable feelings. And she wouldn't, not yet. Not when everything in her heart was so uncertain.

'And what about Barbara?' she asked, suddenly concerned for the paper's secretary. 'Please tell me she wasn't at the office too?'

'No, she went home hours ago, before the raid.'

'Thank goodness. Well, let's hope she's with her family and somewhere safe.'

'I'd better go,' Richard said, gently cupping her face in his hands, his gaze concentrated as though checking her for injury. 'I'm so glad you're all right. I'll see you soon.'

He hesitated before kissing her with such intensity, her knees turned treacherously weak.

And then he was gone.

Less than fifteen minutes later, the city's air raid sirens split through the air, screeching their warning once again, and Freda ran back to the hospital.

9

SYLVIA

Sylvia threw herself across Mrs Golding and did her utmost to protect the poor woman's head without smothering her where she lay on a gurney in one of the basement wards.

'It's all right,' Sylvia yelled as a series of explosions shook the whole building. 'Hitler clearly thinks it's time he reacquainted himself with Bath, that's all. He won't get the better of us.'

Hoping Mrs Golding had heard her words, and that they went some way to bolstering her courage, Sylvia squeezed her body more tightly around her and counted the seconds, trying to stop her panicked heart from beating out of her chest.

Boom!

Boom!

One after the other, bombs exploded followed by machine-gun fire and the most godawful screaming and crying that Sylvia swore would never leave her consciousness for however long she lived. Just as so many of the officers on the ward had predicted, the Germans had returned, and it seemed this attack would put the first well and truly in its place. Sylvia fought her trembling, and not just because of the raid, but more her fear that she was not up to the job being Sister Dyer's second-in-command demanded. She had felt so confident and in control until the first raid hit, but since then nothing but a horrible incompetence rankled.

Boom!

Boom!

For the love of God, woman. Pull yourself together!

Carefully lifting herself off of Mrs Golding, Sylvia looked into the woman's terrified eyes. 'You all right?'

The woman nodded, her entire body shaking.

Sylvia squeezed her hand. As much as she wanted to comfort her, she could not possibly stay with one patient when there were forty or fifty others throughout the wards who needed looking after – not to mention the injured men, women and children who would be arriving at the hospital by ambulance or walked into the hospital by the voluntary first aiders.

'I'm going to have to leave you, Mrs Golding,' she yelled as machine-gun fire sounded along the south wall. 'The shock of another attack is making us a little jumpy, but you'll be safe enough down here in the basement, I promise.'

Mrs Golding squeezed her eyes shut and curled into the foetal position. 'Just go, Nurse. I've very little left to live for anyway.'

Sylvia continued to stare at Mrs Golding as helplessness gripped like a vice around her heart. How was she supposed to argue with her when the poor woman had lost her husband and three children, all under the age of ten, to this bloody war?

She swallowed past the lump in her throat. 'I'll be back to check on you as soon as I can.'

Making her way around the ward, Sylvia reassured as many patients as she could, encouraging the other nurses to do the same. There was no sign of Sister Dyer, which meant – for the time being – the buck stopped with Sylvia as far as supervising the nurses and overseeing patient care was concerned.

'Christ,' she muttered, 'what I wouldn't do for a drink right now.'

The ward hummed with low murmuring, or high-pitched cries depending on how close to the hospital the bombs landed. How was she supposed to keep everyone calm when her own heart was thundering, her nerves stretched so tight she swore they would snap any minute? She had to get herself together; had to find some way to bury the new cowardice that had emerged and taken up residence inside her.

She looked around her and blinked back tears as Jesse's face appeared in her mind's eye. Was he alive? Was he glad he'd signed up? God, she'd give anything to speak to him again, but the reality was, Jesse Howard was just another man she had allowed herself to fall in love with, and he'd chosen to leave rather than stay close to her.

Yeah, because you told him to forget about you! It's your fault Jesse left and put himself on the front lines. Yours.

Jesse Howard. A man she had fallen for but had been too afraid to give a second chance.

Jesse Howard. A man with eyes like melted chocolate and shoulders as wide as an army truck.

Jesse Howard. A man she hadn't introduced to her friends because she didn't trust that they wouldn't reject him because of the colour of his skin.

Sylvia Roberts. Coward. Sceptic. Cynic.

Surely Freda and Veronica would have loved Jesse? They wouldn't have cared if he was black, white or turquoise. And now they might never meet him, and she might never see him again.

No. She couldn't think that way.

When Bath was free of attack, once their lives were back on

as much of an even keel as possible under the circumstances, she would tell Freda and Veronica all about Jesse. From the colour of his skin to the way she felt about him. She had to. God knew the man deserved to be hailed for the glorious human being he was and all the love he had given her when she'd allowed him to.

'Nurse?'

Officer Matthews's croak broke through her thoughts and Sylvia strode to his bedside, quickly wiping the dampness from her eyes with her fingers. 'What is it, Officer?' she asked, gently placing her hand on his forearm. 'Are you all right?'

'This is going to be a bad one,' he said, nodding towards the windows. 'The Germans planned for things to play out like this, and they won't leave until they've made their point.'

'I'm sure you know more about strategy than me,' she said, flinching as a huge explosion sounded in the distance. 'But we'll see it through.'

'We'll fare well enough down here, but what about the poor bastards outside? Do you realise this will be nothing less than a civilian massacre? Bath doesn't even have anti-aircraft protection in place.' His manic gaze burned into hers from between the two-inch gap in the bandages around his head. He shook her hand from his arm and tightly gripped her fingers. 'Is Nurse Campbell still in surgery?'

Her concern about Veronica's relationship with the officer rose once again. The unmistakable protectiveness – love? – in the officer's voice couldn't be mistaken. 'She is, but don't worry. Nurse Campbell is the strongest, most resilient—'

'You don't need to tell me that!' he spat. 'I know just how damn strong that woman is.'

Sylvia stiffened. The entire nursing staff had got used to Officer Matthews's snappishness, but the conviction in his tone sent warning tip-tapping along her spine. How did he know how strong her friend was? Had V told him about her being raped? Surely not. She locked her gaze on his and they silently challenged one another. Over what, she had no idea, but if Veronica had shared the most traumatic event of her life with this man, things had dangerously deepened between them. Was her friend emotionally – romantically – involved with him without even seeing Officer Matthews's face? She wouldn't put such a possibility past her sensitive and thoughtful friend, but...

'You need to change my bandages before she does.' Officer Matthews tightened his grip on her hand, seeming suddenly heedless to the bombardment outside the hospital walls and the undercurrent of fear emanating from the eerily quiet patients surrounding them. 'Nurse Campbell cannot be allowed to do it. Tell me you'll ensure that doesn't happen, Nurse Roberts.' Tears glinted in his eyes. 'Please.'

Please? Sylvia had barely heard the man use a polite word to anyone. Ever. What in God's name was going on between him and V?

She needed to move, help someone else, yet Officer Matthews had stolen her entire attention. She loved the bones of Freda. Her friend was her strength and ally. But Veronica was the one Sylvia felt an innate need to look out for and, right now, Officer Matthews was making her incredibly uneasy.

'Why?' she demanded, pulling back her shoulders and holding his unwavering stare. 'Why don't you want Nurse Campbell to change your bandages?'

A single tear seeped from his eye and Sylvia fought to hide her shock and keep the usually standoffish officer talking. 'Well?'

'She can't know who I am,' he said quietly. 'Please, Nurse Roberts. Promise me.'

Sylvia pulled her hand from his, distrust rearing up inside her as she crossed her arms. 'Once you've told me why she can't know who you are, I'll tell you whether or not I can promise anything. How can you be so certain she doesn't know exactly who you are? How can she not have recognised your eyes, your voice or name in the weeks you've been here?'

His Adam's apple bobbed once, twice as Sylvia's heart thudded in her ears, but she remained rooted to the spot, her entire body rigid with tension.

'I don't know, but I thank God every day that she hasn't. If she did...' He squeezed his eyes shut and another tear rolled over his cheek. He cleared his throat. 'Look, please, will you just change my bandages as I've asked?'

'Not until you tell me why you've insisted over and over again that Nurse Campbell doesn't.'

'Because I can't risk sparking her memory, that's why.'

'About what? What are you talking about?'

His chest rose as he inhaled, his eyes so scarily sad on hers. 'I found her.'

The way he said those three little words sent fear inexplicably skittering along her spine. 'What?'

'It was me who found Nurse Campbell after... something happened, but she can never know. It will ruin everything.'

'You found her after something happened?' Sylvia dropped her arms and frowned. Even though bombs continued to fall, glass smashing and Bath's people running for cover, she could not see or hear anything but Officer Matthews. Then the worst possibility of what he was implying entered her head and stayed there. 'You mean you found her on... *that* day?'

His gaze held hers, his lips a thin, tight line.

She released her held breath. 'Oh, this is not good. Not good at all...'

10

FREDA

Freda hurried downstairs to the basement wards, her heart pounding and adrenaline rushing through her blood. She scanned the panicked and stricken faces of patients and nurses alike as she sought Sister Dyer amongst the commotion. She needed to tell her all she had seen and heard. The information she had gathered might at least go some way to helping the sister decide how best to organise the nursing staff going forward, even if there was little they could do in way of predicting how long this raid would last.

Finally spotting the sister hauling and stacking boxes of bandages and dressings at the entrance to one of the wards, Freda quickly approached her. 'Sister?'

Sister Dyer straightened, the fine lines around her grey eyes prominent with exhaustion. 'Ah, Nurse Parkes. How is it out there?'

'Terrible, if I'm honest.'

The sister fisted her hands on her hips. 'Tell me.'

'The volunteers, firemen and first aiders are working like

absolute troopers, but I'd be lying if I told you it was anything less than complete terror for most out there, Sister. Bombs exploding, shrapnel flying in every direction, homes flattened.'

'My God.'

Freda tucked some fallen hair behind her ear, willing some of the bravery she had witnessed outside into herself and the sister. 'It isn't too bad around the hospital. It seems the Germans are concentrating on the industrial area by the river so I can't even imagine how the poor people living in the slums down there are coping. Access to Gay Street and the Circus beyond is cut off, so I have no idea what is happening around those areas, but I'm sure it's not good.'

Sister Dyer darted glances left and right along the corridor, her brow deeply furrowed. 'We will continue as we are on the wards for now, but make sure we support surgery and Mr Martin as much as possible. As head surgeon, he will be the one under the most pressure soon enough.'

'I did my best to speak to as many ambulance staff and first aiders as I could and told them to head to the Royal United with the injured if possible. I explained we won't have the United's capacity to take in many more people, but the panic is rife, Sister. I have no idea how many of those workers actually listened to me, and I can't say I blame them.'

'No, of course not. Those poor souls will be doing what they can despite witnessing pain and trauma like they've never seen before.' She hesitated, her fearful gaze on Freda's. 'Like any of us have never seen before.'

Freda fought the tiredness bearing down on her; tried to remain unaffected by the sister's unfamiliar compassion. She could not falter. Even though everyone was praying this raid wouldn't last as long as the first, it was already proving much more intense and the damage and loss of life would be so much worse, just as the Germans intended.

She stared at the ward entrance. 'Is Nurse Campbell with Mr Martin? Does he need more nursing staff? Only, I have helped out surgery in the past, but I'm by no means as experienced as Nurse Campbell, of course.'

'I haven't heard from Mr Martin for a while,' Sister Dyer said. 'So until I do, I will keep my staff here. There's so much upset and unease among the patients we have throughout the basement wards and when I last looked, comfort and reassuring those who are suffering is still the job of a nurse.'

'Then I'll go and find where I am needed, Sister.'

Freda entered the ward, but barely had a moment to get a handle on the commotion when Sylvia tightly gripped her elbow. 'I need a word.'

'You're hurting me, Sylv,' Freda admonished, pulling her arm from her friend's fingers. 'What is it?'

'It's V.'

'V?' Immediately concerned, Freda looked around the ward. 'What's wrong with her? Sister just told me she's with Mr Martin.'

'This isn't about work,' Sylvia said, her brown eyes wide with undisguised concern. 'This is about something much worse.'

'Worse than us trying to do our jobs in the middle of enemy attack?' Freda huffed a laugh, disbelief twisting inside her. 'I think you should step outside if you think whatever is going on with V is worse—'

'Officer Matthews was the one who found her after she was raped.'

The floor seemed to tip beneath Freda's feet. Had a real bomb dropped rather than the metaphorical one that had just come out of Sylvia's mouth?

'What?'

'Officer Matthews was the first person to see her after the rape,' Sylvia said quietly. 'Don't you see? It must have been him who V was talking about when she told us she thinks she remembers someone talking to her after the attack but couldn't be sure if she imagined it.'

'But that's impossible.' Freda looked at Officer Matthews where he was sat up on his bed, and her heart leapt into her throat to see him intensely studying her and Sylvia. 'He's staring straight at us.'

Sylvia promptly turned in the officer's direction. 'So what if he is?' she said, holding his stare. 'I am so damn angry that he's been here all this time and not had the decency to tell V who he is.' She faced Freda, her cheeks mottled with annoyance. 'How is she going to feel when she finds out she's been talking to and caring for the man, when he's known about the worst time in her life the entire time? She's going to be mortified.'

'Oh, poor V,' Freda said, care for her friend knotting her stomach. 'This will break her. What with the bombing and her dealing with God only knows what in surgery.'

'Break her? Over my dead body.' Sylvia winced. 'Sorry, I shouldn't have said that when so many... What are we going to do? We have to tell her.'

Boom!

Boom!

Freda gripped Sylvia's arm as they both ducked, an explosion resounding around them. 'I suggest we get through this raid before we do anything,' she said, straightening. 'Who knows how long it will be before we're allowed to leave the hospital, and Veronica will be absolutely exhausted whenever that might be. This is not the time to tell her. We need her to be calm... strong.'

'But we can't keep it from her. She's our best—'

'Talking about Nurse Campbell, by any chance?' Kathy Scott sidled up beside them, her hazel eyes alight with interest. 'What are you keeping from her? I thought I had the sole privilege of being kept out of the loop as far as you two are concerned.'

'For good reason...' Sylvia muttered, her eyes shooting daggers at Kathy. 'Why don't you mind your beeswax and get on with your work?'

'Don't you think that's what you should be doing? Especially as *senior* ward nurse,' Kathy sneered. 'It wouldn't do to have someone tell Sister how you two are standing around whispering and keeping secrets when the whole city is on fire. Shame on you.' She glared at each of them in turn. 'Both of you.'

Sylvia stepped forward. 'Do you know something—'

'Let me deal with this, Sylv,' Freda said, deftly sweeping between her friend and Kathy as the two nemeses locked horns – or eyes. 'I can show Nurse Scott what needs to be done next.'

A few tense seconds passed before Sylvia emitted a rather inelegant snort and strode away.

Hackles raised, Freda immediately turned on Kathy. 'What is the matter with you?' She jumped as another explosion sounded. 'You can see we are in the midst of the worst thing ever to happen to Bath and still you're finding ways to rile Sylvia. Why can't you just leave her be?' Kathy opened her mouth to respond, her eyes flashing with anger, but Freda raised her hand, cutting her off. 'I don't want to hear it, and God help you if I find out Veronica has got wind of me and Sylvia talking. I won't be held responsible for my actions if you're the reason for upsetting her. There's only one person out of me, you and Sylvia who can tell her, so be warned. Now—'

'You really think I care about what you two were talking about?' Kathy gave a wry laugh. 'I only came over here to talk to you because Sister said you'd been outside.'

Freda crossed her arms. 'And?'

'And one, I wanted to make sure you were all right, and two, I wanted to ask if you know the state of Kingsmead. Do you know if the houses there have been hit?'

Ashamed that she'd assumed Kathy's motives for interrupting her and Sylvia were most likely steeped in troublemaking, Freda closed her eyes. Even Kathy wouldn't stoop that low considering what was going on around them.

'Sorry.' Freda opened her eyes. 'And I'm fine, thank you, but it's horrendous outside and I won't tell anyone differently. I know Kingsmead has been quite severely hit. Why do you ask? Do you know someone who—'

'My house is on Kingsmead Street, opposite the school. The likelihood is my parents are still at home. Dad doesn't see the point in using the shelters. Well, he didn't until now maybe.'

'Oh, Kathy...' Freda touched Kathy's arm, sympathy twisting inside her. 'I'm so sorry. Someone told me the bombing there was—'

'I hope most people survived. But truthfully? I hope our house is flattened. Destroyed.' Her eyes flashed with undisguised hatred. 'My mother and father with it.'

Shocked, Freda sucked in a breath and stepped back, struggling with the complete and utter venom with which Kathy had spat the words. But before Freda could find her voice to respond, Kathy turned on her heel and walked away, her chin high and her stride long.

Freda stared after her. What on earth had Kathy's parents done to deserve such loathing from their daughter? Their only child, as far as Freda knew.

'Kathy!' Freda shouted. 'Kathy!'

But the other nurse had rounded the corner and was out of sight. Freda slumped her shoulders. Maybe there was a reason why Kathy was always so nasty and impossible, and maybe Freda and her friends should have taken the time to find out what that reason was before now? Vowing to do something about that sooner rather than later, Freda made for the staffroom to store her hat and coat before returning to her duties. War waited for no one.

11

VERONICA

Veronica wiped the perspiration from her forehead with the back of her hand and stood back. She had finished stitching up an unidentified man who had been brought in with a large piece of metal embedded in his leg and screaming with the horror of it before he passed out. For the last hour, she, Mr Martin and Betty had been working in their usual, perfected synchronisation and now they had done all they could for the poor man whose name they did not know.

'He'll do well enough until we can get him transferred to the United,' Mr Martin said as he re-entered the surgery having cleaned himself up in the washroom next door. 'I'm going to go to the ambulance bay and speak to whatever drivers are there. I won't be doing any more complex surgeries unless absolutely necessary. Not during this raid. It's too time consuming when I could see to ten other cases to every one patient needing surgery. I hate having to make that decision, but it must be the way of it for the time being.'

Veronica exchanged a look with Betty, both of them equally alarmed by the surgeon's obvious exhaustion. Yet beneath the exhaustion, Mr Martin remained calm, his professional conviction to do what he must while Bath was under fire steadfast. Every day Veronica felt more and more honoured to be learning new skills under Mr Martin's tutelage, but working with him during the raids exponentially increased her admiration for the surgeon.

He planted his hands on his hips, his brow creased. 'Once I've spoken to the drivers, I'll go outside and assess the incoming before I telephone my contacts in Bristol and see if there is any more they can do to help.' Mr Martin rubbed his hand over his face, blew out a breath. 'Bath has helped Bristol a lot over the last few months. I can only hope they can spare some of their resources for a while.' He started to walk towards the door and then stopped. He frowned at Veronica and then Betty. 'It's been a while since I've heard an explosion. How about you?'

Veronica realised he was right. She lifted her watch. It was almost six o'clock. 'Do you think that's it? It's only been two hours. Surely they're not done with Bath yet. Then again, they could be back again at nightfall.'

'It feels impossible Hitler's finished with us,' Betty said, but her hazel eyes shone with hope. 'Doesn't it?'

'Who knows?' Mr Martin said, a muscle flexing and relaxing in his jaw. 'Whatever happens in the next hours and days as far as the enemy is concerned is out of our control. All we can do is react.' He nodded at the operating table. 'Take this chap to one of the basement wards for safety. Then I want you both back in surgery. When I get back, I'll know exactly how I want surgery running going forward. All right?'

Veronica and Betty nodded and then Mr Martin swept from the theatre leaving them alone.

'We must do as much as we can before dusk. This morning's raid came before five,' Veronica said, laying a bedsheet over their patient as Betty began checking his vitals before they prepared to move him. 'I'm sure if the Germans strike again, it will be after dark tonight.'

'Have you managed to check on your family yet?'

'My family only consists of me and my mother, and she's fine. What about you?'

'It's just me and Mum, too.' Betty's eyes shadowed with worry and tiredness. 'But I have no idea how she is.'

Veronica fought the urge to take Betty into her arms. 'I'm sure she'll be fine, too.'

'I hope so.' Betty resumed her task of methodically removing various equipment attached to their patient, every piece of which entirely befuddled Veronica. 'Your mother oversees one of the wards upstairs, doesn't she?'

'Yes, and she was all right when I saw her a few hours ago, but I'll go and see her again as soon as I can. For the time being though, our patients take priority. Are you ready?'

'As I'll ever be.'

Veronica backed out of the theatre and she and Betty walked the gurney along a narrow corridor into the main corridor. Momentary silence fell between them, both lost in their own thoughts. Trepidation sped Veronica's heart as her mind drifted to her mother, Freda and Sylvia... to Officer Matthews. She cared about them all so much, yet even with the bombing seemingly stopped for now, she felt a sudden and overwhelming fear of dying without having really lived at all. She had wasted so much time since she was raped. Mark Riley had stolen so much more than her virginity from her; he had made her doubt every decision she'd made from that day forwards, meaning she'd avoided making any significant changes to her life since.

Apart from the decision to trust Freda and Sylvia; that had been the best decision of her entire life.

She and Betty entered the lift and Betty pushed the button for the basement floor. Mr Martin hadn't let them use the lifts during the raids, which was why there were at least five patients lying in beds on the surgery floor that would now need moving downstairs. Veronica glanced at the lift ceiling. Hopefully they wouldn't get stuck now the bombing had stopped.

'Life can be over in a heartbeat, can't it?'

Veronica met Betty's sombre gaze. 'Hmm?'

Betty lifted her shoulders. 'I mean, look at us.'

Us? Veronica swallowed. 'What about us?'

'We haven't even had time to get to know each other properly yet.'

Veronica huffed a nervous laugh. 'Why do you think that?'

'Don't you agree?' Betty frowned, her gaze unwavering on Veronica's. 'We've worked together for a while, but we've not really spent time getting to know one another. Loss of time is so bloody terrifying. After all, our time could be up, just like that.' She snapped her fingers.

'I was just thinking the same thing. Albeit wasting time rather than losing it altogether.' Veronica studied her, looking for something in Betty's eyes – although she had no real idea what. She slumped, struggling to pull her eyes from Betty's. She really was very pretty. 'It's criminal really when you think about how many people have died all over Europe during this war.'

'Exactly. Which is why…' Betty paused and raised her eyebrows. 'If – no, *when* we get through these stupid raids, I'd like us to go out somewhere. Just you and me. Have some fun.' Betty flashed a smile that sent Veronica's stomach into the most inexplicable knots. 'What do you say?'

Self-doubt and loathing immediately descended as Veronica's mouth dried. Go out with Betty? Could she? *Should* she? It was a bad idea, one she was bound to regret. Yet…

'Veronica? What do you say? Do you want to go out with me?'

Veronica swallowed. 'Um... I... We...'

Betty grinned. 'What's the matter? I'm not asking you to dance the fandango onstage at the Theatre Royal! We could go for a few drinks. Have a bite to eat. Come on, V. Say yes. God knows, we only live once. Right?'

Was Betty asking her out as a friend? Something more? Veronica swallowed again. *Why on earth am I asking myself such stupid questions?* 'I...' *Come on, Veronica, time is a-wasting.* 'Yes, all right then. Why not?' She forced a smile to hide the nerves leaping and jumping in her stomach. 'I'd love to.'

'Fabulous.' Betty squeezed Veronica's arm as the lift came to a stop and the doors opened. 'As soon as these raids are over, you and I, Nurse Campbell, are going to paint the town red.'

But as soon as Betty looked away and concentrated on moving the gurney out of the lift, Veronica's smile faltered. What had she just agreed to? Would she never learn? Going out with Betty would only end in disaster.

Doesn't every decision I make on my own go the same way?

12

FREDA

The all-clear siren sounded across the city and Freda pocketed her pen and notebook, smiling as cheers and jubilant applause broke out amongst the patients and nurses. Even though she'd told Richard she wouldn't be submitting anything to the *Chronicle* any time soon, it was hard not to jot down notes about the goings-on in the hospital during a time that would remain in history forever. Yet as much as everyone celebrated, she had no doubt their minds would immediately turn to the safety of their families and friends. Just as hers had. Continuing in the task she should've been concentrating on rather than hastily writing, Freda grabbed another blanket from a nearby cupboard and added it to her pile. For the time being at least, the imminent threat from Germany was over and that was something they could all hold on to for as long as it lasted.

A heavy exhaustion pressed down on her, and Freda purposefully straightened her spine. None of them could trust that Hitler would allow them much breathing space. She knew well enough through her work for the hospital and her reporting at the *Chronicle* that the dictator had not granted Bristol any respite from attack for weeks on end, so why would he for the people of Bath after less than twenty-four hours?

'Nurses, can I have your attention, please?'

Putting the blankets on the foot of a bed, Freda walked closer to Sister Dyer where she stood atop a chair. Sylvia stood beside her, her face grave as she swept her eyes back and forth over the assembled nurses. Concern for her friend once more niggled at Freda. Sylvia looked so unusually pale and unsure of herself. Her shadowed gaze and the high set of her shoulders was the opposite of how her vivacious friend normally looked. Could she be struggling with her new role as senior ward nurse? Something Freda would not have predicted in a million years. Or was it the effects of the raids? Whatever it was making Sylvia doubt herself when she was usually so confident and uncaring of what people thought about her was worrying. Or was it her worry about Veronica and Officer Matthews's confession making Sylvia so ashen?

The sister cleared her throat. 'Right, ladies. First of all, I want to extend my gratitude to all the nurses who have been at the hospital since the first siren sounded late last night. You have all worked phenomenally hard and with complete care to our patients over yourselves.' Her voice cracked and she coughed before pulling back her shoulders. 'So as we now have plenty of nurses arriving ready and willing to take over, I'd like the following nurses to go... home and try to rest for a few hours.'

Freda glanced around her. Sister Dyer clearly hesitated with the realisation that some of them might not even have a home any more.

'I, too, will be leaving for a short time, each of us going home on a rota basis,' Sister Dyer continued. 'But please return to the hospital as soon as you feel able. The nurses who are free to leave first are Carr, Parkes, Roberts, Scott, Taylor...'

The sister's voice drifted as Freda's eyes met Sylvia's and her friend winked, the mischievous glint she loved so much shining in her dark brown eyes. Freda returned her smile. Was she being daft? Seeing something in Sylvia that wasn't there? Surely Sylvia would always be Sylvia? Raid or no raid. War or no war.

'Right then.' Sister Dyer cast her gaze over each of the nurses in turn. 'I wish all of you the best of luck out there and hope to see you back at the hospital later today.'

The implication was clear. What each of them would find once they left the hospital was anyone's guess. Would their homes still be standing? Their loved ones alive?

As the nurses scattered, apprehension swirled inside Freda. She wandered closer until she stood a little distance away from Sylvia where she talked in earnest with the sister, no doubt devising a sketchy plan for their return.

Once they'd finished talking, Sylvia approached Freda and pushed her hand into the crook of her elbow. 'Come on, let's get out of here before anyone has the chance to waylay us.'

'Sounds good to me. I'm so tired, I could just lay down here on the tiled floor and sleep for England.'

They made a whistle-stop to the staffroom, which Freda knew was in partial disarray. Luckily, her, Sylvia and Veronica's lockers were untouched, and she and Sylvia grabbed their coats, hats and bags, each silent in their guilt at being able to do so when others' belongings were ruined. They walked upstairs and out of the hospital's main entrance, their continuing silence speaking volumes when it was usually non-stop chat between them. Their steps slowed when the stone pillars of the hospital entranceway stood ahead of them like a symbol that from that point onwards, there was no telling what each of them would see.

Freda faced Sylvia. 'I hope everything's all right with your mum, Sylv. Would she have gone to a public shelter?'

'God knows. Knowing my mother, she's done the sensible thing and parked herself in the pub's cellar.' She laughed, the sound laced with forced joviality. 'And if that hadn't been an option, she no doubt would have found a way to secure a spot in one of the neighbours' Anderson shelters. Not that she would have been welcomed in all of them.'

'Well, either way, I hope she's all right.' Freda put her arms around Sylvia and squeezed. 'I'll see you back here later. Fingers crossed, V will be allowed a few hours' rest, too. She must be dead...' She grimaced. 'Sorry, on her feet working in surgery for the last few hours. I can only imagine it's absolute hell in hospital theatres all over the city right now.'

They stood back from one another and Sylvia unpinned her cap, stuffed it in her apron pocket. She fluffed out her hair, her brown eyes flashing with determination. 'V will be fine. Especially if we keep what we know about Officer Matthews from her for now, but we'll tell her as soon as the time is right. She'll have more than enough on her plate for the time being.'

'I agree. Officer Matthews and what he knows can wait.'

'Right, then I'll see you back here later. Good luck, Freda. I hope all's well with your family, too.'

Freda stared after Sylvia as her friend walked away. She had been about to mention what Kathy Scott had said about her parents, but then she'd seen the tears in Sylvia's eyes even though she'd tried to hide them. She was definitely taking these raids badly, and memories rose in Freda's mind from a month or so before. Sylvia had been absolutely distraught when Freda had gone to Bristol with Richard to chase a story during a period of severe bombing, and again when Veronica had told them there was a possibility of her working in one of the airfield surgeries at some point. The mere thought of her friends willingly stepping into the breach away from their duties at the hospital had horrified her, and Sylvia had immediately claimed she'd never leave Bath, no matter what. Would that still be the case now that the bombing had come to their city?

Freda breathed deep as confusion mixed with care for Sylvia and she vowed to keep a closer eye on her beloved friend from now on. But, for now, she needed to go home.

It wasn't until she rounded the corner into her street that Freda realised how much dread she had been holding in. Her house and all the others, both sides of her street, were not only still standing but seemingly untouched. Even the windows appeared to be intact.

She smiled and pressed a trembling hand to her heart. 'Thank you, God.'

The bombing had definitely been concentrated in certain areas of the city. The industrial area was understandable, but the apparent devastation inflicted on places like Kingsmead and Oldfield Park made no sense. No doubt all would become clear eventually. There must have been damage to the more elite areas such as Royal Crescent and the Circus, too, but access had been shut off when she'd ventured outside the hospital so she'd had no way of knowing how badly the people there suffered. Freda pulled back her shoulders. For now, though, she couldn't cope with more than knowing how her family fared. She didn't have the heart or head space to think about Richard or anyone else for the time being.

She strode to her front door and hesitated. Suddenly putting her key in the lock felt incredibly poignant when so many citizens in Bath, and over the entirety of Europe, no longer had homes.

Swallowing hard, she entered the house.

'Mum? Dad?' she called as she unbuttoned her coat and hung it on the newel post at the bottom of the stairs along with her shoulder bag. When no answer came, she walked farther into the narrow hallway. 'Dorothy?'

'Freda? Is that you?' her mother cried. 'Oh, thank goodness.'

Freda hurried into the kitchen.

Her mum and Dorothy were sat at the table, their hands tightly clasped, their eyes wide and scared, their faces terribly pale.

'Oh, thank God you're both safe,' Freda said, clasping her arms around each of them and kissing their cheeks. 'Where's Dad?'

'Out there somewhere.' Her mother's voice hitched on a sob. 'I haven't seen him since the first raid. He could be dead, maimed, anything!'

'Mum, please, it's important you keep calm. We have to think positively. Dad is a trained police officer. He stands a better chance than most of keeping himself alive.'

'Not your father. He will put himself in the path of everyone and anyone if it means saving their life.' Her mother shook her head, her eyes red-rimmed and her face pale. 'I can't lose anyone else to this war, Freda. I can't! I have lost one son, the other is still missing with no word from him for months.'

'I know, Mum, I know.' She clasped her mother's hand. 'But you must keep the belief that James is alive. Dad will be fine, too. I'm sure of it.'

She straightened and looked at her sister more closely. Dorothy stared back at her, her eyes shadowed and desolate.

'Dot?' Freda intently studied her. Dorothy didn't look frightened like their mother; she looked strangely... distracted. 'What is it?'

Her sister blinked and then abruptly stood. 'Nothing,' she

said, colour seeping into her cheeks. 'Would you mind making Mum a cup of tea? I'm going upstairs to lie down.'

'Lie down?' her mother exclaimed. 'Lie down? How on earth can you think to do such a thing when your father—'

'Mum, it's fine,' Freda said, smoothing her mother's shoulder, her eyes never leaving Dorothy even as she headed for the door. 'Let Dorothy do what she needs to do. The bombing has terrified us all and we all need to deal with it however we see fit. I'll bring you up a cuppa in a minute too, Dot.' Her sister disappeared into the hallway without answering her and Freda gave her mother another kiss on her cheek. 'I'll be right back.'

She hurried after Dorothy and gently grasped her arm just as she put her foot on the first stair. 'Hey, what's going on?'

'Nothing.'

'You and I both know that's not true. You're acting... I don't know. Strangely.'

Dorothy ran her gaze over Freda's face, a deep, dark sadness filling her eyes as the seconds ticked by.

'I wished it gone, Freda,' she said eventually. 'I wished it had just been blasted out of me.'

A horrible sickness coated Freda's throat, dread burning like a hot coal in the very centre of her chest. 'What are you talking about?'

'The baby!' Dorothy hissed from between clenched teeth. 'I wished the baby dead, and it didn't happen.' She swiped at the single tear that rolled over her cheek. 'Don't you understand anything?'

Dorothy ran up the stairs and Freda stood frozen to the hallway floor, her pulse thumping in her ears as the suspicions she'd had about Dorothy over the last few weeks were proven to be true. She gripped the banister. Pregnant? Her fiancé was serving in France or Italy. Or was it Malta? Well, wherever it was, Robert hadn't been home for months.

Freda closed her eyes and tipped her head back. Her sister was a law unto herself, but pregnant? What in God's name were they going to do now? *Good girls are the best girls.* Their mother's motto echoed in her ears. Freda and Dorothy had barely heard anything else from their mother since they were old enough to walk. Dorothy being pregnant and unmarried – her fiancé out of the country – was more likely to kill her mother than any bomb dropped by Hitler.

13

SYLVIA

The closer Sylvia got to Castle Street, the higher the hairs on the back of her neck stood. Evidence of the bombing showed in the shattered windows, the craters left by machine-gun fire peppering the walls of buildings and the burning debris and bits of furniture looming up from the pavement like lanterns, sickeningly lighting her way.

Her heart pulsed against her ribcage as she gripped the strap of her handbag tightly, her nails cutting into her palms. 'You'd better be safe and well, Mother. I don't want any of your usual bloody carry-on. Not now.'

She stopped at the corner of Castle Street and closed her eyes, shamefully afraid to take the final step into the street she loved and sometimes loathed. For all their faults, the residents of Castle Street were a community – admittedly a community of hard-nosed housewives and a brood of bedraggled, unkempt kids, but still they were there for one another... most of the time. As the war wore on and with the majority of the street's fathers and husbands conscripted, the less the mothers and wives seemed to care about the outward appearance of themselves or their offspring. What they did care about was that their children were fed, warm and as safe as humanly possible, and they did all they could to help one another.

Inhaling a strengthening breath, Sylvia opened her eyes and briskly strode into Castle Street.

'My God...' Hot tears sprang into her eyes even as she broke into a run. 'No, no, no!'

One of the houses on the other side of the street, directly opposite her own house, had been entirely flattened; a house that, months before, had been the home of a man who was now serving his country God only knew where. A man Sylvia believed could have been the love of her life. A man whose mother couldn't stand the sight of her. Yet, how could she hold that against the woman when she looked after Jesse and his four younger siblings with every ounce of strength, care and attention she had since her husband died years before?

Sadness gripped fast around Sylvia's heart. Now the home that had been theirs for all too brief a time was no more.

'Oh, Jesse,' she whispered. 'Where are you, my love?'

Sylvia sucked in a sob as she thanked God Jesse and his family had moved to Wales before the war came to Bath, but her gratitude was swiftly replaced with guilt when there was every possibility the entire Cambridge family who lived there now lay dead beneath the rubble. And what of the Longford and Cotton families? She stared at the two terrace houses either side of Jesse's house, which looked as though they'd been crudely cut in half with a jagged saw, the living rooms, kitchens and bedrooms revealed to the rest of the street, the stark cruelness of it only made worse by the bright morning sun.

This bloody, stupid war!

Pressing her knuckles against her lips to trap the scream that clawed her throat, Sylvia quickly let herself into her house, praying her mother wasn't there and had been somewhere else entirely when a bomb had dropped on Castle Street.

'Mum? Are you here?'

The silence of the Victorian two-up, two-down echoed back at her and Sylvia didn't know whether to laugh or cry as a strange mix of relief and fear unfurled inside her. She slowly walked into the kitchen, unsure what she would find. If her mother wasn't here, where was she? Sylvia swallowed. She'd been joking when she'd said to Freda that her mother would be at the pub, but was it possible she was hunkered down in the Garrick's Head where she worked after all?

She walked into the kitchen and her gaze immediately fell on a scrap of paper propped up against the salt and pepper pots on the small circular dining table. Sylvia snatched it up and quickly read her mother's words.

Sylv,

If you're reading this, then I guess the house is still standing!

Mr Austen, the daft sod, came to get me and refused to leave unless I came back with him to his house. Why he thinks I'll be any safer there than here, God knows, but you know how men always think they know best.

Anyway, make your way over to 15 Audley Grove when you can. I'll be the one sitting on his sofa with a glass of something sweet in my hand.

Love,
Mum

'Bloody woman. There's only one Eileen Roberts.' Sylvia laughed, relief swelling her heart as tears welled in her eyes. 'Go ahead, Mum. A drink sounds just the ticket to me right now.'

Smiling, she left the kitchen and hurried upstairs.

Mr Austen was their local butcher and one of the most decent human beings Sylvia had ever known. But unfortunately, the poor man clearly had a screw loose in that he was 100 per cent head-over-heels infatuated with her mother. Before the war, if he could give Eileen – often via Sylvia, considering she did most of the shopping – the best cut of meat he had, he would. These days, he had to settle for giving her mother the best of what scant pickings he'd managed to procure, but still, the desire to make her happy was evident.

Did Eileen return his affection? It depended on a day-to-day basis as far as Sylvia could determine. Poor bloke.

After a quick wash at the bathroom sink, she changed out of her uniform and pulled a clean one, including an apron and cap, from her wardrobe and placed them in an overnight bag along with a hairbrush and other essentials. Was anything essential any more? The likelihood of her going back to Castle Street tonight were slim to none. Even if there wasn't another raid after dark – which was highly likely considering she could not think of another city that had only sustained three attacks in three years – she would be working at the hospital until goodness knew what time tomorrow. And if, for some unknown reason, she wasn't... well, she'd worry about where she would spend the night later, but wherever that might be, back at home or on Mr Austen's settee, at least she'd have a nightie and toothbrush.

Suddenly scarily desperate to give her mother a cuddle even if the old bag was likely to push her away and tell Sylvia to stop being so soppy, Sylvia rushed downstairs. No matter how much she and her mother might argue and bicker, it had been just the two of them since her father walked out on them four days after Sylvia's ninth birthday. An age in a girl's life when their father was her whole damn world so, of course, her nine-year-old self had entirely blamed herself for his abandonment. Then – as luck would have it – her own fiancé followed suit thirteen years later, leaving Sylvia in no doubt how easy men found it to walk away from her.

But Jesse didn't walk away, did he? You damn well pushed him.

Sylvia left the house, slamming the door behind her. Keeping her gaze steadfastly focused ahead rather than at the devastation across the road, she marched purposefully through the maze of residential streets, some bombed, some entirely untouched or affected by the raids, towards Audley Grove.

Once she was at Mr Austen's black painted door, she lifted her knuckles and rapped a couple of times, looking over her shoulder at the little shop at the very end of the street, its wide front window smashed to smithereens, the sign above it desolate and swinging in the soft April breeze. Scuffled footsteps sounded from behind the door before it swung open and Mr Austen stood on the threshold, an open beer bottle in his hand and his piggy eyes impossibly wide due to the unfortunate magnifying effects of his thick glasses.

His round face immediately reddened as he smiled. 'Sylvia, my darlin'! You're safe and here on my doorstep. What a sight for sore eyes you are!' He laughed and ever so slightly swayed on his feet. 'Come on in and join your mum and me for a drink.'

Sylvia grinned as he stepped aside, his arm swinging out with a flourish. She brushed past him into the house. 'Can I hazard a guess you and my mother started celebrating the minute the all-clear siren sounded?'

He hiccupped and tipped her a wink. 'Something like that. Mrs Roberts? Your one-in-a-million daughter is here!' he announced, leading Sylvia into the living room. 'Why don't you pour her a drink?'

'Sylv!' Her mother got up from where she'd been lounging

on a rather worse for wear settee and sashayed towards her with what looked to be a glass of sherry in her hand. 'It's good to see you, sweetheart.'

Sylvia stared into her mother's slightly glazed eyes and her heart contracted when they shone with tears before her mother blinked, and they were gone. 'Mum, I'm so glad you're all right.'

She clasped her arms around the woman who was more often a pain in her backside than not and squeezed tight. Her mother stiffened in her arms before her body softened and she squeezed Sylvia back.

'Yeah, you too, sweetheart.' They stayed that way for a few seconds before her mother eased Sylvia back. 'Now, what will you have to drink? Mr Austen has a drinks cabinet that wouldn't be out of place in the King's drawing room!'

'Is that right?' Sylvia smiled and looked across the room at Mr Austen, where he proudly stood in front of the open doors of his walnut drinks cabinet and, judging by the breadth of his goofy smile, as pleased as punch to have her mother in his house. 'Then I'll have whatever my mother's drinking, please, sir.'

'One glass of my finest sherry coming right up.'

Sylvia's smile faltered. Yes, she had to go back to the hospital in a few hours, but one drink wouldn't hurt. She could always ask Mr Austen if she could have a quick lie down on his bed before she went back to work.

14

FREDA

It had been exactly four hours since Dorothy had dropped the confession of all confessions that had left Freda reeling with shock. Her sister had promptly retreated into her bedroom, seemingly impervious to the fact that Freda would have to digest the news that Dorothy was pregnant while attempting to assuage her mother's shattered nerves over the raids and their father not yet coming home. Good lord, if their mother uncovered her youngest daughter's condition too, it was entirely possible she would become completely comatose.

For now though, her mother slept, or at least Freda hoped she did.

After a second cup of tea, she had claimed exhaustion and suggested they both go to bed for a few hours in preparation for what could possibly be a third German raid come dusk. Thankfully, her mother had concurred and climbed the stairs ahead of Freda.

But Freda hadn't slept. Or if she had, she hadn't been aware of it. Instead, she'd spent the last few hours tossing and turning, closing her eyes, opening them again and now it was time she returned to the hospital, but how could she do that without further speaking to Dorothy? What were they going to do? A baby was coming whether they were prepared for it or not!

Freda abruptly pushed up from her bed, opened her bedroom door and marched along the landing to her sister's room. She tapped on the door and entered without waiting for Dorothy's admittance.

'I was wondering how long it would take you,' Dorothy said from where she sat up on top of her bed, an open book face down beside her, her expression entirely composed. 'If you are even thinking about giving me a "how could you?" lecture, you might as well leave. There is nothing you can say to me that I haven't said to myself a thousand times.'

The strength of Freda's annoyance caused her hands to tremble and she slowly, silently, closed the door before walking to the bed and sitting down at Dorothy's feet. 'How, Dot? How did this happen?'

Her sister's blue eyes flashed with wry amusement. 'Well, if I have to explain *that*, then—'

'Don't you dare!' Freda snapped. 'Your fiancé is fighting for his country, and you have been carrying on behind his back? I don't even know what to say to you right now.' Freda leapt to her feet and paced back and forth at the foot of Dorothy's bed, her blood boiling. 'You're pregnant,' she said quietly, even though she wanted to scream. 'Pregnant!'

'You think I don't know that? And will you please keep your voice down. If Mum—'

'Mum? Did you think about her when you were getting up to all sorts with the father of your child?'

Her sister's cheeks reddened, and her nonchalance faltered, her eyes glistening with tears. 'You're not the only one who finds Mum's good girl expectations a trial, you know.'

'Clearly!' snapped Freda. 'Yet in all the months and years of you snitching on me, stirring the pot... My God, you have never once spoken up for me during all the rows about my wanting to write, when the entire time you were out doing God knows what, with God knows who!'

'Shh!' Dorothy scrambled off the bed and clasped Freda's hand, tears spilling onto her cheeks, all pretence of indifference vanished. 'Please, Freda, I know what an idiot I am and...'

Freda crossed her arms, angry and unaffected by Dorothy's tears.

Her sister closed her eyes. 'This isn't the first time it's happened, but last time everything worked out.'

Disbelief wound tight in Freda's stomach. She had so wanted to be wrong in her suspicions. 'What are you saying?'

Dorothy opened her eyes. 'I had a pregnancy scare awhile back, but I got away with it and now I've done it again and—'

'Wait.' Freda raised her hands, shock reverberating through her. 'Are you saying you've been pregnant before?'

'Well, yes, at least I—'

'Was this when I kept asking you what was wrong a few months ago?'

Her sister nodded, then drew her fingers under her eyes.

Bile coated Freda's throat. Did she know her sister at all? 'I can't believe this, Dorothy. What is wrong with you?'

'Will you let me finish?'

Still reeling, Freda shook her head. 'And what do you mean "you got away with it"?' She stared wide-eyed at Dorothy. 'Please tell me you didn't lose—'

'No. I got my period. I was lucky.' Dorothy sat down heavily on the bed. 'But this time that isn't going to happen. I've missed two periods, Freda. Two. What am I going to do?'

Freda's mind scrambled with what ifs and maybes before the

weight of her shock and concern pressed down on her. She slumped. 'Oh, Dorothy.' She sat down on the bed next to her sister, took her hand and kissed her knuckles. 'I've got no idea. What this will do to Mum...'

'Don't.' Dorothy sniffed. 'I've thought about nothing else for weeks.'

'Why didn't tell me before now?'

'What would you have done?'

Questions, criticism and exclamations of utter incredulity that would do nothing but make the situation worse battled for release on Freda's tongue, and she pulled her lips tightly together, trapping them inside. Over and over again, she had longed for Dorothy's support when her mother had scoffed at her writing ambitions, and over and over again, Dorothy had not only abandoned her to her mother's rants but relished in them. Now it turned out her sister had been up to far worse that had resulted in a pregnancy.

She shook her head and gently pulled her hand from Dorothy's, her heart bouncing between anger and utter sympathy. 'So, who's the father?' she asked quietly, staring at the wall opposite her.

'You... don't know him.'

'Who is he, Dot?'

'Just a... friend.'

'A friend?' Freda snapped her head around and glared. 'A friend?'

Tears leapt into Dorothy's eyes. 'He's just one of the lads I go dancing with whenever I actually manage to escape mother's net. Me, Franny and Melissa—'

'Who are these people?' Freda cried, her heart thumping. 'You've never mentioned their names before. I feel like I'm looking at a stranger, Dot. My God, all you do is tell Mum how you want to be a good wife to Robert, keep house, have children. I can't even look at you right now.' Freda stood and turned her back on her sister. 'How could you do this to her? Mum's hard to live with, yes, but she doesn't deserve such deceit.'

The silence stretched until Freda felt she would scream.

'What is your plan exactly?' she demanded, spinning around and pinning Dorothy with a glare. She would not take over the responsibility of this. Her sister had done something beyond belief. It sounded like she wasn't in love with the father and didn't want the family to know who he was. Did she even have any intention of telling him about the baby? 'I'll support you, of course I will, but you are twenty years old and clearly old enough to have relations with someone so you need to at least tell him—'

'Freda, please.' Dorothy sniffed, looking at the closed bedroom door. 'Will you keep your voice down?'

Freda crossed her arms, her entire body trembling. Whether with anger or fear for what would happen next, she couldn't be sure. 'Well, what do you plan to do?'

Dorothy stared at her for a moment before a habitual gleam of arrogance shone in her eyes. She tilted her chin. 'You're a nurse. You are in the perfect position to take care of this for me.'

'What?'

'Well, you know…' Dorothy shrugged, the colour in her cheeks belying her clear act of nonchalance. 'You must know people. Doctors who can…'

Freda narrowed her eyes, her heart beating fast. 'Go on.'

'Who can…' The skin on Dorothy's neck shifted as she swallowed. 'Help me.'

'Are you suggesting what I think you're suggesting?'

Her sister shrugged, her gaze unwavering.

'An abortion, Dorothy?' Freda asked incredulously, her voice barely above a whisper. She huffed a laugh, itching to take her sister by the shoulders and shake her. 'You want me to approach a professional doctor and ask him if he would perform an illegal abortion? As what? A favour?'

'I'm just saying... You know people. You could—'

'Stop!' Freda jabbed her hand in the air, her temper snapping. 'Just stop. I can't do this with you right now. I'm tired, I'm hungry and I've got to head to the hospital to help all the poor people caught up in these raids to such a degree a good-time girl like you would clearly never understand!'

Freda stormed from the room, leaving the door wide open, ignoring her sister's muffled sobs as they echoed in Freda's steaming ears.

15

FREDA

Despite knowing she should return straight to the hospital, Freda rushed through bomb-damaged streets towards the *Bath Chronicle* office located at the bottom of Bath's premier shopping street. Between the effects of the raids, concern for her parents' safety, Sylvia and Veronica, not to mention Dorothy's pregnancy, there was something she must do. She had something to say to the paper's editor and Richard immediately, lest she change her mind. She could not worry about her writing work on top of everything else right now. As she walked, Freda looked around in wonder. Upon leaving home, she'd made a horrifying journey through devastation and turmoil, rubble, broken glass and warped metal, yet the entirety of Milsom Street remained intact along with the adjoining streets that housed boutique clothes shops, milliners and haberdasheries.

The complete randomness of what had been damaged and what hadn't really brought home people's fate in war – some survived, others died. It was as simple and as unfair as that. Which only served to bolster her determination to keep any romance at arm's length. Why subject herself to the possibility of falling in love and then losing that man to the war? No, it was too upsetting to contemplate. Shaking off her melancholy, Freda pulled on her strength and determination. One way or another, Bath's people would rebuild themselves and their city even if their hearts would take years to heal.

As she neared the *Chronicle's* office, Freda slowed. She had only ever visited the office's ground floor that opened onto the street, so she couldn't be sure of how many staff writers, advertising staff, printers and goodness knew who else worked on the upper floors but, by rights, the office should be empty. Richard, the paper's editor, William Keating, Barbara, and everyone else should all be lying low and safe with their loved ones. Yet she somehow knew Richard and William would either be in the office or out talking to the people on the streets and in their homes. She really hoped it was the former as she might not have the fortitude to do what she must do come tomorrow.

She slowed her pace as she neared the office, trepidation rippling through her that once she stepped inside, she might not see Richard at all, but instead discover he'd been injured or even killed. Although she'd seen him for all too brief a time in between the first two raids, so much had changed in her world since then – undoubtedly in Richard's, too. For her, her family and the hospital had become her priorities over everything going forward, including her writing and her relationship with Richard.

Tentatively pushing open the *Chronicle's* front door, her suspicions were confirmed when it gave way. The office was open which meant at least one person was at work despite the potential for another bombing. She stepped inside and struggled to adjust her eyes to the gloomy interior, which was always in perpetual semi-darkness due to the height of the surrounding buildings packed tightly together in the narrow street.

Soon enough, her gaze fell on Richard where he sat at his desk, his jet-black hair fallen over his brow in a way she found so endearing as he ferociously attacked his typewriter. Her heart jolted and a soft smile pulled at her lips. He'd looked exactly the same way the first time she'd laid eyes on him in the autumn last year and now, just as then, her attraction was immediate and entirely discombobulating and, if she was honest, not at all welcome.

She glanced at William's desk at the back of the office. Papers scattered its surface, a fountain pen and pencil tossed on top of them, the chair behind it pulled out. But the editor was nowhere to be seen. Her tension escalated. William was clearly around somewhere and even though he was always kind to her, his professional brusqueness still managed to provoke her nerves. She quickly returned her gaze to Richard, her heart jolting a second time to find him intensely studying her, his eyes no longer bright with fervour and excitement as they'd been when she'd last seen him, but dark with something she couldn't decipher.

Pulling back her shoulders, Freda purposefully walked to his desk and put her handbag on top of it. 'Hello.'

His shirt and tie were unusually rumpled, dirt and grime streaked across his forehead and cheek unheeded, and exhaustion showing in the lines around his mouth. Lord only knew when he'd last slept or even rested. Care for him swelled her heart and she silently cursed her weakness. She could not waiver. Her family needed her. The hospital needed her.

He slowly pushed back his chair and stood, his eyes never leaving hers as he walked around the desk. Stopping barely inches away from her, Freda tipped her head back to meet his beautiful blue gaze as it lingered on hers before briefly dropping to her lips and then back to her eyes.

'Thank God.' At last, he smiled. 'You're all in one piece.'

Her body reacted to his soft, loving tone as it always did, betraying her mother's good girl teachings and evoking a powerful desire that – thanks to Dorothy – Freda now knew more than ever she should continue to resist.

Somehow, she managed to coolly return his smile. 'As are you.'

'I'm glad you're here,' he said, looking down and inching his hands closer to hers before he stopped. Maybe her expression was such that it made him think the better of touching her. He met her eyes. 'Have you heard what the London papers are saying about the raids on Bath last night and this morning?'

'No, why?' she asked, trying hard not to be affected by the passion in his eyes as he looked at her – watched her. She sensed things had intensified between them. Like the raids had made everything more urgent – which they almost certainly had. How could the terror not have affected relationships all over the city?

She swallowed. 'How could they have distributed them so soon?'

'They would've run something immediately. Bath being bombed is definitely newsworthy. We're a famous historic city after all.' He drew in a breath, then shakily released it. 'But the capital clearly don't know the extent of things and they've got quite a lot wrong, too.'

'Like what?'

'Well, they've reported that a few Georgian houses have been demolished, severe damage around and about one of our cinemas... all of which barely scratches the surface of the damage. The only thing they've reported that can't be disputed is the bomb devastation around the "working-class areas", as they put it.'

'By the river?'

'Yes.'

'How bad is it?'

Richard looked past her to the window, his jaw tightening. 'Bad. Apparently, one of the London papers reported that a couple of families had been killed, but I went there during and after the raids and a hell of a lot more than that have been killed, maimed or injured.'

Freda's heart ached for the people who had been eking out a living and a semblance of a life in the slums even before the raids. What would happen now for those trying to survive in a place where they lived closely packed and dependent on one another?

What Kathy Scott had said to her once again came to her mind. 'I understand the Kingsmead area was one of the most badly hit through both raids.'

'Kingsmead Street especially. I hate to say it, but I don't have much hope of survivors there and it's entirely residential as far as I can remember.'

Freda's stomach knotted as she prayed for Kathy once she learned of her loss. She might have said what she did, but how could anyone really wish their parents dead? Freda had to talk to her. Maybe she needed help and sympathy that her, Sylvia and Veronica had never been prepared to give her before. Maybe there was something going on in Kathy's life that none of them could even imagine.

Stepping back, Freda opened the distance between her and Richard lest she act on her sudden need to feel the comfort of his arms around her. 'I need to speak to you and William,' she said. 'Is he here?'

'I am indeed, Miss Parkes.'

Freda jumped and Richard blinked before they both snapped their attention to the paper's editor as he approached them.

Richard cleared his throat. 'It seems Miss Parkes has risked life and limb to speak to you this afternoon, William.' He faced her, the heat that had been in his eyes a moment before now replaced with habitual seriousness. 'Although I can't say I'm best pleased she's walking around the city as it is at the moment.'

Freda held his gaze before she slid her focus to William. 'I'm on my way back to the hospital and should be there now, if truth be told, but...' She pulled back her shoulders, determined to say what she had come here to say despite the intensity of Richard's gaze boring into her. 'There's something I'd like to tell you now rather than wait. Especially considering anything could, and most likely will, happen over the coming hours and days.'

William gestured with a wave towards the chair in front of Richard's desk. 'Take a seat,' he said, his brow creased. 'Are you all right? Your family?'

Freda sat and offered him a small smile, touched by his concern. He really was a wonderful man to work for and she would miss writing for the paper terribly. 'They're well enough, considering. My father gave my mother a fright by not coming home for hours, but he's a policeman so his long absence is hardly surprising. He's been home now, which is a relief for Mum. Of course, she's lost one son to the war and her other son is still MIA so her nerves are entirely justified.'

'Indeed. Poor woman.'

'Anyway...' Freda sighed, her mother's suffering heavy on her heart. 'Richard suggested that you might be interested in a piece from my point of view as a nurse at the hospital during the raids?'

William beamed. 'I most certainly would.'

'Well, I hate to disappoint you, but I will not be submitting any more articles to the paper. I must focus all my time and energy on my work at the hospital, and my family.'

William raised his eyebrows and looked at Richard with a clear 'I told you so' look.

Somewhat annoyed, Freda inwardly bristled as she studied him before glancing at Richard. His expression screamed of pure disappointment, nothing more, nothing less. Well, that was too bad. Her loyalty to the hospital and her family would not waver in these desperate times.

She sat up straighter in her seat and addressed William. 'Despite my father predicting these raids months ago, none of us could be sure Germany would attack Bath. However, I've learned from working at the paper that the media often knows more than most, and you would have almost certainly alluded to a possible attack had you known anything.' She jutted her chin, looked between them. 'Our lives and what we can expect going forward has changed for us all. Wouldn't you agree?'

Silence fell, but Freda held her ground.

She would not be intimidated by William's gruff expression, nor allow her feelings for Richard to sway her. She loved writing for the paper, but she also loved her family and as far as her nursing was concerned, that was in much higher need by Bath's people right now than those she was trying to help through her writing.

'I agree the hospital is where you should be right now, Miss Parkes.'

A little of the tension left her shoulders and she nodded at William. 'Thank you, sir.'

'But what of your campaigning with Miss Beckett?' The editor crossed his arms. 'Are you to stop that too?'

Freda hesitated. She had been writing back and forth to a young Bristolian woman who Richard had introduced her to weeks before, aiding Susan as much as she could by raising awareness around her magnificent work helping to rehome orphaned or misplaced children. It was her and Susan's hope that the work she'd begun in Bristol would soon stretch to Bath and beyond.

'For the time being.' Freda sighed, regret winding through her. 'I intend writing to Susan this evening to tell her.'

'Do you think stepping back now is wise? The last thing you want to happen is for the people who have shown interest in supporting yours and Miss Beckett's efforts to forget those children and move on to something else. Little ones up and down the country need the benefits of what you are trying to do. If the rehoming process is successful in Bristol, who knows what the future holds?'

Freda's heart beat faster with the passion she felt for Susan Beckett's work and how she had eventually earned her trust to work alongside her.

'I must dedicate my time to my own family and the hospital right now, William.' Regret twisted inside her and she glanced at Richard, his intensity permeating the air around him. She faced William again. 'As soon as we are certain the raids are over and I have helped Bath's people as much as I can medically, then I will return to my writing if you will have me. Please, all of this would be so much easier with your blessing. I am doing the right thing. Whether you' – she looked at Richard – 'or Richard agree is, quite frankly, not my concern. So...' She snatched her bag from Richard's desk. 'With that said, I'll leave you to your work, gentlemen.'

She turned on her heel, head held high, and strode from the *Chronicle*'s office.

With Richard's obvious disappointment in her choices added to Dorothy's complete disregard to everything and everyone, the fact that parts of Bath lay in smithereens, people dying or injured on almost every street, Freda had just about had enough. From now on, she would stand by every decision she made that felt right to her. After all, her life was her own, no one else's.

16

VERONICA

Veronica caught sight of Freda's blonde hair just as she strode towards the hospital entranceway and sent up a deep, heartfelt hope that her friend's parents must be safe and their home still standing, the same as hers, if Freda had returned so promptly to work. She wasn't sure she could bear it if Freda or Sylvia's parents were hurt or worse, their homes gone, and she still had her mother and a house untouched. Such an outcome would be made especially harder considering she'd spent so much time counting the money in her 'escape tin' which she kept locked in her bottom drawer by the side of her bed, dreaming of the day she could leave the street where she lived with her mother.

Swallowing hard, Veronica prayed God forgave her, but when she had returned home from the hospital after the raids, she had never been so disappointed as when she saw that a certain house farther along the street from hers was still intact. She'd felt even worse upon learning that the neighbour who lived there – Mr Mark Riley – was safe and well with his wife and daughters at his mother-in-law's house in Bradford Upon Avon. Damn the man to hell! She wished no ill on his family, but for Mr Riley, she wished a bomb had fallen directly on top of him.

Before her hatred and bitterness could get a firm grip on her, Veronica picked up her pace and fell in step with Freda as she neared the hospital doors.

'Hey, you.' She touched Freda's arm, drawing her to a stop. Forcing a smile, Veronica searched her friend's face, her smile slowly dissolving and stomach dropping upon seeing the strain lines around Freda's eyes and mouth, her bright blue eyes so very sad. 'Oh, no. What's happened? Please tell me your family are all right?'

Freda briefly closed her eyes before opening them again. 'If you mean are they all right as in are they alive, uninjured? Then yes, they're all fine.'

Relief lowered Veronica's shoulders. 'Good, then has something else happened?' She grimaced. 'Apart from the raids and devastation all around the city, I mean. You look... upset.'

Her friend drew her gaze from Veronica's and looked past her shoulder. 'Everything's fine.'

'Are you sure?'

Freda turned, her smile strained. 'Yes.'

'Have you seen Sylvia?' Veronica asked, knowing Freda was far from all right, but not wanting to press her. She would talk to her and Sylvia when she was ready. 'Do you know if her mother is safe?'

'Not yet, but knowing Sylvia, she would have arrived way before us so she could get on helping—' Freda abruptly stopped talking and narrowed her gaze as she looked at something or someone behind Veronica.

Veronica turned to see Kathy coming towards them with Nurses Carr and Taylor.

Kathy smiled at Veronica and then turned to Freda. 'You look awfully pasty, Nurse Parkes. Is there anything I can do for you?'

Veronica inwardly groaned. Even when Bath had suffered air raids that would have undoubtedly left hundreds of people dead and hundreds more injured, Kathy still had to stick pins into her friends.

'Kathy, stop it.' Veronica glared at her. 'Just go inside, will you? Now is not the time for anyone to put up with your nonsense, including us.'

'It's all right, V,' Freda said, placing a hand on her arm and pinning Kathy with a stare. 'Kathy, there is no need to always—'

'What?' Kathy crossed her arms, her cheeks mottling. 'Be unfriendly? Keep my friendship and thoughts to myself? Is that what you were going to say, Nurse Parkes?'

'No, it wasn't.' Freda sighed and glanced at Veronica before looking at the other nurses and then back at Kathy. 'I was actually going to say, there is no need to always assume me, Veronica and Sylvia go out of our way to purposely annoy you. It might serve us all, not to mention our patients, to show one another some compassion. Especially now.'

Veronica stared at Freda's turned cheek. What was going on? She had never heard Freda speak so kindly to Kathy. She glanced at Nurses Carr and Taylor, and their confused expressions told her they were equally as bemused by the unusual tone of this exchange between their colleagues.

'Fine.' Kathy uncrossed her arms and held her hands up in mock surrender. 'You and I will call a truce, Nurse Parkes.'

'Freda.'

'What?'

Veronica softly smiled. So, this was Freda waving a white flag. A proposal of peace between nurses even if there was nothing any of them could do to incite peace between Germany and the majority of Europe.

The colour on Kathy's cheeks darkened, her gaze tinged with unmistakable relief. 'Freda.' Her eyes locked with Freda's for a moment longer before Kathy faced Nurses Carr and Taylor, who quickly stood to attention. 'Come on, ladies. At least some of us should get to work.'

Once the other nurses had walked a good distance away, Freda blew out a long breath. 'Well, hopefully that will go some way to showing Kathy she does not need to be on the defensive with us every minute of every shift.'

Veronica frowned and stared at Kathy and the other nurses' backs as they disappeared through the hospital doors. 'I'd be lying if I didn't admit your kindness towards her took me by surprise.' She faced Freda. 'Has something happened between the pair of you?'

'She said something to me after the raids that makes me think there is a lot more going on in Kathy's world than we know about.'

'What do you mean?'

'She came to find me when she found out that Sister Dyer had sent me outside to assess the damage and she asked me if I knew the state of Kingsmead.'

'And?'

'It's where Kathy lives with her mum and dad.' Freda's eyes were dark with concern. 'And when I told her it had been severely bombed, she said she hoped her house was flattened, and her parents in it.'

Veronica gasped. 'That's a terrible thing to say.'

'Exactly. Which can only mean her parents must have done something pretty bad to Kathy in the past or else they're still doing it to her. What that could be, God only knows.'

'That's awful.' Veronica stared at the hospital doors. 'Do you think I should talk to her? She seems to get along better with me than she does you or Sylvia.'

'Maybe, but leave it with me for now. I won't be talking to her until I find out what's what on the wards. We've got patients to care for, most likely a lot more than when we left this morning. Not to mention the chance of another raid tonight.'

'Is that what has you looking so worried?' Veronica asked gently. 'You can tell me anything, Freda. You do know that, don't you?'

As Freda stared at her, tears glinted in her eyes. 'It's Dorothy.'

'Your sister?'

'Yes.'

'What's wrong with her? I thought you said your family was all right?'

Freda's cheeks mottled as her gaze suddenly burned with annoyance. 'Dorothy is fine... at least as far as the raids are concerned.'

'Then what—'

'Just forget I said anything for now, V. I just have a sister who thinks she can do what the hell she wants and have someone else deal with the consequences of her actions. Dorothy Louise Parkes is a selfish, selfish young woman!'

Veronica's entire body stiffened. In all the months she'd been friends with Freda, she had never come close to losing her temper, let alone raise her voice and turn the colour of beetroot.

'I'm sorry, V,' Freda said, her gaze furious. 'I can't talk about it now. I'm too mad. Anyway, we should get inside.'

Knowing that once they walked inside the hospital, their time might not be their own for hours, Veronica gripped Freda's arm as she moved to walk away. 'Sister Dyer told us to return when we could. She won't be looking for us. Tell me what's happened.'

Freda remained tight-lipped and as the seconds ticked by, Veronica's concern grew.

'Oh, V.' Freda's voice cracked, and tears leapt into her eyes. 'I have no idea what to do for her.'

Veronica immediately put her arms around her friend and Freda trembled in her embrace. 'Tell me, Freda. Let me and Sylvia help you.'

'Dorothy's pregnant.'

Veronica stilled. Just the word 'pregnant' sent shivers down her spine, sending her hurtling back to the day of her rape and how the consequences of Mr Riley's attack could have been far worse. She swallowed. 'Pregnant? But isn't her fiancé… Oh.'

'Even if the baby was Robert's, my mother would still have likely ended up in one of our hospital beds suffering from shock when Dorothy isn't married, but with the father being "a friend" as Dorothy described him to me, it's likely my mother will end up in an asylum.' Freda pulled from Veronica's arms and shook her head. 'And to make matters worse, Dorothy's hinted at getting an… abortion.'

'What?'

'You should've seen the look in her eyes when she said it, V. I'm scared if I don't help her, she'll…'

'Find her own way of dealing with it?'

'Exactly.'

'Come here.' Veronica pulled Freda into her arms a second time and held her tight. 'You're not on your own with this. Me and Sylvia will help in any way we can.' Her mind wandered to Mr Martin and Betty. Her surgical dream team. She should at least talk to them. 'Let me speak to Mr Martin. Maybe he will—'

'No!' Freda jumped back and gripped Veronica's hand. 'Promise me you won't say anything to him, V. If you involve Mr Martin in this... Abortion is illegal.'

'I know it is, but listen to me.' Veronica tightened her grip on Freda's fingers. 'If Dorothy is that determined to terminate this pregnancy, she will.'

'But—'

'There can be no buts.' Care for Freda and thus her sister burned inside Veronica. 'You and Sylvia have been there for me in ways you will never understand. Just being able to talk to you about the rape... about Riley... has made my life so much more bearable than it was before. Dorothy cannot be allowed to think she has to do something about this baby on her own.'

'She won't think that. She knows I will be there for her. And my parents will have to come around eventually. She just needs to tell—'

'But what if she is too scared to talk to them? What if she wants to terminate her pregnancy more than anything? What if she can't think about anything else?' Passion and pain mixed and swirled inside Veronica. She had a deep suspicion she understood exactly how Freda's sister was thinking and feeling. 'When I think back to the terror, the horror, the self-loathing and fear that ripped through my entire being after my attack, I know there was a small sliver of time when I would have done anything, illegal or otherwise, in my desperation to turn back the clock. Who's to say Dorothy won't deal with this pregnancy in a way that could result in her death?'

'Don't say that!'

'I'm sorry, but—' She cupped her hand to Freda's jaw and looked deep into her eyes. 'Let me speak to Mr Martin, please. He's a good, kind man. He will give us advice if nothing else.'

Tears swam in Freda's eyes until, at last, she nodded. 'All right, you can talk to him, but God only knows what he will say.'

'Just leave it with me.' Still holding Freda's hand, she led her in the direction of the hospital's doors. 'Come on, we've got work to do.'

17

SYLVIA

Sylvia slowly cracked her eyes open to slits and then tried to work out exactly what she was looking at. When had her mother bought such a bloody ugly Toby jug? Moreover, why in God's name did she decide the best place for it was balanced precariously on the edge of their narrow mantelpiece?

Wait.

She'd fallen asleep in Mr Austen's house!

Cursing, she scrambled upright and immediately slapped her hand to the pain that felt like someone was plunging a knitting needle through one side of her brain to the other. Emitting a groan from within the cotton-wool dry depths of her mouth, Sylvia dropped back against Mr Austen's settee, and it creaked its indignation.

What the hell was in that brandy he'd given her? Or was her banging head and swirling stomach a result of accepting the fourth glass she'd laughingly encouraged him to pour her? The phantom shadow of guilt and self-loathing that had started to follow her around after she'd been drinking these days descended. If she'd needed further evidence that she was slowly morphing into her mother, she had it. Becoming Eileen bloody Roberts was something Sylvia had vowed more times than she could count she would never allow to happen.

Yet here she was waking up on a relative stranger's settee and – she squinted at the clock on the mantelpiece next to the ugly Toby jug – almost four hours past the time she'd planned to return to the hospital where Sister Dyer relied on her.

'Get up, you silly mare,' Sylvia muttered through clenched teeth as she pushed unsteadily to her feet. 'There are people dying, people bloody injured, and you...' Tears burned her eyes. 'You are sat here like a complete and utter lush.'

Blurry eyed and her head pounding like a hammer against metal, Sylvia pulled her overnight bag from the armchair where she'd left it earlier, slowly got out of her casual clothes, not giving a damn that she was in Mr Austen's living room and he could walk in at any moment. She had worse things to worry about. Like Sister Dyer...

Getting into her fresh uniform as quickly as her upset stomach would allow, Sylvia then stood in front of the mirror above the mantel and pulled a brush through her hair in an effort to stop it resembling an auburn-coloured toilet brush. Holding her head for fear it might roll straight off her shoulders, she shuffled into the hallway, stopping to grab her coat and handbag from the stair newel post.

The silence of the house echoed around her. Where were her mother and Mr Austen?

A bed spring creaked above her and she glanced up the stairs, her nausea escalating as she shrugged on her coat. Maybe it was for the best she didn't know.

Slinging the strap of her handbag onto her shoulder, she walked into the kitchen and took an empty glass from the counter, filled it with water. Once she had drunk three glasses, she flicked some water on her face, patted it dry with a decidedly whiffy tea towel – drunkards couldn't be choosers – and headed out of the front door.

The hazy afternoon sunshine lit the fallout of the bombings in all their devastating glory.

Sylvia's heart broke a little more with every house she passed that was reduced to rubble, walls littered with craters left from machine-gun fire and blackened roof beams bereft of tiles. The subdued wails and sobs of Bath's people followed her as she walked, the effects of the hours before rapidly receding as her professionalism came to the fore. She instinctively scanned the area around her for anyone in need of medical help.

Blood spattered the pavement, walls and pathways of the houses, causing bile to rise in her throat and her heart ache. How many were dead? She suspected it would be days before they knew the exact number, and there was every possibility Hitler hadn't finished with Bath yet. But why was Bath such a threat? Or did he want its people suppressed for some other reason? Sylvia clenched her jaw and narrowed her eyes. He'd have a long bloody wait if it was the latter.

'Nurse! Please, can you help me?'

Sylvia blinked from her thoughts and raced towards a young mother sat on the pavement, cradling a little girl of about two years old on her lap. The woman's head was bleeding and she had a nasty gash on her neck. Beside her, a little boy of no more than four or five lay on the concrete, clearly struggling to keep his eyes open.

'I can't get him up,' the mother cried, tears spilling over her cheeks. 'Every time I move him, his head falls back, and he groans. I'm not sure he can even hear me. Please, you've got to do something. What's wrong with him?'

Sylvia knelt down beside the boy and quickly carried out all the checks she could without any medical equipment. Ascertaining dehydration and a clear struggle to draw clean air into his lungs, she quickly checked him over for any physical injuries, but couldn't find anything more than a few grazes. Which meant her biggest concern was getting the lad somewhere safe and warm before he went into shock. She had seen more and more cases of acute shock since the start of the war and now she imagined Bath's hospitals would be receiving the same amount of people suffering with debilitating shock as Bristol had before them.

'It's all right,' she said, facing the mother and offering her an encouraging smile. 'I'll get him up and carry him to wherever it is you want to go. He just needs plenty to drink and somewhere warm so he can sleep.' She looked around at Bath's stone buildings surrounding them, each in a differing state of destruction. 'The dust from all the blasted stone is going to cause breathing problems for a lot of people. He's also a little shaken up, but he'll be fine in a while.'

'Are you sure?' The mother's gaze never left her son, the little girl in her arms smiling at Sylvia, blissfully ignorant to the devastation and pain all around her.

Sylvia returned the baby girl's smile and nodded, praying her diagnosis was right and she wasn't in any way misleading this young mother. 'Absolutely.'

God only knew how badly the dust from the destroyed buildings would cause infection to the thousands of people walking around with open wounds.

'What's your name?' she asked the mother gently.

'Joan. Joan Clarke.'

'It's very nice to meet you, Joan. And what are your beautiful children's names?'

Her eyes softened with affection. 'Andrew and Margaret.'

'Well, it's very nice to meet them too,' Sylvia said, winking at Margaret and making her giggle. 'Now, where are we headed?' She pushed to her feet. 'Do you have somewhere to take your children?'

'I hope so.' Joan's voice cracked as she stood. 'My parents live not far from here. I just pray they are all right and the house is still standing.'

'Right then.' Sylvia pulled the strap of her handbag over her head so it lay across her body, roughly shoved the handles of her overnight bag over her shoulder and then leaned down, gently hefting little Andrew into her arms. The banging in her head pierced the back of her eyes, but other than that, she felt as strong as an ox. 'You and Margaret lead the way and Master Andrew and I will follow on behind.'

Their progress to Joan's parents' house was slow on account of them stopping three times so Sylvia could help other people where she could. The nightie she had packed proved useful when she had ripped it into shreds and used the material to bandage some wounds, her cotton wool and face cream coming in handy to clean people up as best she could before directing them to the first aid posts.

Filthy dirty and more exhausted than she'd been in her life, she eventually handed over Joan and the children to Andrew and Margaret's granny and granddad amid an outbreak of tears and gratitude, their house having survived untouched.

Half an hour later, Sylvia arrived at the hospital and made her way downstairs to the basement wards, relieved to see both Freda and Sylvia already hard at work. Thank God her friends were safe and seemingly their families too judging by the stalwart efficiency with which they were working. If they had suffered losses, surely they wouldn't be here at all? Then again, she was talking about Freda and Veronica, so anything was possible.

'Nurse Roberts,' Sister Dyer exclaimed, coming to stand in front of her, her gaze dismayed as she eyed Sylvia from head to toe. 'Have you not been home? Your uniform is filthy.'

Sylvia swallowed against her arid throat, praying she did not stink of booze. 'Um, yes, of course. I...'

'Look at the state of you. Have you even slept?'

The hysteria in the sister's voice was far from her norm and Sylvia guessed Sister Dyer was barely managing her own exhaustion and sorrow at all she had seen and dealt with, let alone having the patience to deal with senior nurses who should have been here hours before supporting her.

'I have, Sister,' Sylvia said, trying to inject as much calmness into her voice as possible in the hope it went some way to appeasing Sister Dyer. 'But on my way here, I had to help get a young mother and her two children to her parents' home and then I stopped to help others along the way. I did not look like this when I left the house, I assure you.'

Sister Dyer stared at Sylvia for a moment longer before she slumped and ran her hand over her face, her grey eyes sad. 'I'm sorry, I didn't mean to snap.'

Sylvia battled to hide her unease. The raids had really rattled the sister. So much so, this new, softer Sister Dyer was more than a little disconcerting, and therefore Sylvia vowed to remain on her guard whenever she was around her usually strict, no-nonsense senior for a while yet.

However, needs must, and although she risked being insubordinate, Sylvia gently touched the sister's arm. 'Don't be. The raids have taken their toll on all of us.'

Sister Dyer sighed as she assessed the ward. 'Indeed they have, Nurse Roberts.'

Guilt writhed inside Sylvia.

The sister had promoted her and she was repaying her trust by struggling to cope, drinking too much, and letting the likes of Kathy Scott get under her skin. Well, no more. It was time to step up to the plate.

'If there's nothing else, Sister?'

Sister Dyer turned and nodded. 'Nothing else, Nurse. But please check the storage cupboards for a spare uniform. Hopefully, you'll manage to find something better than what you're wearing at the moment. Off you go now.'

Sylvia returned her nod before striding forward, stubbornly refusing to acknowledge the voice in her head telling her she wasn't the competent nurse she'd thought she was; that a nursing career had never been on her agenda until the men in her life had shown her that her yearning for a family of her own one day – with a husband who loved her – was little more than a pipe dream.

Her heart constricted. It seemed she'd never have a family or a bloody husband so it was time to stop wishing things were different and deal with the destiny life had dealt her.

18

FREDA

'Nurses Parkes and Scott with me, please.'

Freda glanced at Sister Dyer as she barked her instruction before continuing to march towards the ward exit. Kathy Scott immediately abandoned her task and hurried along behind the sister, while Freda took a second more to stare at Officer Matthews as he slept. So much bothered her about his claim he was there after Veronica was attacked. Why hadn't he said anything to her in the weeks Veronica had been caring for him? Irritation simmered deep inside her. How dare he do that to her! How dare Germany attack Bath! How dare her sister get pregnant! How dare Richard look at her with such obvious judgement because she'd chosen nursing over her writing for now!

'Freda,' Sylvia whispered urgently from the adjacent bed. 'You'd better get moving or Sister will have your guts for garters.'

Freda fought to bury her angry frustration, nodded and strode to the exit where Sister waited for her, her arms crossed and her grey eyes flashing with annoyance.

'Well, thank you for joining us, Nurse Parkes.' She sniffed before looking between Freda and Kathy, who stared wide-eyed at Sister Dyer as though she was the Virgin Mary. 'I'd like the pair of you to go to the ambulance bay and relieve the two nurses who have been there for the last four hours. You will be the final part in a chain of nurses whom myself and Sister Campbell have arranged to work in sequence, so that we can efficiently and safely transfer some of the injured from Bristol who were admitted to us prior to the raids on to Gloucester.'

'Gloucester?' Kathy asked. 'Are all our beds now filled, Sister?'

'Yes. Every one, I'm afraid.' The sister sighed and looked past Kathy along the ward. 'And we still don't have enough doctors to deal with the people coming through our doors despite a good number coming from Bristol to assist us. I've received word that the Royal United is also full, their staff entirely exhausted having had no break or sleep since the first raid. It's time to start transferring patients out to the rural hospitals.' Her eyes turned steely with resolve. 'Let's just hope and pray we manage to do that without the threat of another attack. Now, off you go, it's going to be another long, stressful night.'

'Yes, Sister.'

'Yes, Sister.'

As she and Kathy hurried upstairs and through the corridors to the ambulance bay, Freda braced herself for a cutting remark or otherwise from Kathy, but she remained silent, her face pale, almost grey, her jaw tight. Freda wondered if Kathy thought of her parents and now regretted her outburst about wishing them dead. Yet that seemed unlikely when it had been said with such utter ice-cold conviction. Freda feared Kathy had meant every word.

And now seemed the opportune time to talk to her about it. 'Kathy?'

'Hmm?'

'How are you?'

Kathy slowed her pace and glanced at Freda, her hazel eyes shadowed with suspicion. 'Why do you ask?'

'Well, there's quite a lot going on,' Freda said, trying not to snap as she usually did when met with Kathy's bad attitude. 'And now it's been confirmed Kingsmead—'

'Was practically flattened. Yes.' Kathy stopped, her eyes dark. 'My parents were at home, Freda. They're dead, and even though that won't be confirmed for goodness knows how long, I know they are and I'm glad.'

Unease whispered through Freda and she stepped back. 'How can you say—'

'I say it because my parents were two of the vilest people in the world. They hurt me physically, they belittled me and pretty much treated me like their personal slave.' Her eyes blazed with fury, her cheeks red. 'Nursing was something I made happen by sheer will. I wanted to become a nurse, make something of myself... escape, and I endured all the pain that came with doing that when my parents punished me for daring to have a life past their needs.'

Sickness rolled through Freda's stomach and she touched Kathy's arm. 'Why didn't you say anything to—'

'To you? Or Sylvia?' She huffed a laugh. 'I consider Veronica a little more than a colleague from time to time, but you and Sylvia have never made any effort to get to know me. At least Veronica smiles and talks to me whenever we work together. I'd like to be friends with all three of you, I really would, but it seems that sentiment will never be returned.'

'That's not true.' Guilt writhed inside Freda, heat warming her cheeks. 'From now on, if you need—'

'We'd better get on.' Unmistakable tears glinted in Kathy's eyes. 'I wouldn't want you to say something you'll regret.'

Kathy strode ahead leaving Freda to follow, feeling awful. She swallowed hard, shouldering the culpability that pressed down on her. She and Sylvia had been unduly distant to Kathy. They both should have guessed there was more to her manner than innate spite. The girl had clearly endured a home life Freda and her friends had been fortunate enough to have never experienced.

The ambulance bay was working at full steam and over the next two hours she and Kathy barely had time to look at one another, let alone speak. At last, there was a moment's break and Keith, an ambulance driver who Freda and her friends knew better than any of the other nurses on account of him helping them after a *slight* misdemeanour the three of them had participated in a few months back, came out from the hospital bearing two paper cups of water.

'Here,' he said, holding them out to her and Kathy, his green-eyed gaze as happy as always. 'Have yourselves a drink. You deserve it.'

Freda smiled. 'Thanks, Keith, you're a—'

The air raid siren pealed through the air, making them all jump, the water leaping from their cups to the ground.

'Bloody hell! Not again,' Keith shouted above the noise, hastily putting on his hat. 'Right, come on. Let's get the patients we have just loaded into the ambulance back downstairs and into the basement before all hell breaks loose.'

The three of them worked in tandem and soon the two patients were safely in the basement wards.

Keith slapped his hands together and flashed his usual devil-may-care grin despite the continuing explosions from an endless stream of incendiary bombs and machine-gun fire outside. 'Right, if you ladies have no further need of my services, I'll head back to the bay in case we get any more poor buggers coming in. See you later.'

'God, here we go again,' Kathy said, pushing some of her fallen blonde hair under her cap. 'Let's hope this one is over as quickly as the second raid. Then again, from what I could tell, the second was far worse.'

'Well, I haven't heard any huge explosions,' Freda said. 'But when I went outside, I saw first-hand the damage the smaller bombs can do.' She glanced at Kathy who carefully watched her, her gaze unreadable. 'Kathy, I'm sorry.'

'For what?'

'Everything. Your parents. Me and Sylvia. We should've made more of an effort—'

'Yeah, and maybe I should've been a darn sight nicer to you all.' She shrugged, her gaze softening. 'Maybe we can all make some changes going forward?'

Freda smiled. 'Maybe we can.'

Before they could say more, Sylvia came up beside them. 'Am I glad to see you two,' she panted.

Freda frowned. 'What is it?'

'As you and the other nurses did so well getting patients on their way to the rural hospitals, we have fewer cases to manage now and Mr Martin has even instructed V back on the ward. Therefore' – Sylvia looked at Kathy – 'I'd like you to go along to the basement ward Sister Campbell is overseeing and work with Veronica to do all you can to keep patients calm through this latest raid.' She faced Freda. 'And you and I will do the same here. The hospital is now as safe as it can be under the circumstances and the chance of there being any damage to this floor is highly unlikely.'

'Veronica's working with her mother?' Freda asked.

'I purposely arranged it so she can spend a bit of time with her,' Sylvia said, her eyes showing her anxiety as she surveyed the ward. 'Veronica mentioned more than once about her mother's tendency to fret about her under lesser circumstances so I thought it might help.'

'Lucky for Nurse Campbell that she's got a mother who cares,' Kathy said. 'I'll head off to the other ward now, shall I?'

Sylvia gave a curt nod. 'Thank you for your compliance, Nurse Scott.'

Kathy and Sylvia locked eyes for a long moment before Kathy snatched her hand to her head in a salute. 'Not a problem, *ma'am*.'

She marched away and Freda carefully watched her friend as Sylvia scowled after her.

'Why can't she be nice for once?' Sylvia fumed. 'I just don't understand her. She must be more amiable with Veronica, otherwise how in God's name does she tolerate her?'

'Sylv?'

Sylvia faced her. 'What?'

'We need to talk about Kathy when the three of us next manage to grab some time together.'

'Why? What's she done now?'

'She told me something earlier that makes me feel we're as much to blame for what's gone on between us and her since we started working together. We need to make some changes.'

'What are you talking about? She's not threatening to tell Sister Dyer what she knows about us, is she?'

'No, I think the fact we did a moonlight flit with one of the patients weeks ago is the farthest thing from Kathy's mind right now.' The distant sounds of bombs dropping brought Freda's attention back to where it should have been. 'We should get on with our jobs. I'll tell you everything later.'

'Wait.' Sylvia gripped her arm as Freda moved to walk away. 'You don't look right. If Kathy's upset you—'

'It's not just Kathy, Sylv. Has V spoken to you?'

'I've not had a chance to speak to anyone except Sister before I came to find you and Kathy.' Sylvia's cheeks reddened. 'I... was later getting back to the hospital than planned.' She cleared her throat and tilted her head towards the double doors into the hospital. 'We'd better get the supplies Sister asked me to get. You can tell me what's going on as we walk.'

By the time they had taken as much as they could carry from the supply cupboards on one of the upper floor wards and were on their way back to the basement, their arms full with bandages, gauze and ointment, Freda had told Sylvia about Dorothy's pregnancy.

Sylvia's eyes were wide with disbelief. 'My God, your mother is going to have the turn of all turns.'

'A turn?' Freda laughed wryly. 'This will kill her, Sylv. If not with shock, then certainly complete and utter shame.'

They stopped as they came to the final landing at the top of the stairs that would take them to the basement wards, each flinching as a flurry of machine-gun fire passed by the hospital.

'Bloody hell, that was close,' Sylvia muttered, her eyes squinted. 'What if this isn't the last raid?'

Freda thought about the people in Bristol she had spent so much time visiting, talking to and writing about. 'Then the people of Bath will deal with it. We're all made of stronger stuff than we think.'

Sylvia smiled, her eyes glinting with pride. 'Yes, we are.'

Freda returned her friend's smile and then sighed. 'V is adamant that she should talk to Mr Martin about Dorothy.'

'What? Why?'

Freda's next words stuck like barbed wire in her throat, but she swallowed past them. 'About an abortion.'

'Dorothy can't do that,' Sylvia said quietly, her gaze panicked. 'That's... not even an option.'

'Do you think I haven't said that to her? Not only is it illegal, she could die. I don't know what V thinks Mr Martin is going to say about it or why she insisted on speaking to him.'

'It's a child, Freda. Dorothy can't just get rid of it like it's an inconvenience.' Tears glistened in Sylvia's eyes before she blinked. 'Some people pray for children their entire lives and never get blessed. Dorothy cannot get rid of a baby without thinking of all the women in the world who—'

'Go through life without being a mother when they have wished for nothing more? I know that, Sylv. But we can't judge every situation, can we? We mustn't. Women need to support women. Maybe nurses need to support them even more so.'

Sylvia closed her eyes. 'You're right. Of course you're right,' she said, opening them. 'But we should still do all we can to convince Dorothy to either keep the baby or have it adopted. Abortion is not safe, Freda. Maybe it will be one day, but it isn't right now. Your mum will come around soon enough. This baby is her grandchild. Her *first* grandchild.'

'I'm not sure that will make a blind bit of difference considering how angry she'll be when she finds out.'

Boom!

They both jumped.

'Come on,' Sylvia said. 'Or else Sister Dyer will be on the warpath.'

They grimaced at the poor turn of phrase before Freda drew in a strengthening breath and followed Sylvia down the final flight of stairs and into the ward. Dorothy's pregnancy was a stark and real reminder that women's lives – their bodies – were never entirely their own. This pregnancy was not a reason to celebrate as it should have been, but a gargantuan problem that was likely to ruin her sister's life whatever course of action Dorothy decided to take. Freda pulled back her shoulders. Which only served as a new and stark reminder of why she felt ever more strongly that she must carve out a life of her own making, of doing something she truly wanted to do before she found herself in the middle of a life – a marriage – she didn't want five years from now.

19

VERONICA

Veronica couldn't be sure if the third bombing lasted an hour and a half or two hours, but suddenly it was over, the all-clear siren sounded and, once again, the basement wards erupted with cheers from the patients and staff.

'Oh, my darling, the danger has passed,' her mother said, sliding her arm around Veronica's waist and pulling her close. 'At least for now.'

Veronica smiled at her mother, her heart swelling with love for her. 'Yes, I hope so. Better still, let's hope the Germans have finished with Bath completely.'

Her mother stood back, her gaze on her staff as her smiling nurses returned to the task of making sure those in distress were comforted. Veronica's smile dissolved as she cast a sidelong glance at her mother. They had spoken a few times about Veronica's wish to move out and live independently, but each and every time her mother refused to listen to her. No doubt these bombings and the fact that so many people would now be homeless would be what her mother relied upon for Veronica dropping the issue.

Unfortunately, she would be wrong.

Unless Mr Riley's house was little more than a pile of rubble after this most recent attack and there was nothing for him to come home to from his mother-in-law's, Veronica would be leaving as soon as she was able. Yet still, shame warmed her cheeks that she'd hope for another's home to be demolished. After all, Riley's wife and children were not to blame for Mark Riley's wrongdoing or – as Veronica suspected – wrongdoings. The more she reflected on that awful day, the more convinced she was that his rape of her wasn't the first time he had done such a heinous thing, and she had no reason to think he hadn't assaulted others since. Guilt engulfed her as it always did. She had never reported what happened to her to the authorities; hadn't done anything to stop him doing what he'd done to her to someone else. She hadn't been strong enough and now too much time had passed.

'Right, we should get a move on,' her mother said beside her, bringing Veronica out of her tormenting thoughts. 'Why don't you go back to the other ward and see if Sister Dyer would like you back with her now that the raid seems to be over? If not, I'd love you back working with me for a while. It feels nice to have you close by.'

Veronica looked into her mother's loving gaze. Would she even believe her if she told her the truth about Mr Riley? After all, Veronica had invited him into their home, made him a cup of tea, given him a slice of cake…

'Veronica?'

'Yes?'

Her mother laughed and took her elbow, steering her in the direction of the ward doors. 'Go and see Sister Dyer.'

'Yes. Right. See you later.'

The ward bustled with activity, a sense of celebration in the air, relief that the hospital had not taken a hit since the first raid and everyone on the wards remained unharmed. No word of casualties or fatalities had filtered through from any other parts of the hospital, and Veronica sent up a silent prayer there were none.

Her gaze wandered to Officer Matthews's bed.

She had not spoken to him since leaving for surgery after the first raid over twenty-four hours before. Nerves jumped and leapt in her stomach. The last time they were together they'd had their most heated conversation to date. What started about his reluctance that she removed the bandages on his face had turned into a surety that somehow, some way, she and Eric either knew one another or had at least met before.

She strode forward and his eyes met hers as she came close to the bed, but not before she noticed his bandages had been changed by someone else.

'Hello,' Veronica said, once again looking deep into his eyes, searching for a small trace of recognition. Nothing. 'How are you?'

'Fine,' he said stiffly.

'That's good.'

The seconds ticked by before he cleared his throat. 'I'll wager that raid will be the last,' he said. 'Can't possibly know for sure, of course, and I certainly have no idea what's going on all over Bath, but if they haven't dropped any of their big bombs and only dropped incendiaries, they're done with us. We're clearly not worth wasting their biggest assets on.'

'Let's hope so. I'd rather Bath was worth nothing to them. We all would.' Veronica crossed her arms. 'Who changed your bandages?'

He slid his gaze away from her. 'Nurse Roberts.'

Sylvia. At least she'd be able to ask her friend more about Eric's face later. 'Good.' She smiled. 'And you're comfortable?'

'Yes.'

He met her gaze once more and she held it, her heart thundering. 'Good, then I would say you are as comfortable as you can be. Agreed?'

He lifted his shoulders.

'Excellent.' Her cheeks ached from the strain of her smile. 'Then we'll continue our conversation from before and you can tell me who you are and how I know you.'

Panic flared in his dark blue eyes, his gaze darting over her face, but even as guilt twisted inside her, Veronica did not look away, did not give in. 'Well?'

'Nurse Campbell…' he said quietly. 'Why does it matter to you so much that you know who I am? I will be moved from here soon enough and then you'll never see me again.'

'Why does it matter?' She glared. 'I have been treating you, looking after you, giving you as much extra attention as I can without provoking a telling off from Sister and you ask me why it matters? Tell me how I know you.'

'Well now, what's going on here I wonder.'

Veronica snapped her gaze to Sylvia, who had appeared at her side, her friend's smile far too wide and her cheeks red. 'Everything all right, V? Only Sister Dyer has asked that you—'

'What are you two up to?' Freda asked so cheerfully that it was clearly forced as she joined them and stood on Veronica's other side. 'Is Officer Matthews keeping you captive with one of his stories by any chance?'

Narrowing her eyes, Veronica looked at each of her friends in turn. What were they doing? 'Go away. Both of you,' she snapped. 'Officer Matthews and I need a little chat. In private.'

Freda slipped her hand around Veronica's elbow. 'I can't see what you have to talk about privately.' She laughed, the sound entirely insincere. 'Patient and nurse, nurse and patient. Not allowed, V, you know that.'

Veronica glared, hating the heat that immediately assaulted her cheeks. 'We're not talking... that way.'

'Just as well with me being senior ward nurse.' Sylvia stepped in between her and the side of Eric's bed. 'Now, go along with Freda and I'll get Officer Matthews a cup of tea. Sister Dyer has already asked me twice to prise you away. Go on, V. You don't want to be getting in trouble now, do you?'

Veronica snatched her elbow from Freda's grasp and glared at her friends. 'You two are the worst actresses known to man,' she said. 'And neither of you had better disappear once we're allowed to leave the hospital tonight. We're walking home together. All three of us. Do you hear me?'

Sylvia nodded. 'Absolutely.'

'Sounds good to me,' Freda said, her blue eyes wide with innocence.

'Hmm.' Veronica tossed a final look at Eric before lifting her chin and marching over to Sister Dyer. 'I believe you wanted to see me, Sister?'

'Indeed I do, Nurse Campbell. Now...'

The sister's voice drifted as Veronica looked back at her friends who – unsurprisingly – had both left Eric's bedside now that she was busy with Sister Dyer. What did they know? And why had it caused them to deter her from speaking with Eric? Well, if they thought she was going to accept anything but the truth from them, they had another thing coming.

20

FREDA

Freda sat on a low stone wall outside the hospital entrance and stared blindly ahead at the street, the view blurry through the mist of her tears that she would not allow to fall. She was so frustrated! Everything felt such a mess, so out of her control, and it was not a usual or comfortable place for her to be. Dorothy had barely left her mind for more than a minute, she was incredibly worried – and feeling guilty – about Kathy, and it was also clear that Veronica was as determined to find out how she knew Eric Matthews as she'd been before the raids.

Freda closed her eyes. Not to mention that once again she had to return home and find out whether or not her house was still standing. Sickness rolled through her. God, how she hated this war!

She had such important work – exhausting work – to get done at the hospital. Sister Dyer and Sylvia relied on her to perform with the same diligence and commitment as the other nurses, not be distracted by personal goings-on and problems when the entirety of the city was in turmoil. Her thoughts were such a jumble of what to do for her sister, her patients, Richard, her writing. She had never felt so pulled in so many different directions.

Approaching footsteps had Freda hastily blinking away her tears and swiping her cheeks with her fingers. Sylvia and Veronica's faces were stony as they both stared at her, the foot of space between them telling Freda all she needed to know when the three of them walked with linked arms more often than not. Clearly, Veronica was still not happy about Freda and Sylvia interrupting her chat with Officer Matthews.

Slowly, Freda rose and forced a smile in the hope of evoking the same from one or both of her friends.

'Free at last,' she said, throwing out her arms. 'Sister doesn't want us back for at least twenty-four hours. Let's hope we still have beds to sleep in when so many don't.'

'Indeed,' Sylvia cried far too enthusiastically, her smile wide. 'There will be blessings to be counted, I'm sure!'

Freda glanced at Veronica, who stood a little away from them, her arms crossed and her jaw tight as she stared at something in the distance, almost certainly avoiding looking at them rather than looking at anything in particular.

'V?' Freda asked, throwing a grimace at Sylvia. 'Are you all right?'

Her friend turned her head so slowly, so deliberately, a slight chill ran along Freda's spine, and Sylvia took a step back as though she half expected Veronica to slap her.

'Am I all right?' Veronica threw a glare at each of them. 'Are you really asking me that?'

Freda purposefully pulled back her shoulders, braced for the inevitable onslaught.

Sylvia, on the other hand, thought it would be a good idea to instigate distraction. 'Anyhoo,' she said in a high, sing-song way that was so beyond the norm for Sylvia when her voice was almost certainly the deepest out of the three of them. She looked at Freda. 'I'm sure all our houses are still standing. We deserve that at least when we are doing all we can in the service of others, right? How are you feeling about going home and facing your sister again? Shall we walk while we talk?'

Veronica blew out a loud, exaggerated breath and pointedly brushed past them, leading the way.

Behind her back, Freda quickly looked at Sylvia and mouthed, *We have to tell her. Now.*

Sylvia mouthed back, *I know, and we will. Trust me.*

Freda inwardly groaned. Whenever Sylvia said 'trust me', it more often than not spelt trouble.

'So,' Sylvia said, striding forward to walk beside Veronica and gesturing with a wave to Freda to walk on Veronica's other side, 'what do you plan to say to Dorothy when you get home, Freda?'

Freda sighed, surrendering to whatever it was Sylvia had planned. 'I don't know,' she said. 'There's little chance Dorothy has told our parents she's expecting since yesterday, so I guess the first thing I'll be doing is hiding away with her in her bedroom and making sure she's all right.'

Freda stared at a flock of birds who had settled high above them on the exposed beams of a house's destroyed roof, seemingly unperturbed by the devastation. As they walked, they stepped around piles of bricks, broken glass and people's belongings and clothes littering the streets, everywhere peppered with the blue serge uniforms of the ARP wardens or the darker uniforms of firemen.

'Dorothy might be foolish,' she continued, 'but I love her, so looking after her to the best of my ability is my main concern at the moment. The last thing I want is for her to feel alone and start making hasty decisions. Or worse, deciding to take herself off and do something dangerous.'

'She won't do anything daft,' Sylvia said firmly. 'Now she's told you about the baby, I'm sure she feels like a weight's been lifted.'

'You don't know Dorothy,' Freda said dryly. 'She can be... Wait a minute, considering the circumstances, I'm not sure *I* even know Dorothy.'

'Well, it's understandable you feel that way, but let's give the girl the benefit—'

'I've spoken to Mr Martin.'

Freda whipped her head around so sharply to look at Veronica, something creaked in her neck. 'You have?'

Veronica slumped and stopped walking, her green eyes softening – a little. 'Yes.'

'And?'

'And...' She looked at Sylvia before touching her fingers to Freda's. 'He was not happy I raised the subject of abortion with him. In fact, he implied that I was selfish involving him because now he had knowledge of potential illegal activity.'

'That's rubbish,' Sylvia scoffed and crossed her arms, her eyes alight with annoyance. 'You were merely asking his professional advice, not to carry out the procedure! He's just trying to exert his authority, V. Nothing more.'

Veronica snatched her fingers from Freda's and glared at Sylvia. 'And you always know exactly what's what with everyone, don't you, Sylvia? Me, Freda, Kathy, Mr Martin... You know what's best for all of us.'

Freda stared at Veronica, her heart picking up speed. She had never known her so angry. She was – for understandable reasons – by far the quietest of the three of them, and to see her like this showed just how much she resented her friends' interference with Officer Matthews earlier. God, she wasn't in love with him, was she? She really hoped not. None of them should be exposing themselves to that right now. Falling in love was the last thing any of them needed to add to their growing pile of problems.

Her friends locked glares before Sylvia pointedly snatched her gaze away and stared at a building farther along the street whose upper floor was half blown off, rubble piled high on the pavement in front of it and spilling into the road.

Tension rose, unspoken words hovering between them like they never had before.

Freda scrambled for what to say next and the best course of action to take with regards to protecting Veronica while also respecting her wishes.

'Sorry,' Sylvia suddenly said and faced Veronica, colour staining her cheeks and her eyes sad. 'The truth is, I don't know much about anything most of the time, and what I do know isn't worth listening to anyway.'

'Everything you have to say is worth us listening to and always will be,' Freda admonished, disturbed to hear her vivacious friend talk about herself that way. 'We're all under so much stress and we can hardly blame Mr Martin for snapping at V or anyone else.'

'Exactly,' Veronica said, her gaze irritated. 'He is a wonderful man and he must be beyond exhausted, considering the conditions he's had to work under and the haphazard way he's been forced to pick and choose who should be treated and when over the last twenty-four hours.'

'We all need to take a deep breath,' Freda said, glancing at her friends before staring at Veronica. 'Clearly Mr Martin was far from happy, but did he give you any advice at all?'

'There was no advice he could give,' Veronica said. 'Abortion is illegal, Freda. That's all he said to me… several times, in fact.'

Although disappointed and in desperate need of some direction from someone – preferably from a man who likely knew more about the nature of Dorothy's predicament than most – Freda nodded. 'I understand.'

Veronica touched her hand again. 'We'll find a way to help Dorothy. There will be something we can do.'

Sylvia brushed past Veronica and slipped her arm around Freda's waist. 'We will. None of us, no matter what, are alone with our problems. Right?'

Freda smiled, tears pricking her eyes. 'Right.'

But when Veronica pulled her hand from hers, her expression was not one of mutual agreement.

'Why did the pair of you interrupt my conversation with Officer Matthews?' she demanded, all sympathy gone from her voice. 'It was like you were putting a boundary around him or something. I am so angry you did that, I could—'

'We had to,' Sylvia said, her gaze wary. 'It's better that you hear what he knows from us first, not him. That way, you can react as you will, scream, shout, cry—'

'Wait.' V's eyes widened and her cheeks mottled. 'Hear what he knows?' She snatched her gaze between them. 'You both know something about him and haven't told me?'

Freda reached for Veronica's hand, relieved when she didn't immediately pull away. 'We didn't know how to tell you.' She glanced at Sylvia, who continued to stare at Veronica, her lips pulled tightly together. Freda knew the look on Sylvia's face all too well. She was so angry with Officer Matthews she didn't trust herself to speak. 'We still don't.'

Veronica snatched her hand away and tightly crossed her arms, her green eyes livid – worse, hurt. 'Tell me.'

Freda swallowed against the dryness in her throat, looked at Sylvia and back to Veronica. 'I... he's... Oh, God, V. Officer Matthews found you—'

'He was the one who found you after you'd been raped,' Sylvia blurted, her cheeks red and her eyes bulging with undisguised anger, 'and despite all these weeks you've been caring for him, the sod hasn't said a word!'

Freda felt like the entire city had come to a standstill as she stared at V, waiting for… she really didn't know what. Her friend's face was entirely white, her body trembling. She reached her hand out towards Veronica and then lowered it, thinking touching her might not be a good idea in that moment. 'Veronica?'

'V?' Sylvia asked. 'Did you hear what I—'

'He was there? It was him?' Veronica's eyes shone with tears as she darted her gaze between Freda and Sylvia. 'I didn't know. I wasn't sure. And then you…' She looked between them again. 'My two best friends, my two *only* friends find out, and don't tell me straight away.'

'V, please,' Freda said gently. 'We weren't sure whether you—'

'What?' Veronica cried. 'That I would want to know? That I wasn't strong enough to deal with it? How long have you known?'

'He…' Sylvia stepped closer. 'He told me no more than a day or two ago.'

'A day or two? And you didn't say a word to me?' Veronica brushed away her tears with the tips of her fingers. 'Yet you found the time to tell Freda? How could you?'

Freda pressed her hand to the sickness rolling around in her stomach. 'V—'

'Listen to me.' Sylvia touched Veronica's arm. 'We had every intention of telling you, but we wanted to tell you at the right—'

'The right time? My God.' Veronica stepped back and held her hands out like a shield in front of her. 'Would there ever be a right time to tell me this? You're my friends, you should have told me straight away.' Her voice cracked. 'You should have told me!'

And then Veronica turned and ran along the middle of the cobbled road, disappearing amongst the dust, gravel and broken stone.

'Well, now we've done it,' Sylvia mumbled.

Freda closed her eyes, wondering how much more heartache she and her friends could take.

21

VERONICA

It was just after seven thirty the following morning when Veronica pulled the front door of her house quietly closed and started walking back to the hospital. The entirety of the previous evening had passed with her see-sawing between anger and regret for talking to Freda and Sylvia the way she had. One minute, she felt so angry she'd wanted to march to their houses and shout at them again. The next, she wanted to hang her head in shame for attacking her friends in such a way when, deep down, she knew they would never do anything to purposely upset her.

When she'd finally gone to bed, a fitful night had ensued until she'd tossed back her bedcovers at barely six o'clock that morning. She'd made her way downstairs and sat at the kitchen table ruminating how her friends hadn't told her that it had been Eric she'd sensed beside her at the worst possible time in her life. Or else nearly suffocating under the weight of humiliation wondering what he might or might not have seen.

As the hospital entranceway came into sight, Veronica pulled back her shoulders and jutted her chin despite the butterflies swarming around in her stomach. Arriving an hour before her and her friends' shift was due to start gave her guaranteed time to speak with Eric uninterrupted – or at least she hoped so.

Entering the hospital, she headed straight for the temporary staffroom, the old one no longer functioning due to blast damage. Once she had hung her cape and stowed her handbag in one of the cubby holes that had been hastily put together, Veronica purposefully marched to the basement and wished Sister Dyer a quick good morning as she passed her makeshift desk before heading straight for Eric's bedside.

He was sat bolt upright, seemingly ignoring the cup of tea on the wheeled table beside him, his eyes unwavering on hers as he watched her approach. Veronica resisted the urge to shiver. It was almost as though he'd been waiting for her.

She halted beside him and pinned him with a resolute stare. 'Good morning.'

'Good morning,' he replied, the bandages around his face obscuring his expression, leaving just his eyes for her to judge his frame of mind. 'You're early.'

'Do you have any idea why that might be?' she asked curtly.

'You're angry with me. Want to berate me without Nurses Roberts and Parkes around to stop you.'

She huffed a laugh in what she hoped was a show of nonchalance when inside, every part of her writhed with humiliation. 'Berate you? That's one way to put it.'

Her cheeks burned, her eyes stung. He knew what had happened to her. He knew she'd been raped. He'd seen her on the kitchen floor, her clothes in disarray, her underwear gone...

'All I want from you is the truth,' she said, astounded her voice sounded so in control.

Veronica crossed her arms, guilt niggling her. He didn't deserve her anger. Or did he? She wasn't sure. All she was sure about was that Eric Matthews had been through so much during his time fighting overseas, was still suffering physically and mentally, and most likely always would to some degree. And even though she'd devoted every minute of time she could spare to him, cared for him above and beyond what was usual, she was making him suffer as though he was to blame for everything that unfolded yesterday between her and her friends.

But he was to blame, wasn't he? Albeit to a lesser extent than Freda and Sylvia. Their secrecy had upset her the most.

She drew in a deep breath. 'Tell me how I know you.'

His bright, crystal-blue eyes bored into hers for a long moment before he spoke. 'You don't know? Surely, Nurse Roberts...' His Adam's apple bobbed as he swallowed. 'Didn't she tell you?'

Her friends' treachery punched her heart once again just as it had a hundred times through the night, and Veronica drew in a fortifying breath. 'I want to hear it from you, and if by any chance you are still unprepared to fill in the gaps of how we met – gaps that you seemed to have had no problem sharing with Nurses Parkes and Roberts – then I—'

'I only told Nurse Roberts,' he interrupted. 'I never said a word to Nurse Parkes.'

'Maybe not, but you have commented more than once that myself and my friends are as thick as thieves, so you must have suspected Nurse Roberts would speak to Nurse Parkes – or even me – sooner or later, yet still you didn't do everything possible to ensure I heard what you know directly from you. That, Officer Matthews, is what hurts the most. In fact, it's that that's making me more furious with you than anyone else on the planet right now. Including Hitler!'

Her heart pulsed in her ears as the seconds passed. She squeezed her eyes shut before furtively looking around them, relieved that her voice did not seem to have carried above the hubbub of the ward.

'You know, don't you?' he asked quietly.

Heat travelled up her neck and along her jaw, but Veronica forced herself to meet his gaze. How much of her body had he seen that day? Riley had ripped her knickers, her blouse. Had her breasts been exposed? Yes, they were. She still remembered the shame of trying to pull her blouse closed, half the buttons scattered on the kitchen lino.

Looking away from him, she scanned the ward for the sister. Spotting her deep in conversation with Kathy Scott, Veronica drew up a chair and sat, took Eric's hand in hers. At least if Sister Dyer looked their way, she would assume Veronica was comforting him. Since the raids, the sister had somewhat relaxed her views on the correct way for nurses to comfort patients.

'Tell me,' Veronica said. 'I need to hear it from you.'

Once more, the silence stretched.

Then Eric tightened his fingers around hers, his gaze hard. 'Nurse Campbell... Veronica—'

'Tell me, Eric. Please.'

He dropped his head back against the pillows and stared at the ceiling, his body still. Veronica resisted the urge to tell him not to worry, to forget it. She had never asked anything of anyone that might risk their discomfort – their distress – but this was different. This concerned something that happened to her that sent her life veering in a different direction, changed who she'd been the day before. In just a few minutes she'd gone from being happy, trusting, easy-going and fun to be around to someone quiet, studious, well-mannered and untrusting... of herself and others.

It always amazed her how her mother never seemed to notice the change in her – or did she?

Eric shifted on the bed, breaking Veronica's reverie. She stared at him.

His chest rose as he inhaled. 'I was walking along your street, close to your house, and thought I heard a scream before Mark Riley came flying out of your front door, almost knocking me to the ground. He was... adjusting his fly, his cheeks red, his forehead sweaty...'

Bile rose in Veronica's throat, her stomach churning. 'You knew him? You knew Mark Riley?'

'Not then, no. But I made a point of learning his name afterwards.'

Veronica nodded, her mouth draining dry. 'I see.'

He briefly closed his eyes, opened them again. 'My every instinct told me something was very wrong... I suspected that maybe he'd... so I pushed open your front door, walked into the house.'

'Didn't you think to call out? Wait for someone to answer you?' she demanded. 'You were in someone else's house.'

'I did call out. At least twice.'

Veronica shook her head, her foot bouncing up and down on the tiled floor. 'I don't believe you.'

'Veronica—'

'I would've heard you. I would've had a chance to... sort myself out a little before you came into the kitchen.'

'It was obvious as soon as I walked into your house that no man lived there, or at least that's what I surmised. There was no man's coat or hat hung on the hallway hooks, nothing masculine amongst the feminine, and then I walked into the kitchen...' He shook his head. 'You were as white as a sheet,' he said quietly. 'Sat on the floor, your back against the wall. Your legs were pulled up, your arms wrapped around them...' He closed his eyes again. 'I didn't see anything... you know, that you wouldn't have wanted me to see. I promise.'

The depth of her degradation made the hairs on her arms stand up, her humiliation harsher than ever before. 'Thank you for saying that.'

'It's true. I saw nothing. Honestly.'

'And then what? All I remember is a draught drifting over me and then I seemed to suddenly wake up.' She glared at him, her voice sticking on the lump in her throat. 'I was alone, Eric. I know I was.'

'You would've been. I couldn't rouse you. For a long time, you were just staring blindly ahead, then you looked at me for a long moment before turning away and resumed that horrible, desolate staring. All I could think' – he shook his head, rage darkening his eyes – 'was to go after him, so I did.'

He looked away from her, his hand slipping away from hers, and he curled it into a fist on the bed. 'I don't know if I did the right thing leaving you that way, but all I could think about was putting my hands around the bastard's neck.' He shifted his eyes to hers and they blazed with a terrifying fury. 'And I did, albeit a week or so later because that's how long it took for me to track him down, to find him. I didn't know then that he lived on the same street as you, which explained how he managed to disappear so quickly. He probably ducked straight back into his house. Son of a bitch.'

Veronica flinched, her stomach knotting with a strange blend of hope and dread. 'It was you? You put Mr Riley in the hospital?'

'Yes.'

'Did you... ever come back? To my street?' Veronica asked. 'Back to see Riley again?'

'Several times.'

'But you never knocked on my door or tried to talk to me? Why?'

'How could I? I couldn't be sure you even saw me. Clearly you didn't.'

'But—'

'I didn't want to be a reminder of something I assumed you'd rather forget. Rather no one knew anything about.' Tears glazed his eyes. 'I just wanted whatever you wanted, Veronica. The last thing I wanted was to turn up on your doorstep and force you to recollect something so distressing.'

She nodded. 'And Mark Riley? What did you do when you saw him again?'

'I put him back in the hospital.'

Realisation struck and a weak smile pulled at her mouth. 'So the times Mr Riley has disappeared? That's because of you?'

Satisfaction sparked in his eyes. 'Yes.'

'But... did he know why you kept going after him back then?'

'Oh, he knew.'

She dipped her head, stared at her lap. 'But it doesn't stop him talking to me.' She lifted her gaze to him. 'The man is an animal.'

'He is.' Eric's eyes shadowed with anger once again. 'And I could kill him just knowing he still has the audacity to even look at you, let alone speak to you. Damn my injuries,' he said from between clenched teeth. 'Damn this war. It's been far too long since the last time I paid Riley a visit because of this stupid war. I've been in service since 1939.'

'Of course.'

He glared. 'Please don't give that animal any respect by calling him mister. He's nothing but a damn rapist.'

'Shh!' Veronica looked over her shoulder at Sister Dyer, who was now making her way along the hospital beds, coming ever closer to her and Eric. She quickly stood. 'You should have told me who you were weeks ago, Eric.'

'How could I? How was I supposed to open that conversation?'

'You should have found a way.'

He shook his head. 'Well, I'm sorry, but I'm glad I didn't because what I feared would happen if I said anything to you is happening right now.'

'Which is?'

'You're looking at me differently. Speaking to me differently.' His gaze wandered over her face, lingered at her lips. 'Not that I blame you, I just didn't want everything to change between us.' He met her eyes. 'You're a wonderful woman, Veronica, and I've enjoyed every minute I've had getting to know you.'

Tears burned her eyes and Veronica blinked them away. 'Thank you.' She managed a small smile. 'And you're a wonderful man. And, if truth be told, I understand how hard it must have been to say anything. I should go.' She smoothed the front of her apron, her hands trembling before she met his gaze once more, her heart stumbling to see such pleading in his eyes. She forced a smile. 'I'll see you later.'

She lingered a moment longer as indecision and uncertainty wound through her. What was she supposed to do next? How would anything be the same between them now she had met that invisible something – that invisible someone – she had sensed in the kitchen with her that day?

Turning, Veronica quickly brushed past the sister and headed towards the ward exit, needing a moment to calm her thundering heart, to cry a few tears so that she could contain the rest until after her shift. Because there would be more. A lot more.

22

FREDA

Freda looked out of the tearoom window for the fourth time since she and Dorothy had arrived twenty minutes before. She scanned the street looking for Sylvia and Veronica, her nerves stretched to breaking. Still no sign of them. She glanced across the table at Dorothy, who was tucking into a currant bun as though she had no problems or strains in her life at all.

'Are you enjoying that?' Freda demanded, barely managing to keep her voice down.

'I am as it happens,' Dorothy said. 'After all, I'm eating for two, right?'

'That is not the slightest bit funny, Dot.'

Her sister shrugged.

Freda glared. 'My friends are coming here to help us. Veronica most of all, and she is only just speaking to Sylvia and me again.'

'What? Why? What have you done?' Her sister's blue eyes brightened with interest. Even with the seriousness of her own issues, it seemed Dorothy cared more for gossip than anything else. 'The way you talk about them I'd assumed you three to be the Three Musketeers, entirely unbreakable and all that.'

'You don't need to know what's happening between me and my friends, all you need to know is that it is thanks to Veronica's close working relationship with a surgeon at the hospital that, after he said he wasn't willing to talk to her about your situation, he changed his mind and gave her some advice.' Freda worried her bottom lip, her nerves jumping. 'God knows we need it. Or at least I do, whereas you don't seem to give a fig what happens next!'

'Of course I do, but I'm not having this baby so it's neither here nor there.'

Freda stared at her in disbelief, her heart picking up speed. 'If we were alone right now...'

'Well, we're not,' Dorothy sneered. 'So you can't do whatever it is you want to do to me, can you? The fact of the matter is, sister dear, you shouldn't have said anything to your friends without my permission.'

'Is that so?'

Dorothy's eyes flashed with anger, colour darkening her cheeks. 'Yes.'

'Well, I have no regrets asking for their help. We need it, and you more so than me. Sooner or later, Dorothy Parkes, you'll realise just how much!'

'I don't think so.'

Freda glared at her sister's bowed head as Dorothy resumed devouring her currant bun. Where were her friends? She'd soon need them here to prevent her committing murder, let alone anything else.

The bell above the door tinkled, the jauntiness of it so erroneous amid a city where parts were blown to pieces even though others remained untouched like the street housing the tearoom.

Committed attempts to clear the devastation had already begun with hundreds upon hundreds of Home Guard, ARPs, firemen, doctors and nurses, both from within Bath and volunteers coming to help from outside the city, spending hours clearing and searching for survivors and recovering the dead.

'I think your friends are here,' Dorothy mumbled around a mouthful of bun. 'And don't they look pretty?'

Freda turned and despite her need to throttle Dorothy, she softly smiled, her tense shoulders relaxing – a little. Sylvia and Veronica did look nice, and they almost certainly wouldn't be aware of it. Well, Veronica wouldn't be. It was possible Sylvia did, of course. Out of their uniforms, their hair curled and left to flow from beneath their hats to their shoulders, her friends looked young and beautiful, like a pair of women who shouldn't have a care in the world, yet they did. A lot of cares.

She raised her hand, gesturing them over.

Sylvia and Veronica joined her and Dorothy at the table and, as they lowered into their seats, they both looked at Dorothy, who continued to eat her bun as though they weren't there. Practically humming with suppressed annoyance, Freda deliberately sat back. She would not intervene. She knew Dorothy well enough to know that this silly show of nonchalance was far from genuine and why her sister wasn't acknowledging her friends' presence was because she didn't know how to under the circumstances.

Sylvia held out her hand. 'Dorothy, I presume?' she said. 'It's nice to finally meet you.'

Freda bit back a smile. Sylvia could always be relied upon to be the one to step front foot forward and centre.

Dorothy looked up and tentatively took Sylvia's hand. 'You, too.'

'Sylvia.' Sylvia flashed a smile, her eyes shining with the

epitome of friendliness. 'And this' – she waved towards Veronica – 'is Veronica. We're Freda's friends, but I'm sure you know that already. What you might not know is that we are here for Freda. No one else right now...' She pinned Dorothy with a glare that had her sister swallowing and pushing the last of her bun to the side. 'Is that understood? Loyalty from us is earned, not presumed.'

Freda itched to say something to help Dorothy, but her sister needed this talking to, and having it delivered by Sylvia would be a darn sight more effective than it would coming from her.

Dorothy nodded. 'I understand.' She hesitated before warily looking at Veronica. 'Pleased to meet you, too.'

Veronica's smile was distinctly warmer than Sylvia's. 'How are you feeling?'

Dorothy managed a weak smile. 'Fine, thank you.'

A waitress came to the table and took their order for another pot of tea and two flapjacks for Sylvia and Veronica. Once the waitress had retreated, Freda cleared her throat and leaned forward, feeling a little sorry for Dorothy even if she didn't deserve her sympathy.

'Thanks for coming, ladies,' she said, smiling at the best friends a girl could ask for. 'It might not seem like it, but I'm sure Dorothy appreciates your support.'

'Oh, I do.' Dorothy sat straighter in her chair, the shine of tears in her eyes belying her previous indifference. 'I'm sorry for being... you know.'

Relief and a little pride swelled Freda's heart, knowing how much it would've taken for Dorothy to admit such a thing.

'Well, you can thank us if we manage to make a difference to your current situation,' Sylvia said with her usual frankness. 'The fact of the matter is' – she made a show of looking over her shoulders before lowering her voice – 'that baby in your belly is coming out one way or another, whether you like it or not.'

'It is, indeed,' Freda agreed, staring at Dorothy and fighting the need to comfort her. Sylvia's heart was bigger than an ocean and Freda had no doubt she was stepping up as the hard one of her friends so Freda wouldn't have to. 'And that's why Dorothy is willing to listen to everything we have to say and will make her future decisions on fact, not misplaced pride.' She raised her eyebrows at Dorothy. 'Right?'

Dorothy nodded, her face pale.

'Good.' Freda turned to Veronica, whose brow was creased as she carefully watched Dorothy as though gauging her from a medical point of view, which Freda had no doubt she was. 'Why don't you tell us what Mr Martin had to say, V?'

Veronica blinked from her contemplation and immediately flashed Dorothy an encouraging smile. 'Well, I very much doubt what he said will be what you want to hear, but as you are Freda's sister, that means you matter to us – all of us – more than you realise.'

Two spots of colour darkened Dorothy's cheeks. 'Thank you.'

'Therefore…' Veronica sighed. 'I will tell you the truth of what my boss, who happens to be one of the top surgeons in Bath, had to say when I' – she furtively glanced around her and lowered her voice – 'asked him to talk to me about the alternatives available to pregnant women should they not wish to keep their child.'

Everyone around the table knew what 'alternative' they were really there to discuss.

'What he said,' Veronica continued, 'shocked me more than words can say, so I want you to listen very carefully. All right?'

Dorothy paled even further and nodded, whereas Freda

suddenly felt incredibly sick. She glanced at Sylvia, who gave her an encouraging wink.

The waitress chose that moment to return to the table and took her merry time laying out the teapot, cups and saucers until Freda feared Sylvia would snatch their flapjacks from the poor girl's hands. At last, the tea was poured and they were left alone once more. No one seemed keen to eat.

Veronica cleared her throat and spoke directly to Dorothy again, succinctly layering as much warning into why abortion was a bad idea, the dire and frequent resulting consequences, and that Mr Martin advised against it completely. However, it was what she finished with that had each of them, Freda included, sitting stock-still and silent in their seats.

'Sorry,' Sylvia eventually said, breaking the silence and staring wide-eyed at Veronica. 'He wants to see Dorothy at home? *His* home?'

Veronica nodded.

Dorothy's eyes widened. 'Well, does that mean he's willing to—'

'I've no idea,' Veronica interceded, her face etched with concern as she looked nervously around the table, her gaze settling on Dorothy. 'And it will do you no good to assume anything at this stage.'

'She won't,' Freda said, grasping Dorothy's shaking hand where it lay on the table. 'She won't assume anything. No doubt he just wants to speak to her somewhere privately.' She looked around the tearoom. 'Which is exactly what *we* should be doing.'

'Well...' Sylvia picked up her teacup and took a hefty sip. 'There's nothing like a bit of personal drama to put pay to Hitler's tantrums, is there? Come on, girls, let's talk about something else for a while, shall we?'

Freda picked up her tea. 'In that case, I think this is as good a time as any to tell you what has been going on with Kathy.'

Sylvia groaned. 'Why are you so determined for us to get along with that woman? She's a pain in the—'

'She's *in* pain, Sylv,' Freda snapped. 'We need to change the way we are with her. Ask her to join us now and then when we go out and see how we go along.'

'Why?' Veronica asked. 'Is this about her parents?'

'Yes.' Freda looked between her friends and glanced at Dorothy, who stared blindly ahead, lost in her own thoughts. 'If what Kathy told me is true, which I believe it is, she needs our friendship.'

Sylvia slumped, her gaze softening. 'Go on then. Let's hear it.'

'Well…' Freda exhaled a shaky breath. 'It seems her mum and dad…'

23

SYLVIA

Five hours into yet another harrowing night shift, Sylvia tentatively touched the letter in her apron pocket as though making sure it was still there and not a figment of her imagination. Nurses brushed past her, some walking alone, some pushing bloodied and bandaged patients in wheelchairs or else helping others to walk, each of them in a near-comatose state, especially the mothers who had lost children.

A few days had passed since what everyone prayed was Germany's final attack on Bath, but Bath's people remained in a state of semi-shock, even if most were making a good show of stalwart bravery – or maybe defiance. Sylvia drew in a long breath, slowly releasing it. She had no doubt the shock, trauma and heartbreak would go on for months, maybe even years.

She stopped and leaned her shoulder against the corridor wall, doing her best to make herself as inconspicuous as possible – a pretty tall order considering the godawful brightness of her auburn hair. She put her lunch box and flask on the windowsill beside her and then slipped the letter from her pocket, began to reread it again for what felt like the fiftieth time since she'd found it waiting for her on the doormat when she'd returned home from the previous night's shift.

Dear Miss Roberts,

There is every chance you have done all you can to forget me, but I hope you at least remember my son with fondness.

Sylvia huffed a laugh. She'd never held any animosity towards Jesse's mother, it had been much more the other way around, but it was good the woman had managed to hold on to a sense of humour. Most hadn't.

Jesse has been proclaimed unfit for service (not that the powers that be know what they're talking about, I'm sure), and he will soon be home where he belongs. I have no idea what has happened to him and pray, by the grace of God, it is something I will be able to manage well enough. The reason I am writing to you now is that Jesse wants to return to Bath and where Jesse goes from now on, the entire Howard family goes. I suspect this wish of his has something to do with you. Therefore, I hope you will find it in your heart to at least pay him a visit once we're settled. I will write again with our new address.

Yours sincerely,
Corinne Howard (Mrs)

Sylvia closed her eyes.

I suspect this wish of his has something to do with you.

Could she dare to hope Mrs Howard was right? Hope that Jesse really wanted to see her – maybe even wanted her back – after the way she'd cut him off?

'Sylv?'

She jumped and turned, hastily stuffing the letter in her pocket. 'Hey, you two,' she said, flashing a shaky smile at Freda and Veronica as they came to stand in front of her. 'Joining me for a bite of lunch?'

'Is everything all right?' Freda asked, concern showing in her blue eyes. 'You looked so worried just now. You didn't even hear me tormenting you.'

Sylvia's smile strained. 'What did you say?'

'It doesn't matter.' Veronica touched Sylvia's elbow. 'What's wrong?'

Sylvia looked between her friends as shame descended. She hadn't been honest with them about her feelings for Jesse, how badly it had affected her when he'd signed up to fight, or even the fact he was black.

She cleared her throat. 'I've got some things I need to tell you. Things I should've told you ages ago.' She picked up her lunch box and flask from the windowsill. 'Come on, let's grab a table in the canteen.'

Once they had opened their packed lunches and each poured a cup of tea, Sylvia shifted uncomfortably in her seat. Freda and Veronica had barely stopped watching her since they'd entered the canteen and it seemed they wouldn't until they had heard what she had to say.

'I've received a letter. From Jesse's mum.'

A moment or two of silence and then...

'Oh, Sylv,' Freda said. 'He's not... is he?'

Veronica clutched Freda's hand. 'What does she say?'

'He's not dead, he's coming home. To Bath,' Sylvia said, sighing. 'He's unfit for service, whatever that means. Not that it's stopped me imagining every possible scenario, each one worse than the one before.' She closed her eyes. 'We're hardly ignorant about what this war is doing to our service men and women, are we? We also know "unfit for service" could mean anything.'

Freda took her hand. 'We also know not to jump to any conclusions about anything until we know the facts. Jesse might be perfectly all right to resume his job on the railway. Don't go upsetting yourself by thinking the worst.'

'Anyway,' Veronica said, smiling, even though sadness lingered in her eyes, 'he's coming back to Bath, rather than returning to Wales where he's been living for months. That's good news, right? You want him back here, don't you?'

'You're forgetting it was me who called things off between us, V.' Sylvia sighed. 'I'm still halfway convinced it's because of me that he signed up in the first place.'

'Maybe, maybe not,' Freda said sharply. 'Either way, Jesse made the decision to go, not you.'

Sylvia squeezed Freda's fingers before she picked up her cheese sandwich and then tossed it back onto the greaseproof paper she'd wrapped it in, her stomach turning over just from the smell of it. 'From what his mother says in the letter, I can only presume she wrote to me under duress of doing her best by Jesse. Which is the most pleasing scenario, or' – she blew out a breath – 'she's so worried about him medically, she wants a nurse on hand.'

'And would it be so bad if it's the latter?' Veronica asked. 'You still care for him, don't you?'

'I care for anyone injured in this bloody war, V. You know that.'

Veronica picked up her Spam sandwich, took a bite and chewed, put her fingers to her lips. 'Well, I'm neither stupid nor blind, Sylvia Roberts,' she said, swallowing and dropping her hand. 'This letter has put the wind up you because you regret losing Jesse, regret him signing up and regret not telling the man how you really feel about him despite the fact it's always been written all over your face for the whole world to see.' Veronica raised her eyebrows. 'Including Jesse, I'm sure, which most likely would have only confused the poor man even more.'

Sylvia stared at Veronica's turned cheek as she continued to tuck into her sandwich. 'Well, you've got a lot to say for yourself, haven't you?'

Veronica shrugged.

Freda laughed, her blue eyes twinkling with pride as she looked at Veronica and then Sylvia. 'I think V has voiced the crux of it to a T, don't you, Sylv?' she asked, raising her eyebrows. 'Jesse's coming home. That can only be a good thing. What happens next is up to you.'

'But what if he—'

'No ifs or buts allowed,' Freda said, lifting her finger. 'If this war has taught us anything, it's that nothing can be assumed. Not any more.'

Sylvia watched her friends eat before slowing picking up her sandwich and taking a bite. It was like chewing rubber. She forced the morsel down. 'There's something else I should've told you about Jesse. Something I was scared to tell you when he and I were courting in case you... disapproved.'

Freda and Veronica exchanged a cautious look before slowly putting down their sandwiches and simultaneously picking up their teacups. The synchronisation of it would've been laughable had Sylvia's stomach not been in knots and her mouth drained dry. What in God's name did they think she was going to tell them? Then again, Jesse was black, she was white, and it was likely two-thirds or more of the country would have a problem with them being a couple.

She pulled back her shoulders and held her friends' expectant gazes. 'Jesse is black.'

Freda and Veronica stared back at her as the clamour in the canteen continued, shouting and jeering, laughing and chatting, crockery clattering and glass clinking. Sylvia tried and failed to decipher the look of absolute shock on Veronica's face and the look of utter, instantaneous concern on Freda's.

'Well?' Sylvia forced a laugh. 'Say something. V has already proven once today that she's broken through the timidness she used to carry around like a lead weight!'

The silence continued, their gaze flitting over Sylvia's face like she had been pebble dashed or something. Oh, to hell with this...

'Fine,' she cried, pushing to her feet. 'Forget it. I'm glad I told you, now it's up to the pair of you to deal with—'

'Sit down,' Freda said quietly. 'Just... give me a minute.'

Sylvia vibrated with the strength of her defensiveness and snatched her gaze to Veronica. 'Anything to say, V?'

'Plenty,' Veronica snapped back. 'But I'd rather you took a seat before I share it.'

The horrible insecurity Sylvia had around abandonment reared its ugly head again as she slowly sat. Was this the moment their beautiful friendship severed, never to be put back together again? Was she going to lose the two most wonderfully strong women with whom she wanted to be friends for the rest of her life? All because the colour of Jesse's skin was too much for them to accept? Well, if that was the case when they knew she damn well loved him, then...

'Is this why we never met him before he went away?' Freda asked, her blue eyes flashing with undisguised annoyance.

Sylvia swallowed. 'Partly, yes.'

'And the other part?' V asked quietly. 'What was that?'

'That I love him so much.'

'What are you talking about?'

'I was embarrassed. You both assume me so happy-go-lucky, but the truth of the matter is sometimes I want to be a wife and mother so much it hurts. And when I fall in love I fall hard, and by now I should know better having been dumped more times than I can count. I didn't want to look pathetic in front of you when you are both so amazing at dealing with everything and anything that's thrown at you.' Sylvia looked at them, tears threatening. 'I didn't want to admit how much it mattered to me that you liked him, accepted him. But now Jesse's coming back to Bath and I'm not sure I'll be able to let him go a second time... if he still wants me, of course.'

'Of course he wants you.' Freda smiled. 'The man could return to any part of England, Scotland, Ireland or Wales but – for some reason – he's coming back to Bath. Back to a city that the whole country knows is now on Hitler's radar.'

Confused by Freda's smile, the twinkle in her eye, Sylvia looked at Veronica only to see the same happy expression on her face.

'What?' Sylvia smiled. 'Why are you both looking like a pair of loons let out of the loony bin?'

'Because,' Freda said, laughing as she got up from her seat and put her arm around Sylvia's shoulders. 'Why in heaven's name did you think that the colour of Jesse's skin would matter one jot to me and V? Don't you know us at all?'

Veronica came around Sylvia's other side and slipped her arm around her waist, squeezing her close. 'You love him, Sylv,' she said. 'Do you know how wonderful that is after everything you've been through, everything the whole of Europe is going through? You love the man! I couldn't care if Jesse was bright pink with lilac spots, love is always something to celebrate. Always!'

Laughing, Sylvia kissed each of her friends on the cheek and then pulled them into a hug, heedless to the heckles from their fellow nurses.

24

FREDA

Tired to the marrow of her bones, Freda left the hospital, pleased that she had nothing more to do for the next few hours other than sleep. She just wanted to take some time to recharge so she'd be able to work as hard as possible the next day. With the bombings over – at least that was what everyone was saying – a semblance of procedure and process was being re-established on the ward, overseen by Sister Dyer and Sylvia.

She walked along the street, surveying the damage in the grey, early morning light and marvelling at how Bath's people had banded together to clear rubble and temporarily rehome those in need. Never before had the home front felt so necessary – yet still her need to do more, be more, niggled. Germany's attacks had undoubtedly changed the hearts and minds of almost all in Bath, and heaven knew they had changed hers, too. What she would do over the coming weeks and months, she did not know, but the one thing Freda was certain of was that there wasn't room in her heart and mind for a man and she had no idea if or when that would change.

She liked Richard. She liked him a lot. But she refused to allow her care for him to influence or alter what really mattered to her. And sooner or later she would tell him as much. But for now, she would concentrate on what needed to be done at the hospital. First thing tomorrow, she would help get the last of the patients from the basement wards onto the original wards where most of the blast damage had been sufficiently cleared that patients and nurses alike would be able to respectively recuperate and work.

'Good morning.'

She stopped walking and looked straight into Richard's ridiculously blue eyes, her treacherous heart promptly turning over. So much for her pep talk!

'Hello,' she said, purposefully averting her gaze from his. 'You do know it's barely seven o'clock in the morning, don't you?'

'I do. I've been at work since six.'

'So, what are you doing here?'

'Do you really need to ask me that?'

She turned and her cheeks warmed at the way his study grazed over every inch of her face to linger at her lips. 'Stop it,' she said.

He smiled. 'Stop what?'

She laughed and shook her head as they resumed walking again.

Richard cleared his throat. 'I left the office in the hope of buying something for my breakfast, but my feet took me to the hospital on the off chance you were on a night shift last night.' He winked. 'My instincts never let me down, you know that.'

She tried to suppress her smile, but it was hopeless. Her determination to remain stalwart against her growing feelings for him and her work at the paper always proved harder than she thought. She dragged her gaze from his and stared at the heavy machinery lining the street, ready to move rubble and stone once it reached a reasonable hour.

'So, how are things at the paper?' she asked.

'Well, for one, we're all missing you coming in and out of the office,' he said, frowning at a house completely cut in half, its interior exposed like a doll's house. 'I think it would be a good idea if you popped in for a chat with Barbara when you can.'

'Oh?'

He glanced at her, his care for the paper's secretary clear in his eyes. 'Her brother wasn't doing so great in his mind before the raids, now he's even worse.'

Affection for the woman who had become more friend than associate twisted Freda's heart. 'I will when I can.' She blew out a breath, her mind immediately drifting to Dorothy. 'Between work and home, it's all a bit...'

'Of course. No need to fill in the blanks.' His jaw tightened as he continued to stare ahead. 'The entire city daren't make any promises at the moment. We're all doing as much as we can. I really hope the articles I'm writing are hitting the right tone and hold the content the *Chronicle*'s readers need right now, but Lord knows if they are. How do we really know, as journalists, what our readers want in these times?' He looked at her. 'You always seemed to strike a chord with our women readers, though.'

'Thank you. And...' She softly smiled. 'You always get it right.'

Their eyes locked for a moment before Freda looked away.

'I don't suppose I can persuade you to consider writing a piece about the effects of the raids on the hospital's nurses?' he asked.

Freda frowned, her eyes drawn to a young woman pushing a

pram filled with a hodgepodge of meagre belongings, a small, upturned side table, a tin bucket, her toddler daughter balanced on her hip and sucking a lolly. 'Don't you think it will be a little crass to do that? People don't want to know what it was like for hospital staff when they are struggling so much themselves.'

'People want distraction. No matter what guise that might come in. Which' – he smiled and stopped – 'brings me to the next article pitch I have that I'm sure will tempt you from exile, so to speak.'

She stopped and laughed. 'Exile? Really?'

'Have you heard who's visiting Bath tomorrow?'

'Who?'

'None other than King George and "the most dangerous woman in Europe" herself.'

Freda grinned. 'Queen Elizabeth? Wow.'

'Exactly.' He laughed. 'Hitler's summary of her is one thing, but to see her here in Bath alongside the king will be something to behold.' His excited gaze burned into hers. 'Will you be able to carve out some time to see them doing their rounds? I know they're scheduled to first sign the official visitors book at the Guildhall and then tour the city. Lord knows how long they'll spend here, but the *Chronicle* will cover every minute and with the healthy female readership who follow you, then—'

'Follow my work, you mean! You make it sound as though I have a line of women following me to and from the hospital doors.'

'I'm surprised you haven't!' He winked. 'So, Miss Parkes, will you be joining me to see the king and queen?'

Temptation pulled at her, but Freda shook her head, burying her passion for reporting as she had hundreds of times before. 'I'm sorry, Richard, I can't. And anyway, you and I both know there will be others at the paper who will jump at this opportunity!'

'Fair enough. It was worth a shot... Which brings me onto my next attempt to lure you to the dark side...'

She smiled, cursing the way her gaze kept falling to his mouth, his strong jaw... 'Which is?'

'A drink. Coffee. A meal. A bloody sandwich.' His smile dissolved. 'I want to see you, Freda. Properly. Not snatches here and there.' He gently touched her fingers, his blue eyes intense on hers. 'Things were going well between us before these raids. I thought – hoped – they might continue. Please, come out with me. I don't care what we do, I just want to spend some time with you.'

Oh, how her body reacted to him when he looked at her that way! The desire to kiss him, touch him, and have him touch her stirred inside her. No, she couldn't weaken. She didn't want to become any more attached to him; to establish a him and her. It wasn't just her patients; too many other people she loved – cared for – needed her time and energy right now. Dorothy, her mother, her best friends...

'I'm sorry, Richard,' she said, easing her fingers from his. 'The hospital needs me. My sister, too.'

'She's all right, isn't she?'

Freda's heart beat faster to see such genuine care in his eyes. 'If you mean is she hurt or worse, she's fine. It's... something else.'

'I see. Can I help?'

She smiled softly. 'I wish you could, but no.' She stepped back. 'I should go, but I'll come by the office soon. I promise.'

Just as she moved away, he grasped her arm, stared deep into her eyes before lowering his head and covering her mouth with his. A low moan escaped her as Freda pressed against him, her entire body and soul betraying her as she scored her fingers into the hair at the back of his neck. He kissed her harder, deeper, his tongue touching hers until Freda forcefully stepped back.

'Bye, Richard,' she said firmly. 'Stay safe.'

And then she hurried away, leaving him – and her heart – on a bomb-blasted street in the very centre of Bath.

25

VERONICA

Veronica should not have been surprised to discover Mr Martin lived on The Circus, one of Bath's most affluent streets, yet his down-to-earth manner and how he so naturally conversed with working-class girls like her and Betty made it just as easy to imagine him living in a two-up, two-down on the outskirts of town.

As she entered The Circus from the top of Gay Street alongside Freda and Dorothy, Veronica's breath caught, her companions' gasps sounding beside her.

'I knew The Circus had escaped the worst of it,' Freda said, her eyes wide. 'But the damage looks bad enough.' She nodded towards Bennett Street, one of the side streets visible from where they stood. The carnage there was evident in the piles of rubble, still smouldering buildings and rows upon rows of volunteers clearing and searching. 'I heard the Regina Hotel took a direct hit, the blast setting fire to the Assembly Rooms across the road. They'll be dealing with that for weeks.'

As they walked, Veronica stared at the crater in the grassed area in the very centre of The Circus where an unexploded bomb lay, the edges of the enormous hole lined with firemen and servicemen as they yelled and shouted instructions to one another. Her stomach tightened. Neither she, Freda nor Dorothy could possibly know if they were in imminent danger, but they could not falter or allow the 'Beast of Berlin' – as some now called Hitler – to frighten them from following through what they'd come here to do.

'Mr Martin told Betty and me that his home escaped with nothing more than a few shattered windows so it must be along this row somewhere,' she said, peering along the houses' short pathways. She stopped by a house with a vase of blue flowers in the window and smiled. 'This is his. He told me to look for the flowers.'

She led the way to the front door, which was caked in thick yellow dust, and lifted the knocker, her back straight and turned against the turmoil and destruction behind her. She tilted her chin and fought the weakness that ebbed and flowed inside her whenever she allowed herself to think about the overwhelming suffering and loss that was happening all over her beloved city.

The door opened and a pretty woman of about thirty years old stood on the threshold, her smile uncertain but her brown eyes warm. 'Hello. You must be Nurse Campbell.' She held out her hand. 'Mrs Elspeth Martin. Please, won't you come in?'

Veronica returned her smile. 'Thank you,' she said, stepping into the house. 'This is my colleague Nurse Parkes and her sister, Dorothy.'

'Pleased to meet you.'

Mrs Martin's gaze lingered on each of them in turn, a little longer on Dorothy. Even if her husband hadn't told her why they were here this morning, the fact Dorothy wasn't wearing a nurse's uniform made her all the more conspicuous.

Mrs Martin coughed and dragged her gaze from Dorothy to

Veronica. 'My husband is waiting for you in the back parlour,' she said, gesturing with a wave towards a room on the left at the end of the hallway. 'Why don't you go on in and I'll see about making some tea.'

Veronica nodded, her stomach knotting with a sudden attack of nerves. She had thought they'd be ushered into the drawing room at the front of the house. The back parlour spoke of secrecy, broken propriety...

'Thank you.'

Mrs Martin continued along the hallway, turning through a doorway on the right which presumably led downstairs to the kitchen. Veronica turned around. She had never seen Freda look so anxious and poor Dorothy looked awfully pale, like she might faint at any moment.

'Right,' Veronica said, pulling herself up to her full five foot five inch height. 'Are you ready? Everything will be all right, Dorothy. Mr Martin is not only a magnificent surgeon, but a truly compassionate man. He will not stand in judgement so, please, try to relax.'

Hoping she hadn't just lied to the poor girl about how Mr Martin would treat her, Veronica turned to Freda. They held one another's gazes for a moment before Veronica gave a curt nod. They were as ready as they'd ever be.

She knocked on the closed door.

'Come in.'

She entered the room which, despite it being after noon, was in shadow due to the curtains being drawn, the only light coming from the three or four lamps dotted about the intimate space. Veronica's gaze fell on a day bed covered with a white sheet, two pillows neatly stacked at its head. Her stomach dropped. Did Mr Martin mean to examine Dorothy?

'Nurse Campbell.'

Veronica jumped and snatched her gaze to Mr Martin as he came forward, his grey eyes shining with kindness, his mouth curved with a smile.

He nodded at Freda. 'It's nice to see you again, Nurse Parkes, and this' – he turned to Dorothy, who visibly trembled – 'must be Dorothy. Hello.'

Veronica's heart ached with sympathy for the young woman as she offered Mr Martin a shy smile.

'Hello.'

'Why don't we all take a seat?' he asked, waving towards a row of three chairs set out against one of the walls to the side of the day bed. 'We'll just get settled with some tea and—'

As if on cue, Mrs Martin came in with a tea tray laden with a teapot, cups and saucers.

Her husband immediately rushed to take the tray from her and put it on a table on the opposite side of the room. As Mrs Martin served the tea, asking who wanted milk and sugar, Veronica and Freda exchanged strained smiles of encouragement while simultaneously glancing at Dorothy, who didn't seem to be able to look at anything but the day bed. Unsurprisingly, she had refused a cup of tea. Veronica wasn't sure she would be able to drink her own, she was so nervous.

Mrs Martin didn't say a word for the entire time she served them, but her gaze constantly hovered on Dorothy. Veronica studied the surgeon's wife, her curiosity piqued. Mrs Martin's eyes were shadowed with a strange sadness as she stared at Dorothy, and Veronica prayed Dorothy didn't notice how Mrs Martin watched her. It was obvious she knew exactly why they were there, and that Dorothy was pregnant.

Veronica's stomach knotted. Had Mr Martin also told his wife that Dorothy wanted to abort the baby? She really hoped he hadn't, but was finding it increasingly difficult to believe anything else when Mrs Martin continued to study Freda's sister so earnestly.

Warmth seeped into Veronica's cheeks as culpability whispered through her. The last thing she had predicted when she'd volunteered to speak to Mr Martin was that even more people would learn of Dorothy's situation – of her intention. She prayed Freda and Dorothy wouldn't be angry with her when her genuine purpose had been to help them. Self-doubt and judgement niggled and Veronica shifted uncomfortably on her seat. Her record of successful decision-making away from her work was poor at best and now she feared this visit with Mr Martin would prove she'd made yet another bad choice.

Mrs Martin silently left the room, softly closing the door behind her.

'So...' Mr Martin cleared his throat and his gaze turned sombre as he looked at Dorothy. 'Miss Parkes, it is probably best that I jump straight in with what I'd like to say and what I'd like to happen today.'

Dorothy nodded. 'Yes, sir.'

'I understand you do not wish to keep your baby?'

Veronica stilled and couldn't fail to notice that Freda seemed to have stopped breathing entirely. Mr Martin's demeanour and tone was entirely no-nonsense. He was a surgeon of the highest calibre and they were here to discuss abortion. None of them should have expected anything else other than his complete professionalism.

Dorothy sat straighter in her seat. 'I can't have this baby.'

'Can't or won't?'

'Pardon?'

'There's a difference, Miss Parkes. I can see no reason you *can't* physically have this baby, at least at face value, but I can imagine a few reasons you might give me why you *won't* have this baby. So, which is it? Can't or won't? I'd appreciate your honesty.'

Veronica sipped her tea, steadfastly looking at neither Dorothy nor Freda, knowing however discomforting this was for her, it must be a thousand times worse for them – Dorothy especially. Yet, Mr Martin really was her best bet for receiving sound advice and help right now. Dorothy was not an innocent bystander in creating her current circumstance and now she would have to step up and face the consequences – whatever they might be.

'I won't have this baby, sir.'

'Right, then I know what I'm dealing with,' Mr Martin said.

He stared at Dorothy a moment longer before he glanced at Freda and then Veronica, his gaze not exactly angry, but neither was it happy.

He faced Dorothy, his gaze softening slightly. 'Would you allow me to examine you, Miss Parkes? Your sister can stay or leave. Whatever will make you feel the most comfortable. I think an examination is necessary so that I might advise you properly.'

Veronica hastily put her teacup on a bureau beside her and stood. 'I'll wait outside.'

Mr Martin nodded. 'Thank you, Nurse Campbell.'

She walked to the door and pulled it open.

'I'd like my sister to stay, please.'

'Of course.'

Softly closing the door behind her, Veronica walked into the hallway and gratefully lowered onto a fine upholstered, high back chair placed by a side table holding a phone, notepad and pen. The wealth of the Martins was obvious – and it felt oddly improper when chaos reigned the other side of their front door.

The next fifteen minutes felt more like fifteen hours as Veronica intermittently paced and sat, the odd feminine cough or clink of china that came from behind the closed drawing room telling her Mrs Martin remained at home. Veronica had no doubt she was as tense with nerves not knowing what was happening in the back room of her house as Veronica was.

The murmuring of voices snapped her to attention and Veronica halted her pacing as Freda emerged from the parlour first, followed by Dorothy and then Mr Martin. Freda's gaze locked on Veronica's as she walked ahead of her sister, her cheeks flushed and her jaw tight. Veronica knew her friend's look all too well. A cloak of determination had descended over Freda and whatever had provoked it, it seemed she was preparing for a fight.

Veronica inwardly grimaced. Poor Dorothy.

'Well now, Nurse Campbell,' Mr Martin said as they came to a stop in front of Veronica. 'I have spoken to Miss Parkes as you asked and given her my advice. What happens next is up to her. Let me show you ladies out.'

'Thank you so much, Mr Martin,' Veronica said as they walked to the door.

'You're welcome.'

Freda and Dorothy thanked the surgeon and then followed Veronica outside, the front door closing behind them. For a long while, they walked along the pavement without saying a word until Veronica began to wonder if she should say something – anything – when Freda broke the silence.

'I don't care if you'd prefer Veronica not hear this, Dot,' she said gruffly. 'But I pray you heed what Mr Martin said. You are almost three months pregnant. An abortion will be dangerous at best, fatal at worst. You cannot even think about it as a course of action. You have to speak to Mum and Dad.'

'I can't.' Tears ran down Dorothy's cheeks and she swiped at them. 'The baby isn't Robert's, Freda. What on earth do you think Mum and Dad are going to do? Tell me all is forgiven, and they can't wait to meet their grandchild?'

Veronica pulled her lips tightly together. This was a conversation that she had no intention of getting involved with. Freda was the kindest, most sensible, level-headed person she had ever met and she loved her sister. She would do what was right by Dorothy... whatever she deemed that to be.

'You must tell them. They need to know,' Freda said firmly. 'As Mr Martin said, you won't be the first woman to have a baby out of wedlock or fathered by someone else other than her husband, fiancé or boyfriend during this war.'

'But what of Robert? He will kill me.'

'You don't know what he'll do. The only thing you do know is he will shortly be home on leave and then he'll have to be told either way.'

'But—'

'No buts,' Freda said, taking her sister's hand and lifting it to her heart as they walked. 'We are telling Mum and Dad. Together.'

Veronica walked slightly behind them, her gaze on the back of Freda's head. Whatever happened next, Dorothy had Freda by her side and, come what may, she would be all right.

26

FREDA

Freda glanced at Dorothy from the corner of her eye.

They stood at the kitchen counter plating up the dinner they had prepared for their parents. Food rations were getting worse, but they had somehow managed to cobble together a decent cottage pie with the family's meat allowance, stuffed full with homegrown vegetables and topped with mashed potato. She had also bought their dad a couple of bottles of pale ale in the hope a touch of alcohol might go some way to relaxing him enough that he didn't completely lose his wits when Dorothy's expectant state was revealed.

'Right.' Freda blew out a breath, picked up two of the plates and ran her gaze over Dorothy's pale face. 'Are you ready?'

'No,' her sister said glumly. 'But I don't think I ever will be so we might as well get it over with.'

Freda flashed her a sympathetic smile and led the way from the kitchen into the living room where their dining table was nestled beside the window that looked out onto their small back garden.

She put two laden plates in front of her mother and father.

'Here you go,' she said, her voice sounding far too cheerful to her own ears, let alone her parents'. 'I hope you enjoy it!'

Her mother arched an eyebrow, her blue eyes amused. 'Well, someone is feeling rather jolly this evening.'

'Not at all,' Freda said. Clearly her amateur dramatics had a long way to go. 'I just enjoyed preparing this meal alongside Dorothy, that's all. It's been too long since we cooked for you and Dad.'

'Hmm.' Her mother studied her for a moment before turning to her plate. 'Well, let's eat before it gets cold.'

Dorothy suddenly jumped up from the table, her nervousness obvious. 'We forgot your beer, Dad!' she exclaimed. 'Freda pushed the boat out and treated you. I'll go and get you one. They're in the kitchen.'

She swept from the room and Freda kept her gaze steadfastly on her plate, forcibly swallowing a mouthful of pie, her stomach churning. She and Dorothy had agreed that it would be Freda who told her parents about the baby as Dorothy would have more than enough to deal with afterwards.

'Here you go, Dad,' her sister announced as she returned with the bottle of beer and a glass, which she placed in front of their father. 'Cheers!'

Freda closed her eyes. If her acting hadn't roused their mum and dad's suspicions that this dinner was not about a sudden wish to cook for them, Dorothy's 'cheers' almost certainly would. Her sister had never said anything so pithy, not even when she usually behaved like the good girl their mother insisted upon. Of course, until recently, the entire family had been blissfully ignorant to the fact that Dorothy abandoned that mentality at the front door whenever she left the house.

'What's going on?' Her mother laid down her knife and fork, her canny gaze sweeping between her daughters. 'First Freda and now you, Dorothy. It's like the pair of you have taken some happy medicine.'

Dorothy laughed. 'Oh, Mum. Aren't we allowed to do our best to be happy while we can? The bombings have left the entire city in a state of distress. Freda and I are merely counting our blessings and—'

'Dot, stop.' Freda's heart beat fast. She might not have wanted to tell their parents about the pregnancy any more than Dorothy wanted her to, but keeping up a pretence that all was well would only anger her parents more once the truth was revealed. 'Just stop.'

Silence descended and tension immediately shrouded the table.

It all too often felt like their mother's sole priority in life was to keep up appearances, whether that be with regards to the cleanliness of her house, the perfection of the sewing work she took in for extra money or the impeccable appearance and behaviour of her family – her daughters especially. In fact, her obsession that 'good girls are the best girls' had been so drilled into Freda and Dorothy, it had backfired entirely. It seemed her mother's 'drilling' had burrowed a hole so deeply into her daughters that the 'good' had seeped out, leaving behind stalwart, *unseemly* writing ambitions in Freda and pregnancy from a tryst with a relative stranger in Dorothy.

'Freda?' Her father studied her, his brow creased with a frown. 'What's going on?'

Freda swallowed, her mouth dry. The bond she had with her father was far closer than she had with her mother and a horrible shame came over her. The news she was about to deliver would undoubtedly be deemed as a gargantuan disappointment of conduct. That unforgivable behaviour might not be hers, but she shared everything, good or bad with Dorothy –

despite their frequent and sometimes heated differences, they loved one another deeply.

She looked across the table at Dorothy, sorry she could not hold her hand. Tears glinted in her sister's eyes, but Dorothy's chin was tilted as though braced for the inevitable. Maybe she wasn't as helpless as she liked to make out to her parents and fiancé and this pregnancy would be the making of her.

Freda cleared her throat and faced her father, the easier of their parents to look at. 'I have something to tell you and Mum,' she said. 'Something that neither of you will care to hear but you must be told.' Steam from their plates rose between them, the smells of cooked beef and vegetables hovering in the strained atmosphere and turning Freda's stomach. 'Dorothy is pregnant.'

There was no need to add the further blow that the father wasn't her fiancé considering they knew well enough that Robert had been thousands of miles away serving his country for months.

'Well, heavens above,' her mother cried. 'You must be three or four months along. Robert hasn't been home since Christmas. Oh, the pair of you!' Her cheeks reddened. 'What were you thinking having... relations before you are married?'

'Mum.' Freda swallowed and glanced at Dorothy, who appeared to be entirely frozen and mute. 'You don't understand.'

'Oh, I understand perfectly! Well, there's nothing for it, Dorothy.' Her mother waved her hand dismissively. 'You and Richard must marry the next time he's home.'

Freda glanced nervously at her father, who was yet to say a word and only glared at Dorothy, his eyes dark with anger.

She stared at her sister. 'Tell them, Dot, or I will.'

The silence stretched and Freda risked another look at her father. His face grew more and more pale, a sure sign that he was beyond angry. Clearly, he had already concluded Robert could not be the baby's father even if it seemed his wife hadn't.

Freda placed her hands on the table either side of her plate and braced for whatever happened next. 'Robert isn't the father, Mum.'

'What?' her mother screeched as she snapped her gaze to Dorothy. 'What on earth is Freda saying?' She looked at Freda, her husband, back to Dorothy. 'Tell your sister she's wrong, Dorothy. Right now!'

Freda touched her mother's hand where it lay fisted on the table. 'Mum—'

'Don't you dare Mum me!' Her mother snatched her hand away, her blue eyes blazing with anger, her cheeks mottled. 'I should wash your mouth out with soap for saying such disgusting lies about your sister.' She glared at Dorothy. 'Tell her. Tell Freda to stop her filthy lies!'

Any bravado Dorothy might have been battling to maintain dissolved and she sucked in a sob, her tears bursting like a breaking dam from her eyes. 'I'm sorry, Mum,' she cried. 'I'm sorry, Dad.'

Freda looked at her father again as he stared unblinkingly at Dorothy, his face now beetroot red, his gaze unreadable and his lips drawn into a thin line. Sickness coated Freda's throat. She had never seen her father look at anyone with such undisguised fury, nor had she ever known him to be lost for words in a crisis.

'Oh, the shame!' her mother wept as she put her hand to her throat, her eyes glistening with tears. 'Robert... he loves you... How could you do this to him? How could you do this to us?'

'I...' Dorothy visibly trembled. 'It just hap—'

'Don't you dare!' her mother screamed. 'And who's the good-for-nothing beast who has done this to you?' She looked at her husband. 'You must hunt him down, Clive. Make him marry her. Threaten him if you have to.'

'I am not marrying the father, Mum. He's... he's not a man I wish to spend my life with.'

'Not a man you wish to spend your life with?' Her mother's eyes bulged. 'He's not good enough to marry, but he's good enough to... Oh, the shame of you!'

'I want to marry Robert!'

'How much do you think my heart can take?' her mother asked, her hands shaking. 'First your brother is killed, the other is missing and we have no idea if he is dead or alive, your sister goes along her own merry way with little thought for anyone but herself... and now this!'

Freda closed her eyes. Now was not the time to contradict her mother. Then again, could she really argue with her when – from her mother's point of view, at least – what she said was all true. Freda was resolutely pursuing her own life rather than the one her mother had mapped out for her.

She opened her eyes just as her father abruptly stood with such force that everyone else around the table jumped. His chair toppled to the floor behind him as he glared at Dorothy. Freda's heart raced, waiting for his anger to unleash. His eyes burned with a livid rage, his face white. Time suspended as he stood there, the mantel clock counting the seconds before he strode to the living room door, yanked it open and then slammed it shut so violently behind him that they all jumped a second time. Freda's heart thundered. Why had she been focusing on her mother's anger when all along it was their father's they should have prepared for?

'Now you've done it, my girl,' her mother exclaimed. 'I have never seen your father so angry or disappointed. Woe betide you when he has managed to calm down enough to actually deal with you.'

Dorothy emitted a horrible yelp before covering her face with her hands and beginning to cry.

'Well, one thing's for sure,' her mother said firmly. 'He must never know.'

Freda dragged her gaze from Dorothy to her mother. 'Who?'

'Robert, of course.'

'What?' Dorothy dropped her hands and laughed, the sound hysterical. 'What do you expect me to do when he comes home on leave?' She sniffed, wiping her finger under her nose in a far from ladylike way. 'Hide in the closet? Dress in a bedsheet?'

Freda grimaced. Now was not the time for Dorothy to start defying her mother with such flippancy after all her years of adhering to her every command – at least, superficially. It seemed who Dorothy was in reality, nobody knew.

'You, my girl,' her mother said quietly, her gaze cold, 'will do exactly as I demand from this moment forward. You are not the daughter I thought you were, Dorothy. You have clearly been lying and scheming, cavorting with God only knows what sort of young men while pretending you are a child I could be proud of. I no longer trust you...' Her mother swiped at the tear that rolled over her cheek. 'I'm not sure I even particularly like you right now.'

Dorothy emitted a strangled sob and Freda winced.

'Mum,' she said quietly. 'I think it's best Dorothy is honest with Robert. How can any of us know how he will react to this news? Yes, he'll be shocked and angry to begin with, but the war has changed everything. It's almost certainly taught us how fragile life is. How nothing is guaranteed. He might—'

'He might what? Accept a bastard as his own?' Her mother sniffed. 'Don't be so foolish, Freda.'

'I'm not being foolish,' Freda said slowly, fighting to hold on to some rather flimsy remnants of calm. 'I've seen enough through my work at the hospital and, dare I say it, the paper, to know nothing and nobody is the same as they once were.'

'Poppycock!' Her mother waved dismissively and stood, pacing back and forth. Her forehead furrowed in concentration. 'No, the only thing to be done is to send Dorothy away. She can have the baby and put it up for adoption. Yes, that's what we will do.' She stared at Dorothy. 'You can go and stay in Cornwall with your dad's sister.' Her mother sniffed. 'She'll know how to deal with your situation only too well.'

Not even bothering to ask her mother to clarify her blatant insinuation against their Aunt Maureen, Freda sighed.

'I've made my decision. Now, I'll go and see your father.' She glared at Dorothy. 'My girls are good girls, young lady.' She pointedly looked at Dorothy's stomach even though it was half-hidden beneath the table. 'This pregnancy is not happening as far as the rest of the world is concerned. Not a word of what happened here tonight leaves these four walls. Ever. Do you understand?'

Dorothy nodded, her eyes red-rimmed.

Their mother snapped her gaze to Freda. 'And you, do *you* understand?'

Freda defiantly held her mother's glare. She would not agree to remain silent. This baby was coming one way or another and her mother banning Dorothy from talking about it – talking about how she felt about everything that would unfold over the coming weeks and months – wouldn't solve anything in the long term.

She continued to lock eyes with her mother.

'I'm warning you, Freda,' her mother continued, her voice shaking with anger. 'No one outside of this house is to know about this. You are no stranger to upsetting me. After all, you were the first to fall from my expectations with your writing nonsense and trips back and forth to that damnable newspaper office, but now it seems your sister has followed your example and further pierced my heart.'

Her mother swept from the room and Freda looked at Dorothy, who stared back at her, her eyes wide, not with fear but with an unexpected cold and hard determination. Yet, rather than pride, dread ran through Freda's veins. In that moment, she had every belief Dorothy held more intent than ever to deal with her pregnancy in her own way.

27

SYLVIA

Sylvia walked along Castle Street towards the house she shared with her mum. It was her day off and two weeks since she'd received the letter from Jesse's mother. Barely an hour had passed without Jesse floating into her thoughts throughout that time. His sexy half-smile and warm, chocolate-brown eyes tiptoeing into her dreams, causing her to wake in a state of semi-arousal, her body aching for his touch. They had courted on and off for weeks and it had become impossible to resist being with him in every way. But when they'd split up and he'd gone off to serve at the front, she'd regretted her impulsiveness, her sexual desire to have him, his absence making the void he'd left behind all the harder to close.

Her regret stank of hypocrisy though, made her a charlatan who had turned her back on the best thing – the best man – to ever walk into her life and wrap her heart in soft comfort. A comfort that also had the potential to explode whenever they'd stolen moments of complete and utter physical surrender.

She swallowed around the lump that rose in her throat, steadfastly avoiding looking at the gap on the opposite side of the road where Jesse's house and its neighbours had once stood. Was it too late to wish she could turn back time? Was she living in futile hope that Jesse wanted to come back to Bath to court her again?

Reaching her house, she pushed the key into the lock. She'd barely hung her handbag on the banister newel post when her mother came barrelling out of the kitchen into the narrow hallway, her face fully made up and the requisite cigarette sitting on her bottom lip as she poked the metal handle of a comb through her platinum blonde curls.

She snatched the cigarette out of her mouth. 'There you are!' she cried, her eyes alight with feverish excitement. 'Are you trying to kill me? How long does it take to walk around the shops?'

Sylvia slipped off her cardigan. 'I'm no Sherlock Holmes, but I'm guessing something has happened since I've been gone.'

'I should say so! You'll never guess who graced our doorstep less than twenty minutes ago.'

Sylvia's heart beat faster. It couldn't be. Surely, he wouldn't just...

'Mrs bloody Howard!' her mother exclaimed. 'Remember her? Bold as brass she was. Just strolled right up to the front door and spoke to me as though she was someone I'd pass the time of day with. Bloody nerve of the woman, after the way she treated me when she lived across the street.'

'Jesse's mum?' Sylvia gripped the newel post, her knees ever so slightly trembling. 'She was here?'

'Yes! Do you need your ears cleaned out or something?'

'Well... what did she say?'

'She came here asking for you.'

'And?'

'And I told her you weren't here, but I'd gladly take a message if she was so inclined to tell—'

'Mum!' Sylvia's patience snapped. Her mother would happily draw out her dramatics into the early evening given half a chance. 'What did she say?'

Eileen Roberts snapped her mouth shut and narrowed her eyes before taking a long, purposeful drag on her cigarette, turning on her heel and striding back into the kitchen. Sylvia glared after her. *For the love of God...*

'I'm sorry for snapping, all right?' she said, following her mother into the kitchen where she now sat at their small table, mashing out her cigarette with unbridled gusto in a half-full ashtray. 'But you know I care about Jesse and if his mother was here, then...'

Her mother slowly lifted her head and met Sylvia's eyes, her gaze suspiciously less annoyed than Sylvia had expected, which only made things worse. Her mother was always easier to tolerate when she was waist-deep in narcissism rather than ankle-deep in maternal care. It was a state Sylvia so rarely witnessed, it was guaranteed to knock her off-kilter every time. It also meant emotional pain for her was imminent.

'They're back,' her mother said, picking up a lipstick and unscrewing the lid. 'The Howards. They've found a place across town.'

'Across town?' Sylvia's mouth drained dry. 'Where?'

'No idea. She didn't say.'

'So what did she say?'

Her mother took her time slicking on a coat of bright red lipstick, her eyes never leaving Sylvia's. She theatrically shook out a tissue and blotted her mouth before returning the tissue to the table and replacing the lid of her lipstick.

She cleared her throat. 'Well, it wasn't long before all the bluster went out of the woman. She might have a mother's pride, but if that woman ain't grieving, I'll throw my fags on the fire.'

'Grieving?' Sylvia's stomach tightened. 'You don't mean she came here to tell me Jesse—'

'Hold your horses.' Her mother pinned her with a protective glare. 'Don't go running headlong along a path when you've no idea what's what.'

'Mum, please! Did she mention Jesse or not?'

'No, not a word.'

'Then—'

'Bloody woman wouldn't tell me a damn thing despite me asking more than once. Said she'd talk to you and only you.' Her mother stood, tossed her bits and pieces into her make-up bag, picked up her cigarettes and matches. 'She said that if you were back in the next half an hour or so, you were to meet her in the tearoom on Abbey Street.' She glanced at the kitchen wall clock. 'You'd better get a move on if you want to catch her.'

'For God's sake, Mum! I've wasted five minutes just trying to get some basic information out of you,' Sylvia said over her shoulder as she rushed into the hallway.

She snatched her handbag from the banister and yanked open the front door, slamming it behind her. She could damn well swing for her mother sometimes, even if it was likely her mother had delayed her because she was worried what Mrs Howard had to say.

Sylvia picked up her pace, hurrying across town as fast as her high-heeled shoes would allow. Once she arrived at the tearoom, she fought to catch her breath and pushed open the door before she could surrender to the fear galloping through her heart. The bell above the door announced her arrival and she scanned the scarved and hatted women sitting at the dozen or so tables, the volume of chatter hushed and polite when Sylvia felt like screaming inside. She stepped forward, but then hesitated when her eyes met Corinne Howard's where she sat alone at a table at the back of the small shop.

Battling to keep breathing, Sylvia walked forwards and slipped onto a white-painted chair opposite Jesse's mother. 'Mrs Howard.' She smiled. 'It's lovely to see you again.'

'I was just about to leave,' the other woman said bluntly, her eyes unreadable as they grazed over Sylvia's face, a flash of distaste in their brown depths as she noted Sylvia's red-painted lips.

'Can I get you another cup of tea?' Sylvia asked, nodding towards Mrs Howard's empty cup. 'I know I could do with one after practically running all the way here. My mother likes to make a song and dance about everything and by the time—'

'I didn't ask you here for no good reason, Miss Roberts. Nor do I have time for chit-chat.'

Sylvia pressed her lips together, trapping inside her natural instinct to retort, gathered herself and forced a smile. 'I see. Then might I ask why you wanted to see—'

'Jesse hasn't said as much, but I'm here because I know he loves you, Miss Roberts.'

Sylvia stilled. 'What?'

'You heard,' Mrs Howard said, a little of the hostility leaving her eyes as her shoulders lowered. 'He's released from service and the first thing he asks is that we move back to Bath. When I asked him if it was for you that he wanted to come back here, he denied it and said he wants you to know he's alive, but has no wish to see you again.'

Sylvia swore she heard the splinter that cracked along her heart, but said nothing.

'But I don't believe him,' Mrs Howard continued. 'I look at my son and I can pretty much guess every secret he carries, and every regret or loss that burdens him is somehow connected to you.'

'I never intentionally set out to burden him,' Sylvia said, swallowing against the lump in her throat. 'Far from it.'

'I know that.'

Surprise jolted through her and Sylvia vowed to remain silent lest she undo the unexpected progress that seemed to be taking root between her and Mrs Howard. A woman she had assumed couldn't stand her.

Mrs Howard cleared her throat, looked around the tearoom as though struggling to meet Sylvia's gaze. 'In the brief time you and Jesse spent together, my boy was truly alive.' She turned, met Sylvia's eyes. 'I'm woman enough to admit that now, even if I couldn't at the time. I was scared of losing him to you, Miss Roberts. I now know I was foolish to fight the love between the two of you and maybe I should have embraced it' – she studied her – 'possibly.'

'I... don't know what to say,' Sylvia said quietly. Her heartbreak suddenly felt insignificant compared to the deep regret reflected in Mrs Howard's eyes. 'I love him too, Mrs Howard. I never should have called things off between us. I was hurt when he left and then he came back, and I wanted to protect myself in case he went away again. Then he signed up and—'

'All of that was my fault. I was – still am – in a bad place, Miss Roberts, but I'm doing all I can to get better.'

Sylvia swallowed against the ache in her heart for the woman's grief, knowing the loss of her husband at the very beginning of the war had taken its toll on Mrs Howard, manifesting itself in her obsessive cleaning and over the top care for her five children. It was an affliction that affected her entire family, but Sylvia suspected it tormented Jesse the hardest because he couldn't fix the problem.

'Is Jesse back working at the railway station?' she asked, subtly changing the subject. 'He was a fine worker. I imagine they'd be glad to have him back.'

'No, he's not. His brother Johnny is though.'

Sylvia smiled. 'I bet he's proud to be following in Jesse's footsteps.'

'I leaned on Jesse too much, Miss Roberts, made it hard for him to love you how he wanted and...' Tears leapt into her eyes. 'Now he's—'

'Afternoon, ladies,' said the far-too-happy waitress who bounced up to their table, all bright green eyes and shiny white teeth. 'Can I get you some tea and cake today?'

'No, thank you.' Sylvia's eyes never left Mrs Howard's. 'We're fine.'

'But—'

'You need to go away, girl,' Mrs Howard said firmly, her eyes locked on Sylvia's but her words meant for the waitress. 'We don't need anything right now.'

The girl hesitated before huffing and leaving them alone.

'Now Jesse's what, Mrs Howard?' Sylvia asked softly, not entirely sure she was ready to hear the answer. 'You said now Jesse's...'

Corinne Howard closed her eyes, curled her hand into a fist on the table before slowly opening her eyes again. 'Jesse's blind, Miss Roberts.'

The floor seemed to tilt left and right and Sylvia gripped the edge of the table. 'Blind?'

'Blind.'

Mrs Howard eased her hand across the table, gripped Sylvia's hand with tears glinting on her lashes, before she stood and made for the door, leaving Sylvia stunned and alone, her own tears spilling onto her cheeks.

28

FREDA

As Freda pulled her house key from her handbag, trepidation rippled through her.

Dorothy had been told by their mother that she was not to leave the house under any circumstances since the pregnancy confession. It was just as well her sister had only pursued avenues of marriage and homemaking rather than a career, otherwise Freda wasn't sure what her mother would have done had Dorothy had a job.

What had become clear, with Dorothy being confined to the house, was just how often she'd managed to successfully leave it – day and night. Her sister's stories to her parents and Freda about visiting friends, finding a knitting circle and a myriad of other 'good girl' pastimes had been plausible and ingenious, the entire family believing whatever reason or excuse she had fed them. Or maybe each of them had been too wrapped up in their own lives to notice what Dorothy was up to, or be concerned about her obviously growing need for escape. Why wouldn't any young woman – with a fiancé who had been serving overseas for the last eighteen months and only been home half a dozen times throughout that time – want some fun? The trouble was, Dorothy had taken her fun too far. Not only had she slept with another man behind Robert's back, but she had also told Freda the man in question was a playboy of the highest order and there was little to no chance of him giving a stuff about honouring his mistakes.

When Freda entered the house, the first thing that struck her was the silence.

She lifted her nurse's watch pinned to her chest. Four thirty-three. It was still too early for her mother to have begun preparing the evening meal and, as a policeman, her father could be absolutely anywhere as the clean-up of the city continued. But where was Dorothy? Unless their mother had relented and allowed her sister to go for a walk with her somewhere, yielding on her insistence that sitting in the back garden was ample fresh air for a harlot.

Anger towards her mother and the way she had been treating Dorothy over the last couple of weeks simmered deep inside as Freda walked into the living room. She dropped her handbag on the arm of the two-seater settee before falling back onto the cushions. She closed her eyes and fought the headache beating at her temples. It had been a hard shift at the hospital with more and more people coming in with respiratory problems caused by the volume of dust and fumes the bombs had provoked and infections caused by the dirty debris, glass and metal strewn here, there and everywhere. Sister Dyer and Sylvia were doing all they could to return the ward to some sort of a methodical state, but getting things back to the way they were before the raids would take a while yet.

It felt such a long time since those two awful days in April, but as time edged towards the middle of May, the warmer weather brought a quiet but resolute optimism – or maybe defiance – amongst Bath's people. It echoed silently along the hospital corridors and the city's streets, in the faces of men and women and the continued play of children. It made her damn proud to be British and to stand alongside all those remaining stalwart against Nazi invasion across Europe.

Freda inhaled deeply and opened her eyes, her gaze falling on the latest issue of the *Bath Chronicle* where it lay on the coffee table in front of her. She picked it up, her head and heart filling with thoughts of Richard and the last time she'd seen him – the last time they'd kissed. She still felt she was needed at the hospital more than the paper and even though sometimes she longed to see him and spend some time with him, it wouldn't be fair to do that when she wasn't ready to commit to him romantically – and wasn't sure she ever would be. What made things worse was that she suspected his feelings for her ran decidedly deeper than hers for him. On top of that, they were both fervently ambitious and there was no doubt in her mind that writing and journalism would always be smack bang in the middle of any personal relationship that might develop between them.

How was she supposed to be around him, listen to all the exciting, potentially dangerous things he was doing in pursuit of a story when her decision remained that, for now at least, her nursing had to come first? It was the fact he was such a fantastic writer that drew her to him; the fact he believed in her and encouraged her in a field that everyone else around her claimed to be unladylike or fanciful was what made her fear she could love him. But she would not fall for him. What if they ended up getting married and he then expected her to give up everything in her life to stay at home?

She leafed through the pages, looking for his byline, eventually finding a piece he'd written on the rescue of four children and their mother from one of the many collapsed houses in and around Kingsmead. As she read, Kathy Scott and the worrying thing she'd said about her parents sat front and centre in Freda's mind. The bombings of the Kingsmead area had been intensive and widespread, leaving very few buildings standing, and those that were had been severely bomb-damaged and left mostly uninhabitable. There was little chance Kathy's parents had survived unless they'd found shelter elsewhere through the raids. Yet Kathy had not taken any time away from the hospital. In fact, she'd worked more hours than most, including Freda. Surely she wouldn't have been able to work as she had been if she was now an orphan? Her dislike of her parents had been unmistakable, but if they had been killed, her taking some time away from work would be expected. Wouldn't it?

Deciding she would make a concerted effort to talk to Kathy tomorrow now that things were so much calmer at the hospital, Freda continued to read as she stood from the settee and walked into the hallway and then the kitchen. The silence of the house echoed around her. Where were her mother and Dorothy? She tossed the newspaper on the counter and took the matches from the top of the stove. She was just about to turn on the gas to boil the kettle when a loud strangled yelp came from the outside toilet just beyond the kitchen window.

'For goodness' sake.' She smiled and shook her head, putting the matches on the side and heading for the back door. 'That cat next door is forever getting stuck in...'

As she reached for the handle on the back door, she realised the door was already ajar. Tension inched across her shoulders. The family often left the back door unlocked when no one was home, that was commonplace in the street, but it was never left open. Picking up a wooden rolling pin as a potential weapon, Freda tentatively stepped outside and stared at the brick toilet building. She had been home for at least fifteen minutes. If there was someone in there, they should have come back into the house by now.

The grunting and stumbling coming from inside the toilet was distinctly human rather than feline. There was a soft whimpering, followed by a hitched breath and then whimpering again, the sound so agonised, it made Freda's blood run cold.

'Dorothy?' She tapped on the door. 'Is that you?'

The whimpering stopped.

'Dorothy?'

She was just about to shove the door open when—

'Freda!' her sister wailed. 'Help me!'

Freda shoved open the door and her heart leapt into her throat. 'Oh, my God! Dorothy! Mum! What are you doing?'

The rolling pin clattered from her hand to the stone floor as Freda ran forward and gripped her mother's arm and then Dorothy's, trying to pull them apart as they fought and scratched and screamed at one another in a tussle of the likes Freda had never seen before.

'What are you doing? For crying out loud,' she yelled. 'Mum, stop it. Dorothy!'

'Give it to me, Dorothy!' her mother screamed. 'Right now!'

Suddenly her mother ripped something from Dorothy's grasp and tossed it away. Freda stared at whatever landed with a light clatter on the stone floor. A knitting needle? A knitting needle!

'Oh, Dot,' she breathed. 'No.'

Her sister let out a sob and her mother quickly and firmly pulled her youngest daughter into her arms. 'Now, now, you silly, silly girl,' she said, her voice cracking. 'Whatever were you thinking?'

Freda stood back and stared in almost morbid fascination as

her mother rocked Dorothy in her arms, whispered indistinguishable words of comfort against her daughter's hair. Sickness unfurled in Freda's stomach. *My God, is Dorothy really so desperate to be rid of her child?*

After a long moment, her mother straightened and held Dorothy at arm's length before lifting her fingers to her daughter's eyes and thumbing away her tears. 'Now, you listen to me, young lady, and you listen well. Do you hear me?'

Although her mother's voice quaked a little, it was clear the commencement of normality had returned, her mother's tone firm and determined. 'We are never going to see anything like what just unfolded ever again. Do you understand? You are carrying a baby, Dorothy, a life. I might be disappointed that you have conceived this child under such appalling, shameful circumstances, but that baby is not to blame, and you *will* give birth to it.'

Her heart aching with love for her mother, Freda lifted her fingers to her cheeks, surprised when they came away damp. 'Mum...'

Her mother lifted her hand to silence her, her eyes never leaving Dorothy's. 'Do you accept what I'm saying, Dorothy?'

Dorothy nodded, hiccupping another sob before crossing her arms as though protecting herself or maybe even the baby. 'Yes.'

'Good. Then...' Their mother walked a slow circle in the centre of the small toilet block, her forehead deeply creased in a frown, and then she suddenly stopped, looking first at Freda and then Dorothy. 'Right, here's what happens next,' she said, her blue eyes glittering with determination. 'You are going to write to Robert, pleading with him to put in for some leave. You need to tell him about the baby as soon as possible. But not by letter.'

'I'm scared, Mum,' Dorothy wailed, her eyes wide and red-rimmed. 'He's going to be so angry.'

'Scared? Scared?' Her mother gave an inelegant snort before leaning down and snatching the knitting needle from the floor. 'The time for cowardice has passed, my girl. You will soon be a mother and that means you will need courage every day for the rest of your life! Now then, let's get back into the house and pretend what happened here today did not happen at all.'

Freda pressed her hand to her stomach, still feeling nauseous about what could have happened had her mother not got to Dorothy in time. 'So, you aren't going to send Dorothy away?' she asked. 'You mentioned her going to Aunt—'

'It seems your sister still wants to marry Robert.' She glanced at Dorothy. 'If he'll have her. So, for now at least, Dorothy remains at home.'

And with that, their mother marched towards the door behind Freda and she stumbled back lest her mother storm straight through her.

Left alone with Dorothy, Freda tentatively approached her and gently put her arm around her shoulders. 'Everything will work out in the end, Dot. You'll see.'

But her sister only continued to cry, soft sobs escaping her as Freda led her from the toilet into their small back yard, clenching her jaw against the threat of her own tears. If she had needed any more proof of how readily she needed to avoid romance, love or even physical entanglement with the opposite sex, she'd most certainly received it now.

29

VERONICA

'Hey, V. Have you seen Nurse Parkes this morning?'

Veronica looked up from her task sorting out a pile of newly delivered suture kits as Betty walked into the small room adjacent to one of the hospital's operating theatres. 'Oh, hello. No, I haven't. Why?'

The anaesthetist frowned, her pretty eyes shadowing with concern as she tucked a long tendril of her dark auburn hair beneath her cap. 'I know I don't know Nurse Parkes anywhere near as well as you do, but I exchanged a few words with her in the corridor just now and she doesn't look at all well.'

'Really?' Immediately troubled, Veronica stopped what she was doing, her gaze going to the door. 'In what way?'

'Well, she's really pale, grey under the eyes like she hasn't slept for a couple of days.' Betty brushed past her to the sink. 'In fact, I'd go as far as to say she looked better when the raids were going on and it was absolute bedlam everywhere.'

'I should go and make sure she's all right,' Veronica said, untying her apron and tossing it in the laundry bin behind her. 'Was she heading to the ward?'

'I assume so. She barely said two words to me, if I'm honest.' Betty winked, her gaze amused. 'I was doing all the jabbering as usual.'

Ignoring the inexplicable loop the loop in her stomach that Betty's wink evoked, Veronica cleared her throat and looked again at the door rather than at Betty. 'She has a lot on her plate right now. If Mr Martin comes in asking for me' – she forced her gaze to Betty's – 'can you tell him I had to go back to the ward for a few minutes and I'll be straight back?'

'Aren't you back there after lunch anyway?' Betty glanced at the clock. 'It's your lunch break in half an hour. Just go now and if he comes back, I'll make your excuses.'

'Thank you.' Veronica smiled, cursing the strange, frightening feelings she had for Betty that tumbled through her. 'You're a pal.'

'A pal?' Betty grinned. 'Well, that's an improvement on colleague, I suppose.'

Veronica's cheeks heated as Betty's gaze bored into hers, something blatantly flirtatious in her eyes.

Veronica turned away. 'I'll... get going then.'

'Of course. Hey.' Betty clasped Veronica's arm as she moved to walk away, her gaze soft as she studied her. 'I didn't mean to worry you. I'm sure Nurse Parkes is fine. No doubt she's just exhausted like the rest of us.'

'Maybe.'

Veronica stared at Betty for moment longer before flashing her a half-smile and rushing from the theatre into the corridor. Once alone, she exhaled a long, shaky breath, waiting for the awareness that had been roused all over her body to subside. What was wrong with her? Confusion rose and she blinked back the tears that sprang into her eyes. Mark Riley and his actions had put pay to her even testing the idea of romance, of love, and now she seemed to be in the throes of a schoolgirl crush on a woman, no less! Why was her life so often beleaguered with stupid, dangerous thoughts?

Hurrying along the corridor, Veronica entered the ward and scanned its length and breadth looking for Freda. She had just spotted her at the far end when Sylvia came up beside her.

'I need to talk to you and Freda,' she said urgently as she looked around them at the hustle and bustle. 'Are you in any hurry to get home tonight?'

Veronica grimaced as she kept her eye on Freda. 'Am I ever in a hurry to go home?'

Sylvia grinned. 'Me and you both, my friend. Me and you both. Right, then what do you say about a quick drink after work?'

'All right.' Veronica smiled. 'I need to speak to Freda so I'll ask if she can join us, shall I?'

'Yes, but be careful to not talk too loudly. Kathy has been hinting at wanting to join us. And she can another time. I stand by my promise to Freda to include her more often from now on, what with everything she told us about Kathy, but not tonight. There's stuff I need to tell you both that is not for Kathy's ears. It's too… personal.'

Veronica nodded. 'All right. Not this time.' She looked at Freda as she helped Mrs Fisher into a wheelchair, her face solemn. 'Does Freda look all right to you?'

Sylvia frowned as she followed Veronica's gaze towards their friend. 'A bit peaky maybe. She's been working as well as she usually does this morning. Why?'

'Nurses Campbell and Roberts!' Sister Dyer said loudly from across the ward. 'Do you two think this is the time to be gossiping? Get to work. Both of you.'

'Oh, bloody hell,' Sylvia muttered. 'That's us in the doghouse for the rest of the day, but I'm kind of grateful that at least some things around here seem to be returning to normal. See you later.'

Taking a deep breath, Veronica marched forward, intent on speaking to Freda, but then faltered, having made the mistake of looking at Eric Matthews. His gaze bored into hers, his face, free of its bandages since two days before, sombre. The crisscross of welts and gashes, puckered and stitched skin, caused her heart to constrict painfully behind her ribcage. The man had done all he possibly could to help her – to defend her honour – on the worst day of her life and punished her assailant how he thought best several times afterwards.

And now she knew what Eric had seen and done, the connection that had been between them from the moment she had laid eyes on him had deepened. Yet she had no idea what to do or feel about it. She glanced again at Freda as her friend sat down next to Mrs Fisher and picked up a hardback novel, seemingly preparing to read to her. Freda did not look herself at all. Ashen faced, her shoulders drooped. Her whole demeanour was far from usual.

'Nurse Campbell? Could I have a quick word?'

Blinking from her contemplation, Veronica faced Eric Matthews. How could she ignore the hope in his eyes?

Swallowing hard, she approached his bed. 'Officer Matthews.' She forced a smile, aware of how little time she'd spent with him after making a point of spending every spare minute she could at his bedside before finding out how he knew her. 'How are you? It's good to see your bandages have been removed.'

'I'm all right.'

His sad blue gaze travelled over her face, his study intense as though trying to gauge her feelings.

'The sister has told me I will be transferred to one of the rural convalescent homes in the next few days,' he said. 'I was hoping to be reassured things are better between us before I go.'

Veronica held his stare. More than once her friends had inferred that Eric's feelings towards her surpassed care, but she did not feel anything romantic towards him at all. Which, if she was honest, was entirely unfair. After all, Eric had proven himself a better man than any she had ever met before.

She touched her fingers to his where they lay on the bed and smiled, tears pricking her eyes. 'We're in a good place, Eric. I promise,' she said quietly. 'What you did for me that day... it was so good of you, and I never should have been angry with you. I was just shocked and ashamed thinking you knew and... saw things.'

'I only wanted to do right by you then and when I arrived here, Veronica. Sometimes knowing what to do for the best isn't easy.'

'No.' She sighed. 'Not for any of us.' They stared into each other's eyes and Veronica felt the kinship between them strengthen even more. 'Write to me here, at the hospital, once you're settled and I'll come and visit you. How will that be?'

He smiled as best he could considering his facial injuries, tears glinting in his eyes. 'That would be more than I could've hoped for.'

She grinned and squeezed his fingers before leaving his bedside and approaching Freda where she still sat with Mrs Fisher.

'Hello, Mrs Fisher,' she said as she reached the bed. 'Do you mind if I have a quick word with Nurse Parkes.'

'Not at all, my dear.' She closed her eyes. 'Pretend I'm not here.'

Veronica looked at Freda. 'Sylvia's suggested we go out for a drink tonight. What do you say?'

Freda nodded, blew out a tired breath. 'I say yes as long as we make it more than one.'

'Something's happened, hasn't it?'

'Yes, but I can't talk about it now.' Freda briefly closed her eyes before opening them again. 'I'll tell you and Sylvia everything later. All right?'

Veronica nodded and slowly walked away.

Whatever happened in Freda and Sylvia's lives, she would be there for them, just as the three of them had been for each other over and over again in the short time they'd known one another. This war had broken so many things, so many people, all over Europe, but it would never break her friendship with Freda and Sylvia. She prayed nothing would.

'Nurse Campbell!' Sister Dyer boomed. 'I've told you once, I will not tell you again. Will you please move yourself!'

'Yes, Sister. Sorry, Sister!'

30

FREDA

Freda smiled as she watched Veronica practically run along the ward in answer to Sister Dyer's command. Her friend really was one of the most sweetest—

'She's one of the special ones, isn't she?' Mrs Fisher gave a weak smile. 'Nurse Campbell.'

Freda met Mrs Fisher's shadowed gaze, pleased to see the first hint of happiness in them that she had seen for a while. 'She is. Veronica is very special indeed. A wonderful friend and a brilliant nurse.'

Mrs Fisher coughed, held a cotton handkerchief to her mouth and stayed like that for a moment to compose herself. She lowered the handkerchief and closed her eyes. 'You all are. You, Nurse Roberts, even Nurse Scott can be a good 'un when she puts her mind to it.'

Freda smiled, her fondness for the older woman who had lost her husband, two sons and two grandchildren to this war warming her heart. Somehow over the last couple of weeks, Mrs Fisher and her wise words and amusing stories had come to matter to Freda. This force of a woman – nearing her sixtieth birthday just next month – had managed to hold on to her only daughter through sheer luck because she had been cleaning someone's house when the raids struck rather than with her children where they lived in the slums. Had she been, Mrs Fisher's daughter would have almost certainly perished alongside her children. Possibly something Mrs Fisher's poor daughter now wished had happened...

'What have you got planned over the coming months then, Nurse?' Mrs Fisher asked, her eyes slowly closing. 'Personally, I mean. Not your work, that side is sorted well enough.'

If only I knew... Freda drew in a long breath. 'If you are trying to ask me about my love life, there's nothing to tell you.'

'Why not?' Mrs Fisher squinted one watery eye open. 'Surely you had a line of young chaps wanting to court you before this damn war took most of them away?'

Freda huffed a laugh, Richard filling her mind's eye. 'Hardly. There is one chap who manages to distract me from time to time, but no one serious.'

'Manages to distract you?' Mrs Fisher closed her eyes again. 'It certainly isn't love then if you call him a distraction. I know you're not asking for it, but let me give you some advice from a woman who's been on this earth for a good time longer than you.'

'And a good time longer yet I hope.'

Freda fought to maintain her smile, knowing that Mrs Fisher grew weaker every day from the dust and dirt caking her lungs, the trauma of a broken hip and damage to her pelvis. God knew she had put up a good fight, but it was a fight Freda feared Mrs Fisher was losing despite all what Freda and the other nurses had done for this wonderful woman.

'Ah, get away with you. My only regret is I'll be leaving my beautiful Jenny behind...' Mrs Fisher screwed her eyes more tightly shut as though she didn't want to open them and have Freda witness her grief. 'Some people say regrets are futile, Nurse Parkes, and maybe they are, but there aren't many people who get through a life lived without a whole list of them, myself included.'

Dorothy and her pregnancy came to Freda's consciousness, Robert, too. Lord only knew what lay ahead for them...

'Now, you listen to me, Nurse, and heed what I say.'

Freda's heart swelled with relief to see a blessed spark of determination shining in Mrs Fisher's dark brown eyes. She smiled. 'I'm listening.'

'Give me your hand.'

Freda slid her hand into Mrs Fisher's and she gently clasped it, her thin skin smooth as glass against Freda's. 'I want you to promise me something.'

Tears pricked Freda's eyes. Why did she feel like this was a final farewell? 'Mrs Fisher—'

'Ah, no, you promise, Nurse, that from this day forward, you will live your life to the fullest. Hitler and his cronies are wreaking havoc over half the world and who knows when anyone will manage to stop him. Life is for living now, war or no war. You find a way. Do you hear me?'

Freda frowned. 'A way to what?'

'If you want to stay in nursing, nurse like you never have before. If you want to get married, marry good and quick. If you want neither of those things, then leave, go, find what it is that makes your heart sing and makes you feel like you're ten feet tall. Nothing else will do.'

Freda's pulse beat faster, her mouth drying. That was it! That was what she was looking for. She wanted her heart to sing; wanted to stand ten feet tall!

'I will.'

'Pardon me?' Mrs Fisher quirked an eyebrow, her canny gaze boring into Freda's. 'I didn't quite hear you.'

Freda smiled, her heart beating fast. 'I said, I will. I promise.'

'Good.' Mrs Fisher blew out a heavy breath, released Freda's hand and collapsed back against the pillows, her eyes closing. 'Now, go on with you. I need to sleep.'

Freda stood and stared down at Mrs Fisher. 'I'll see you later.'

But Mrs Fisher didn't answer, and somehow Freda knew that she wouldn't.

* * *

A few hours later, Freda walked into the Garrick's Head pub behind Sylvia and Veronica, trying not to screw up her nose against the smell of unwashed bodies and cigarette smoke as the men they passed blatantly appraised her and her friends. With its dark wood panelled walls, sticky floor and nicotine-stained ceiling, the Garrick's Head was a far cry from the quieter, more female friendly pubs the girls met at for a drink now and then, but with so many streets closed and buildings considered unsafe, they'd opted to go to the pub where Sylvia's mum worked in the hope she'd find them a corner where they could talk privately.

However, from the few times Freda had met Mrs Roberts, she wasn't holding out much hope she'd comply with Sylvia's request and was more likely to laugh them out of the pub. Privacy did not seem to be a high priority amongst the Garrick's Head patrons.

'You two wait there,' Sylvia said, her eyes narrowed against the screen of grey cigarette smoke hovering all around them, and surveyed her mother where she held court behind the bar. 'I'll speak to Mum and be right back.'

Freda exchanged a subtle grimace with Veronica as Sylvia

left them alone. Tension emanated from her friend, her face pale. Veronica didn't like pubs at the best of times, grubby, lecherous-eyed men even more so. Freda fought not to slip a supportive arm around Veronica's waist, knowing there was a good chance the gesture would not go unnoticed and would undoubtedly be crudely commented upon if any of the drinkers saw it.

'Right,' Sylvia yelled as she emerged from the throng carrying a tray of three vodka and oranges. The crash of a smashed glass sounded a few feet away, making them flinch, and Sylvia scowled at the offender. 'Mum has come up trumps for once. She said we can take our drinks into the backyard. It's small, but there's a couple of tables and chairs out there. The evening's warm enough. Come on.'

Freda and Veronica dutifully followed Sylvia out of the bar and along a narrow hallway lined with barrels and boxes of every imaginable size. They came to a door that opened onto the promised back yard, a couple of rickety-looking wooden tables and chairs set out along one side. Freda breathed deep, welcoming the open air even if it was far from springtime fresh when it was peppered with smoke and ash from the continual clean-up work going on around the city. Either way, it was a lot better than the fetid air inside the pub.

They sat around one of the tables and clinked glasses, each of them taking a hefty sip before returning them to the table with satisfied sighs.

'I guess you two needed a drink as much as me for once.' Sylvia grinned. 'Well, there's plenty more where that came from.' She wiggled her eyebrows. 'One of the perks of having a mum working as a barmaid and her being the landlord's main draw for his punters is the free drinks she has no problem providing me with. She might not be mother of the year, but she has her uses.'

Freda shook her head. 'You do like a drink, my friend.'

Sylvia laughed and lifted her glass in a toast. 'I do.' She took a couple of sips. 'So, you go first, Freda. What's wrong? You didn't seem yourself today.'

'No,' Veronica said, her green eyes shadowed with concern. 'Not at all. Has something happened? Is it Dorothy?'

Freda sighed, somehow not surprised that Veronica assumed the issue was with Dorothy. After all, she had orchestrated Mr Martin's involvement in the crisis. 'Partly. She's agreed to keep the baby.'

'She has?' Veronica grinned. 'Well, that's a relief, isn't it?'

'Yes, it is. 'Course it is,' Freda said, squeezing her friend's hand. 'But she also has to tell Robert, so the crisis isn't over yet.'

'No, I can't imagine he's going to be very happy about it,' Sylvia said before taking a large sip of her drink. 'What man would be?'

'Exactly. Mum seems to think everything will work out, but I'm not so sure.' Freda sighed. 'On top of that, I'm pretty sure I'm going to be greeted with the news Mrs Fisher has passed away when I arrive at the hospital for my shift tomorrow.'

'Why do you say that?' Veronica asked.

'I don't know.' Freda took a fortifying gulp of her drink. 'It was the way she was talking to me earlier. It's just a feeling.'

'Bloody hell, Freda. You love the bones of her, don't you?'

Freda nodded, any further words lodged behind the lump in her throat.

'Right then.' Sylvia stood and focused on the pub's back door. 'I think we're going to need another drink. Especially when you've heard what I've got to say. I'll go and get another round.'

She glanced at Freda and Veronica's half-filled glasses. 'Don't rush.' She winked. 'I'm just thirsty.'

She disappeared inside, a cacophony of male shouting and swearing from inside the pub filtering into the yard as the door opened and then vanished again as it closed.

'Are you all right, Freda?' Veronica asked, her beautiful green eyes filled with care. 'You really don't look it.'

Freda leaned forward on her elbows, put her head in her hands. 'I don't know how I am, V,' she said, feeling her friend's hand on her back. 'I'm so tired. So fed up with this war. With the pain and suffering.' She straightened and looked into Veronica's eyes. 'Sometimes I so desperately want to write, other times I just want to have a career away from the hospital and I know it's selfish to feel that way when my skills are needed here, but the feeling I should be elsewhere just won't go away.'

'Your skills are needed wherever you can give them,' Veronica said, pulling a tissue from her bag and handing it to her. 'You are more than a nurse, more than a writer at the *Chronicle*, Freda. Look at the amazing work you're doing with that woman in Bristol. What's her name?'

'Susan. Susan Beckett.'

'Susan, that's it. You have such huge ambitious changes you'd like to make through your writing. You might have to stay at the hospital awhile longer yet, but this war can't go on forever and then you can do whatever work you feel the most called to do.'

'Maybe.'

'Not maybe. All of us must believe we'll get to do what we want with our lives.' Veronica held Freda's gaze. 'I have every intention of moving out of my mother's house sooner rather than later and finding my own place. But with half the buildings in the city demolished, God only knows when that will happen now, but it will happen. Everything we want will come to all three of us eventually. I know it will.'

Freda managed a small smile, pride filling her heart as she studied her wonderfully kind, ridiculously strong friend. 'You're the best out of the three of us, V.'

She grinned. 'We're all the best.'

'Cheers to that!'

Laughing, they spun around as Sylvia came back into the yard, her tray duly replenished. She set it down on the table and picked up one of the glasses.

Holding the glass aloft, she made a show of taking a good long drink and smacked her lips together. 'Now, are we ready to hear my godawful news?'

31

SYLVIA

Once she had her friends' attention, Sylvia set her glass firmly on the table and blew out a breath. 'I've spoken to Jesse's mum.'

'What?'

'When?'

'A few days ago,' Sylvia said, taking another mouthful of her drink. 'And I still haven't worked out what I'm going to do about it. Not that there is anything I can do. But you know what I mean.'

'I haven't got a clue what you mean,' Freda said with a frown. 'You haven't worked out what you're going to do about what? What did his mum say exactly?'

Sylvia looked between her friends, suddenly afraid to tell them about Jesse's blindness. If she said it out loud, that made it real. She'd said it countless times in her head, tossed and turned for the last few nights trying to comprehend what Jesse must have been through, what his blindness would have done to him, how it would have changed him...

'Sylvia?' Veronica said quietly. 'What is it?'

She inhaled a long breath, shakily released it. 'Jesse's blind.'

In the sudden silence, the banter and cat-calling from the pub faintly sounded in the small back yard.

'I have no idea what he's going to be like now. What he's going to feel about himself, I mean,' Sylvia said, taking a drink. 'Jesse is... so proud. A protector and a provider. He is his mother's everything. He's a guardian and teacher to his younger brothers and sisters.' Tears filled her eyes and she angrily swiped them away. 'This could destroy him.'

'You don't know that,' Veronica said gently. 'From what you've told us about Jesse, he's strong. He'll find a way to live without his sight just as we've seen other soldiers at the hospital do. Human beings are so resilient when they put their minds to it. We know that more than most.'

'I'm not so sure.'

'Of course he will,' Freda said decisively as she picked up her drink. 'And if he doesn't, you can be with him every step of the way. If that's what you want, of course?'

Sylvia met her friend's questioning gaze and fought the urge to crawl into Freda's arms. She was her strength and stay, whereas Veronica was her softener, the one who calmed her. She needed them both right now, but if she surrendered to V's love and care, she'd be too weak to be of any use to Jesse. It was Freda's strength she needed to concentrate on for the time being.

'I don't know what I want,' she finally said, closing her eyes, self-loathing twisting inside her. 'And I don't know what kind of person that makes me or what it says about me.'

'It says you're human,' Freda said, pinning her with a no-nonsense stare.

'Maybe.' Sylvia drained her drink before returning the empty glass to the table. 'But Jesse's mum asked that I leave him be for the time being anyway, and I'll respect her wishes. Well, I will until I know what to do next. Right now, I haven't got a bloody clue.'

'So you're not going to try to see him at all, regardless of what his mother says?' asked Freda. 'That doesn't sound like you!'

'Plus...' Veronica exclaimed, her green eyes wide. 'You love him.'

Sylvia swallowed, her throat parched. She glanced at her friends' glasses and saw they hadn't even touched their second drink yet. She clenched her hands together on the table and fought her impatience to return to the bar.

'We've seen so much devastation, heartbreak and terror at the training school and hospital since the start of this war,' she said. 'Yet we always find the right words to comfort and support our patients. Now, with Jesse, I just feel numb.' She closed her eyes. 'No words of encouragement are coming to me that will bolster him. No plan or process that will help him.'

'The words will come, Sylv,' Freda said firmly. 'They will come if you want to find them badly enough. Where is Jesse now?'

Sylvia opened her eyes. 'I don't know.'

'Do you want to know?'

'Yes, but that doesn't mean I'm not scared to death about actually seeing him.'

'That's completely understandable,' Veronica said quietly. 'Do you think his mum will write to you with their address soon? Invite you to their home?'

'I've no idea, but I'm not sure I'm prepared to just wait around until she dictates what's going to happen next either.' Sylvia wiped away an errant tear. 'I might be terrified of seeing Jesse, but I won't turn my back on him. I need to find out where the Howards are living and then when I'm ready I'll decide what to do.'

Freda smiled. 'That's my girl.'

Sylvia sat a little straighter, embracing her friends' warmth and the bravado her alcohol consumption provided. 'Maybe I just need to see him. See what's what. Tell him... I love him. After that, who knows?'

'Knowing you still love him is enough at this point, Sylv,' Freda said. 'The next step will become clear in time.'

Sylvia stood and picked up her empty glass, tipped it from side to side. 'I'm just going to grab another. I won't be a tick.'

Before Freda or Veronica could respond, Sylvia hurried inside the pub, ignoring the little voice in her head telling her she was turning into her mother, that her fondness for the bottle was becoming a problem. That little voice needed to learn to keep its mouth shut because, one, she was nothing like her mother, and two, she had a responsible job and practically ran their home life. On the other side of the coin, her mother was so drunk half the time she wasn't capable of a responsible job or doing as much as flicking a duster around the house.

'Ah, here she is, my wonderful daughter!' Eileen Roberts shouted across the bar as Sylvia approached and put her glass on the bar. 'Another round, is it?'

'Just one for me will do for now.' She held her mother's canny gaze. 'The other two have got things on later.'

'Whereas you'll just fall into bed when you get home?'

'Something like that.'

Her mother reached up and selected a glass from the rack above her head, poured a liberal splash of vodka followed by a far less liberal dash of orange cordial.

She pushed it across the bar. 'You all right?'

'Aren't I always?' Sylvia forced a smile, winked. 'I'm my mother's daughter, after all.'

Her mother studied her. 'Hmm, that you are.'

Lifting her glass in a toast, Sylvia slowly made her way back through the pub, sipping her drink and fighting to keep control of the horrible vulnerability twisting inside her as it threatened her enforced and necessary bravado. Jesse's face swam in and out of her mind's eye, his beautiful brown gaze meeting hers. Would his eyes be the same now? Or would they be marred by his blindness? She had nursed long enough to know blindness afflicted the sufferer in any number of ways and his eyes could easily look just as they always had. Either way, that didn't matter to her in the slightest. She just wanted him to be all right in himself.

She purposefully burst through the back door into the yard with aplomb, trying to re-establish the façade she wore like a second skin most of the time these days. 'And I'm back!'

'So you are,' Freda said, studying her. 'I really need to go, Sylv. Once you've finished your drink, we'll walk out together. I was just saying to V that maybe after a good night's sleep everything will look a bit brighter for all three of us.'

'It's a crap show, isn't it?' Sylvia drained half her drink, wiped a small dribble from her chin with the back of her hand. 'But it's up to us to change things if we're not happy and the first thing I'm going to do when I leave here is head to the station.'

'The railway station?' Veronica's eyes widened. 'Why?'

'Because Jesse's mum mentioned his younger brother is working the railway now. If I can find him, I'll get their address out of him soon enough. You see if I don't.' She downed the rest of her drink and stood. 'Come on then, if we're going.'

32

FREDA

Freda fought her tears and hardened her heart. *I'll keep my promise to live my life to the fullest, Mrs Fisher. You see if I don't.*

'I really am sorry to be the bearer of bad news, Nurse Parkes. I had expected Mrs Fisher to rally when we moved her to her own room earlier today, but it seems the move gave her the privacy to pass peacefully away instead.' Sister Dyer flashed a fleeting tight-lipped smile. 'I wanted to let you know at the earliest opportunity. I know you had come to like Mrs Fisher very much, and she you.'

'Yes, we did have an... understanding.'

'Indeed. I have also been meaning to extend my appreciation for your hard work over these past weeks. In fact, I have mentioned your bravery and willingness in going to investigate the situation outside during the bombings to the hospital powers that be. I think your courage should be justly acknowledged.'

To say Freda was taken aback by the sister's compliments would be an understatement of epic proportions, and she couldn't help but wonder if Mrs Fisher's passing had contributed to them. 'Well, that's very kind of you, Sister. It was the least I could do.'

'Now, now,' the sister said, her eyes softening. 'Credit where credit's due.' She glanced at her watch. 'And you are half an hour over the end of your shift. Why don't you get yourself home? I believe you're due in at six o'clock tomorrow morning?'

'I am, Sister.'

'Very good. Run along then.'

Sister Dyer stood from her desk, gave a curt nod and then marched away, her stout shoes striking the floor tiles with their usual military precision. Freda stared after her before continuing on to the staffroom, her mind reeling with what she could or should do, what she must or mustn't do. The sister's words were kind and well meant, but she had also suggested on numerous occasions that Freda's mind was more often elsewhere other than on her nursing. Something which had only led her to suspect Sister Dyer had come across Freda's byline more than once in the newspaper.

It was no good. She had to take some inspired action as her soul was calling her to do.

Once she was out of the hospital grounds, she walked across town, marvelling at how much of the city's destruction had been completely cleared in places and then plunged into sadness again when she came across buildings and homes reduced to mountains of rubble and glass. A group of children played atop a pile of bricks, pretending to shoot one another with broken planks of wood, their innocent screams and cries poignant, yet strangely heartening that they remained unaffected by the devastation all around them – at least, it seemed that way on the surface. No one could know what the consequences of this war would make to Europe's children's future health and happiness for a long while yet.

Picking up her pace, Freda suddenly knew with complete clarity what she needed to do to shake off her frustration. She arrived at the *Chronicle*'s office and confidently pushed open the door before she could change her mind.

Richard was sat at his desk, his fingers moving rapidly over his typewriter keys, his brow creased. Her stomach knotted with desire like it did every time she saw him hard at work. She hugely admired the man and, right then, wanted to be with him so much, but she would not sway in her decision to steer clear of any notion of a serious relationship.

'Freda! It's so good to see you!'

Freda jumped, her smile instantaneous as she faced the paper's bubbly, totally wonderful, secretary, Barbara Dean. 'Barbara!'

They embraced and Freda locked gazes with Richard over Barbara's shoulder. His ridiculously blue and broody eyes burned into her... Through her.

She quickly drew back and smiled at Barbara. 'You look so well,' she said. 'How are your family? Your brother? Was he all right during the raids? I know some returning officers struggled with the explosions after serving on the front lines.'

'My family are all good and my brother is doing as well as can be expected. He knows he's lucky to be in one piece and with his family so that's what he tries to focus on.'

'That's what we should all be focusing on.'

'Hmm.' Barbara looked between Freda and Richard. 'But I think you and Richard are more often thinking about others than you are yourselves.' She lifted her eyebrows. 'I assume it's the man himself you're here to see?'

'It is.'

Richard rose from his chair but didn't come closer; he just

stood there, carefully watching her, his hands in his pockets and his gaze indecipherable.

Freda pulled her gaze from his and she smiled at Barbara. 'I'll see you again soon.'

'Do you want a cuppa?'

'No, I'm fine. Thank you.'

With a squeeze of Freda's hand, Barbara returned to her desk even if Freda felt the secretary's eyes on her all the way to Richard's desk.

She stopped in front of him, tried and failed to get her disloyal heart under control. Looking into his questioning gaze, she immediately knew coming here had been the right thing to do, that he wouldn't let her down.

'I need you to drive me to Bristol,' she said.

'When?'

'Now.'

They stared at one another and as much as Freda instinctively sensed Barbara would feel the tension emanating between her and Richard, she did not look away from him.

'Let's go then,' he said, his study gliding over her mouth before he snatched his keys from his desk. 'After you.'

He gestured with a wave for her to lead the way from the office and Freda walked ahead of him, nodding at Barbara as she passed her desk, smiling widely when the secretary grinned and winked.

Within twenty minutes, she and Richard were leaving Bath behind and were on their way to Bristol. They had barely spoken a word, the taut atmosphere escalating along with Freda's need to touch him, but she refrained, knowing it would be unfair to encourage him when she could guarantee nothing happening between them when she felt so torn and discontent.

'What are we doing, Freda?'

Richard continued to stare ahead, his jaw tight and his knuckles showing white as he gripped the steering wheel.

'I need to see Susan. I want to see how she's going along. How the children are.'

'I see.'

Disappointment laced those two little words and a horrible guilt brought warmth to her cheeks. 'I need to see something worthwhile that I'm – or rather *was* – a part of, Richard. A patient that I had come to care for passed away today and the loss has left me feeling more than ever that nothing I do makes a difference at the hospital, but when I was writing, when I was working with Susan campaigning to rehome the children, everything felt so exciting, so valuable and right.'

'Your work at the hospital is valuable,' he protested. 'How can it not be?' He glanced at her, his eyes dark. 'When I saw you back there, standing in the office and looking so resolute, I'd hoped' – a muscle flexed and relaxed in his jaw – 'that you'd come to see me.'

She looked at her lap, wanting to give him so much more than she had to give, but it was impossible. 'I came to you, Richard. I wanted your help above anyone else's.' She looked at his handsome profile. 'I hope that means something even if I can't be with you as you'd like.'

'You can, but you won't.'

Tears pricked her eyes and she looked away. 'I'm sorry.' She faced him, her stomach knotting at the sight of his hard, tight jaw. 'I won't make promises to you I can't keep. I won't say what you want to hear to keep the peace between us. I really wish things were different...'

'But?'

'But...' She sighed, stared ahead through the windscreen. He deserved her honesty. 'I'm not ready to commit to anyone right now – including you. I need to experience more, live more. Then, and only then, will I truly know what I want.'

The car's engine rumbled, traffic and noise from the street filtering into the car through the open windows, but Freda refused to add another word more. If he could not accept what she'd said, then—

'I appreciate you being candid with me.' He turned, met her eyes and gave a wry smile. 'Even if your words have made a few cuts across my pathetic heart.'

She blushed at the charming sparkle in his blue eyes and dropped her gaze to her lap.

Seconds of silence passed before he cleared his throat.

'Susan is doing well,' he said, his focus back on the road. 'She's in lodgings and has secured the backing of a rich philanthropist who is heavily involved and hands-on with the kids. From what little I know of Mr Steven Audley, he seems like a good chap.'

'Chap?' Surprised, Freda smiled. 'Is he young?'

He glanced at her, didn't return her smile. 'He's around my age, I'd think. Maybe a little older.'

'So early thirties? Well, it's certainly encouraging to hear someone, a youngish man no less, taking an interest in those poor children.' She smiled again, trying to tease the same from him even if she knew it was a hard task. 'Or maybe it's Susan who's caught his interest.'

'Either way, his money is welcome.'

The rest of the journey passed mostly in silence, the odd remark shared about the clean-up operation in Bath, family and friends, bits and pieces that skirted around the subject of them.

At last, they pulled up outside a townhouse in one of Bristol's cobbled side streets and Richard cut the engine.

He turned in his seat. 'I respect everything you've said to me about us, our future... any commitment, but I want you to know I've fallen in love with you. You *need* to know that.'

Freda stared at him, her heart pulsing in her ears. 'What?'

A ghost of a smile lifted his lips. 'I said I love you. Do with that what you will. I just want you to know.'

And with that, he pulled on the car door handle and stepped out onto the pavement.

33

VERONICA

After a good night's sleep, Veronica walked onto the ward ready to start her shift, a slight spring in her step and feeling more than a little proud of herself that she'd gathered the courage over breakfast that morning to raise the subject of her moving out again with her mother. Of course, the conversation had been far from congenial, her mother barely holding back her tears, but at least Veronica had held her ground.

It was now the beginning of June, and she had every intention of being away from her street – away from Mark Riley – come winter. Whether her mother came to terms with her leaving between now and then, who knew? But she'd be leaving either way. Over and over again, she'd tried to reassure her that she would regularly come home for a visit, have the odd Sunday lunch with her, but her mother appeared determined to keep hold of her fervent displays of emotional blackmail. Well, she could carry on that way all she wanted; it would be to no avail.

Veronica pulled back her shoulders. Maybe Eric would like a cup of tea and she could tell him all about it. He seemed to always be happy to listen to her even if she never really had much to say. She walked along the ward, nodding and smiling good morning to a few of her favourite patients, but when her gaze turned to Eric's bed, her stomach dropped.

A gentleman she'd never seen before lay, pyjama-clad and asleep, where Eric had lain for weeks. The convalescent home. Had he been transferred already?

Her heart stumbled and Veronica pressed a hand to her chest as she frantically scanned the ward looking for Sister Dyer or Sylvia, an unexpected wave of loss washing over her. She spotted Sylvia across the ward as she said something to Mr Harkness that made him roar with laughter and then clutch the wound on his torso.

'Knock it off, Nurse Roberts,' he said, coughing. 'I'll pop my stitches if you carry on with that nonsense.'

Sylvia laughed and turned, her smile faltering as her eyes met Veronica's. 'I'll go and see about that toast,' she said. 'Be back in a jiffy.'

Striding towards Veronica, she frowned. 'What's up?'

'Officer Matthews,' Veronica said. 'Where is he?'

'He's been transferred to the convalescent home.'

'Already?'

'Hey.' Sylvia touched Veronica's arm. 'What is it? You knew he was being moved this week.'

'Yes, but...' Veronica looked again at Eric's newly occupied bed. 'I just thought... I need to...' Veronica pressed her hand to her mouth and rushed towards the exit.

'V! Where are you going?'

Ignoring Sylvia's call and praying her friend didn't follow her, Veronica jogged along the corridor, a deluge of emotions threatening to overcome her. Loss, sadness, anguish. Eric had been a familiar presence on the ward for so long. From the moment he'd arrived at the hospital, they had spoken to one another as much as possible throughout every shift before, during and after the raids that had brought the city to a standstill.

He hadn't just done all he could to help her the day she was raped; he had been a quiet, non-assuming strength to her ever since he came to the hospital. Now she felt a huge, inexplicable grief. She was being irrational. She could write to him, visit him. What was wrong with her? A sob caught in her throat and Veronica slapped her hand to her mouth as she entered the staffroom, relieved to find it empty.

Looking left and right, her breath rasping against her throat, she hid out of view behind a row of metal lockers, not wanting anyone to see her crying. She squeezed her eyes shut and images of Mark Riley's grinning face, his maniacal eyes, spittle on his lips as he puffed and panted on top of her as she lay helpless and unmoving on the cold kitchen floor, played behind her closed eyelids. Panic rolled through her and gathered in her chest, perspiration bursting onto her forehead and upper lip. With trembling fingers, Veronica grappled to get the top buttons of her dress undone and then collapsed her head against the locker behind her, waiting for the pulsing in her temples to ease.

Then, for the first time, she saw Eric's face on that day so clearly in her mind's eye that she felt faint. His crystal-blue eyes dark with protective anger, his handsome face free of blemish or scar, his dark hair hidden beneath a flat cap. There he suddenly was, hunched down beside her, wanting to help her – wanting to avenge her.

Shame and hatred for Mark Riley curled like hell's flames around her heart as Veronica fought back the scared, timid, trusting young woman she'd been that day compared to the strong, wise and savvy woman she liked to think she was today... She swallowed. But was she really?

Hurried footsteps tapped this way and that across the tiled

floor before they abruptly stopped. Veronica held her breath and squeezed her eyes shut. The last thing she wanted was for anyone to see her like this...

'There you are.' Sylvia's voice sounded above her. 'Oh, V.'

Her friend sat on the floor beside her, her arms coming around her in a firm embrace.

'I don't know what's wrong with me.' Veronica sniffed. 'It's as though with Eric gone, I'm entirely exposed to Mark Riley's abuse again. It doesn't make sense. I went years without even knowing Eric existed and now...'

'Now what?'

'Now it's as if I came to rely on him to keep me safe.'

'Oh, V. Maybe you unconsciously did and that is completely understandable. There must have been some recognition or connection between you.'

'It doesn't make sense.'

'Nothing about what you went through makes sense. It never should have happened and...' Sylvia cupped her hands to Veronica's jaw, her brown eyes bright with anger. 'That monster should be dead, or at least behind bars, as far as I'm concerned. Let's hope and pray one day he will be. But in the meantime, V, please know you're safe. Freda and I will never let anything happen to you, you know that.'

Not wanting to point out that none of them could be there for each other twenty-four hours a day, Veronica pulled her lips tightly together, her tears spent and her breathing slowly returning to normal.

'Officer Matthews went after him,' she said quietly.

'What?'

'He put Riley in the hospital again and again until he was conscripted.'

'I knew there was reason to like the man,' Sylvia said, slipping her hand from Veronica's face and dropping back against the adjacent locker. 'He certainly wanted to do anything he could to put things right. It's just a shame he didn't kill Riley.'

'Don't say that. Would you really have wanted Eric to be a murderer?'

Sylvia sighed. 'No, I suppose not.'

'One day…' Veronica exhaled a shaky breath. 'I'll make sure Riley pays for what he did to me and no doubt other women, too. I should have done something by now, put a stop to…' She shook her head. 'What if there were more women and I could've done something to—'

'If there are others, that is not on you. Do you hear me?' Sylvia glared at her, her cheeks red. 'Anything Riley has done before or since he attacked you is on him. All of it.'

Veronica nodded, but a horrible, gnawing culpability lingered that she might have prevented further attacks, and she knew it wouldn't disappear until she did something to atone for her inaction.

'Listen,' Sylvia said quietly. 'If or when you are ready to do something about that bastard, just say the word and we'll see what we can do, all right?'

'We?'

'Yes, we.' Sylvia's eyes burned with a discomfiting fury. 'All three of us. Possibly four, if Kathy comes to prove her worth.'

Before Veronica could respond, more footsteps sounded across the staffroom floor before Kathy Scott appeared in front of them.

She narrowed her eyes. 'Were you talking about me, Nurse…' Her eyes widened as her gaze swept over Veronica's face before she frowned, concern replacing the suspicion in her hazel eyes. 'Is everything all right, V?'

'Clearly not,' Sylvia snapped.

'Sylvia, stop it,' Veronica said wearily as post-breakdown exhaustion pressed down on her and she met Kathy's eyes once she'd dragged her glare from Sylvia. 'Whatever you two need to do to work things out, do it because I consider you both my friends and I'm fed up with the bickering between the pair of you.'

Kathy's eyes lit with a flash of undisguised happiness for a brief moment and then they shadowed with concern once again. 'Can I do anything for you?'

Before Veronica could tell Kathy she was fine, Sylvia cleared her throat. 'Yes, you can find Nurse Parkes, relieve her of whatever it is she's doing and tell her to come to the staffroom, quick smart. You do that and we might see about you joining us for a drink after shift. How's that?'

Kathy grinned. 'Well, that would be grand. I'll go and find her.'

She raced from the staffroom and Veronica blew out a breath. 'I'm not sure I'll be in the mood for a drink after work, but I appreciate you trying to make an effort with Kathy.'

'Yeah, well, needs must I suppose.' Sylvia sighed. 'And of course you'll want a drink considering the day you're having. We all will.'

They lapsed into silence and Veronica held on to her concerns about Sylvia's noticeable fondness for a glass or two of gin and tonic, or vodka and orange these days. She hadn't said anything to her or Freda because she felt a little naïve about what pertained to normal alcohol consumption and what didn't. Maybe the next time she was alone with Freda, she'd mention it. No doubt her friend would put her mind at rest.

A few minutes later, Freda rounded the lockers and immediately sat down by Veronica on her other side, put her hand on her leg. 'You all right?'

'I will be.' Veronica managed a tired smile. 'I always am with you two either side of me.'

'What happened?'

Veronica reiterated her reaction to seeing Eric no longer in his bed and how everything about the most awful day of her life had come flooding back.

'Could it be possible you have feelings for Officer Matthews?' Freda asked. 'That could go some way to explaining why you'd be so upset about him being transferred.'

Betty immediately came into Veronica's consciousness and so did the habitual warmth at her cheeks whenever she thought about her. 'No, it's nothing like that.'

Sylvia leaned forward and looked Veronica in the face. She laughed. 'Are you sure about that because you're blushing well enough.'

Freda grinned too, her blue eyes sparkling with amusement.

'I don't like him that way,' Veronica protested.

'Hmm, come on, V, you're amongst friends.' Sylvia nudged her. 'With those bandages gone, you can see what a handsome man he is, even with the scars.'

Annoyance simmered inside her. 'I am not attracted to him!'

'Leave her alone, Sylv,' Freda said, even if she was still smiling.

'Look at her!' Sylvia grinned. 'Her cheeks are all rosy, her eyes all misty. I'll bet you a round at the pub later that our beautiful V is halfway to falling head over heels.' Sylvia stood and held out her hands. 'Come on. Let's get you out of here.'

Veronica slipped her hands into Sylvia's and let her friend pull her to her feet, entirely relieved that Sylvia had moved on from Veronica's imagined love life.

34

SYLVIA

As Sylvia clutched a bag of pear drops and a bottle of pale ale, standing two doors down from the house where the Howards now lived, anyone would have the right to ask her how the hell she'd got herself in this predicament. But the simple truth was, she'd got three sheets to the wind the night before and somehow managed to tell her mother about Jesse's blindness, which had resulted in her mother calling her a complete and utter chicken if she didn't go around to his house and visit him the next day.

Sylvia cursed. No one called her chicken. Not even her damn stupid mother.

Grasping the sweets and beer tighter in her hands, Sylvia pulled back her shoulders and strode purposefully towards the address she'd obtained from Jesse's younger brother with little to no trouble at all when she'd accosted him at the station. It seemed he was as much of a sucker for her face as Jesse had once been. Tentative confidence inched over her as a small smile pulled at Sylvia's lips. Tilting her chin, she pushed open the garden gate of 41 Powlett Road. The small front garden could've done with a bit of attention which, considering how completely obsessive Mrs Howard was about cleaning, proved all too clearly that the family were not going along in the same vein as they'd been when they had lived in Castle Street.

How the Howards had been granted such a nice house when so many of Bath's families were now homeless was something to find out another time. Right now, all she needed to concentrate on was seeing through her mission to see Jesse today.

She knocked on the green painted door and respectfully stepped back, concluding that if Mrs Howard answered she'd not be best pleased to see her and was likely to throw a scrubbing brush or something similar at Sylvia's head. A little distance might be her saving grace. Yet even the potential for violence wouldn't put her off. Now she was at Jesse's home and with the possibility of him being a mere few yards away, Sylvia's uncertainty about seeing him again had vanished, leaving behind the overwhelming need to throw herself into the man's arms and kiss him like she had months before.

The question was, would he want to do the same?

She was about to step forward to knock a second time when the door opened and Patricia, Jesse's lovely youngest sister whose pretty face Sylvia hadn't seen for far too long, stood on the threshold.

The little girl gasped, her dark brown eyes lighting up. 'Miss Roberts!'

'The one and only.' Sylvia smiled and held out the sweets and bottle of beer either side of her to execute a semi-curtsy. She bowed her head. 'Miss Howard.'

Patricia giggled. 'Are you here to see Jesse?'

'Yes, but is your mum home? It might be best if I speak with her first.' Sylvia grimaced. 'You and I both know I'm not her favourite person and considering that the last time I saw her things went reasonably well between us, I really don't want to—'

'She's not here, so the coast is clear.'

And with that, Patricia whipped her hand out, grabbed Sylvia's wrist and propelled her inside the house with considerable and unexpected strength.

Stumbling on her high heels, Sylvia righted herself and feigned a glare. 'Well, that's not a very polite way to behave, is it?'

'I don't want you to disappear again,' she whispered.

'I've never disappeared. What are you talking about?' Sylvia whispered back. 'And why are we whispering?'

'Because I don't want Jesse to hear us talking or he might send you away.'

Dread knotted Sylvia's stomach and she looked to her right at a closed door that she presumed led to the living room, the tinny chatter of the wireless playing behind it. She wasn't going anywhere until she'd seen Jesse, who she suspected was behind that door, but having his little sister know there was potential that Sylvia wouldn't be wanted stung more than it should.

'I see,' she said quietly.

'You have to speak to him now you're finally here, Miss Roberts.'

Sylvia faced the little girl. 'What do you mean finally here?' she whispered. 'And before, you said I disappeared. Where were you told I've been, Patricia?'

'Mum said you took off some place and wouldn't be back, and Jesse told me that you didn't want to see him, and you weren't friends any more, so I thought you'd moved away.' She looked up at her with undisguised annoyance in her eyes. 'I didn't believe them, but I thought you might have been looking after all the hurt soldiers around the world. You know, like a heroine in one of my story books.'

Sylvia swallowed past the lump in her throat. 'Nothing so

grand, I'm afraid,' she said, smiling. 'I've been in Bath all along, sweetheart.'

'It doesn't matter. You're here now.' She took Sylvia's hand from her face and held it, urging her towards the closed door. 'Go on. He's in there.'

Sylvia stared at the door but didn't move. 'Aren't you coming in with me?'

'No, the last thing Jesse will want is me there, too. Best I leave you two alone.'

Smart girl...

'Wish me luck,' Sylvia muttered.

She twisted the doorknob and stepped just inside the door, her gaze immediately landing on Jesse where he sat a few feet away in a winged-back chair wearing dark glasses, a white cane propped up against the arm of his chair. He didn't move or give any indication he knew she was there so Sylvia took a moment to take in the beauty of him, her heart pounding.

She ran her gaze over his handsome profile, the curve of his ear, the jaw she'd kissed a hundred times, the perfect lips she'd kissed a hundred more. She lowered her study over his shoulders and chest. He'd lost a lot of weight. Lower to his hands laying on the armrests. His hands... Those skilful hands.

She flitted her gaze back to his face, her gaze automatically drawn to his mouth—

'Are you just going to stand there all day staring at me, Sylvia?'

She jumped. 'I... How did you know—'

'I can still hear.' He smiled wryly. 'And I can still smell... and I'd recognise the way you smell anywhere.'

Her heart constricted, her hands immediately itching to touch him, her lips to kiss him – God, she'd missed his deep, husky, toe-curling voice so much.

She stepped forward and smiled, blinking back the tears that leapt into her eyes. 'Jesse—'

'No.' He shot his hand into the air. 'There's no need for you to come a single step closer.'

Her smile vanished, her heart aching. 'What do you—'

'You need to go. Don't come near me, Sylvia. Don't touch me. Please.'

'But—'

'I don't want you here. I've got no idea how you got our address, but I'm pretty damn sure you didn't get it from my mother which means—'

'Damn right she didn't get it from me!'

Both Sylvia and Jesse flinched, and Sylvia spun around to look straight into the furious eyes of Mrs Howard. 'Mrs Howard, there's no need for you to—'

'To what, Miss Roberts? Smack you upside the head, to pull you out of my house by your hair?' She glared at Sylvia, her cheeks bright red and her body trembling. 'How dare you come here uninvited?'

'But at the tearoom you said—'

'I said I'd be in touch. How dare you upset my boy after everything he's been through?'

'Mum, that's enough,' Jesse growled behind her. 'I've asked Sylvia to leave and she's going.' His voice softened. 'Go, Sylvia. Now. And don't come back here again. I mean it.'

Sylvia faced him, her heart breaking all over again. 'Jesse, please. These months you've been gone, being without you, not seeing you, were so hard. Too hard. I can't give up on you, Jesse. I won't...' She swallowed. 'Just as you promised you'd never give up on me. Remember?'

She swiped at the tears rolling over her cheeks as he turned away from her, his hands tightly clasping the chair's armrests.

'Jesse?'

'Go, Sylvia. Leave.'

She stared at his handsome profile, the firm set of his jaw, and knew there would be little chance of him going back on his words. Burying her dented pride and newly rebroken heart, Sylvia lifted her chin and brushed past a glowering Mrs Howard.

'I'll see myself out.'

Sylvia walked into the hallway and nodded at Patricia where she sat as still as a statue on the stairs and then strode through the open front door and along the Howards' short pathway into the street.

But then she took a deep breath and smiled. Jesse was back. And for now at least, that was enough.

35

FREDA

'You could always stay here, Mrs Farnham. In Bath?' Freda suggested as she passed the young woman of twenty-five – just two years older than Freda – a cup of tea. 'You could stay with one of the many mothers in the same position as you, who have opened their homes to other women.'

'Bereaved women, you mean. Widowed with their kids gone?'

Freda swallowed, once again at a loss for the right thing to say or do in the face of a mother who'd lost everything. 'It might be the first step,' she said. 'Won't it be easier to stay with women somewhere less likely to be bombed? With women who understand what you're going through? Rather than go back to Bristol where all your memories are and a city that Germany targets over and over again?'

Mrs Farnham sipped her tea, her cheeks mottling. 'They're the reasons I want go back.'

'I don't under—'

'Hitler's not chasing me away from all I've known my entire life, Nurse.' Mrs Farnham's eyes were dark with loathing. 'He's not gonna make me leave the place my babies were killed and he's not going to make me think I'm anything less than a strong, brave Bristolian. Bath has been good to me.' Her gaze marginally softened. 'You've been good to me, but I want to go home.'

As Mrs Farnham sipped her tea, Freda drew in a long breath, admiration for the other woman filling her chest. How alike she was to Susan Beckett. Bristolians indeed held some of the strongest fortitude Freda had ever seen considering all they'd been through since Hitler turned his attention on the city just one year into the war. Since then, the murderous maniac had barely left them alone.

'In that case, I will do all I can to support you,' Freda said firmly. 'When you get to Bristol, if you want to do something more, something that will help the hundreds of children in the city find homes, let me know.'

Mrs Farnham frowned. 'What are you talking about?'

'Before the raids, I was working with a friend in Bristol helping her as much as I could to rehome orphaned kids or kids separated from their parents. Eventually we hope the scheme will be widespread in Bath too.'

'There's someone doing that in Bristol? I haven't heard anything about it.'

Freda smiled, pleased by the spark of interest in Mrs Farnham's eyes when they had been so empty of anything for so long. 'Her name is Susan Beckett and she's incredible.'

'Nurse Parkes!' Sister Dyer's voice boomed across the ward. 'A moment of your time, please.'

Freda grimaced. 'I'd better go.'

'I'd love to know more about this Susan Beckett when you have a spare minute or two, Nurse.'

'Of course. I'll be back as soon as I can.'

Freda hurried to Sister Dyer's desk and waited as the sister signed a paper with a flourish and put it on the top of her stack of trays. She replaced the lid of her fountain pen and pinned Freda with a stare.

'I've just been informed that Nurse Scott is in the staffroom comforting a young woman who claims to be your sister. I've not seen her myself, but I understand she is in quite a state of distress.'

Sickness unfurled in Freda's stomach. 'Dorothy? She's here?'

'I believe that was the girl's name. Yes.' Sister Dyer frowned, but her grey eyes softened with sympathy and concern, which only made Freda's sickness grow. 'It appears she's been attacked. Beaten.'

Freda froze. 'What?'

'Nurse Scott is taking care of her, but I think it best you go to the staffroom right away, don't you?'

Freda took off like she had fire on her heels, her heart thundering and her mind racing. Dot had been attacked? Attacked how? Like Veronica? By whom? A sob caught in Freda's throat, her knees threatening to crumple as she rushed along one corridor after another. How little any of them knew about the people Dorothy had been associating with – presumably for months, if not years. Never before had the staffroom felt so far away from the ward. At last, she shoved the door open and burst in to find Dorothy sitting on one of the armchairs and Kathy handing her a cup of tea, which her sister refused.

'Dot?'

'Oh, Freda!' Dorothy leapt up, almost knocking Kathy off her feet as she stumbled backwards, tea slopping onto the patterned rug. 'Look at me. Look at what he did!'

'Who?' Freda gently put her finger and thumb to her sister's chin, turning her head left and right as she examined Dorothy's split lower lip, the graze on her cheek and what looked to be a nasty bruise developing along the side of her eye and cheekbone. 'Dot, answer me. Who did this to you?'

'Robert.'

Shocked, Freda released her sister's chin and stepped back. 'Robert?'

'Yes,' Dot cried, sniffing, her fingers shaking as she swiped away her tears. 'Apparently, he was on his way home on leave anyway. He'd left before he even received my letter and someone told him about the baby. Oh, Freda, he was so angry. I didn't even recognise him. His eyes were manic. He wouldn't listen to me.'

'But who would've told him about the baby? Did you tell someone outside of the family?'

'Of course I did! I have friends, you know.'

Freda closed her eyes. 'Ah, yes, your mystery friends.' She opened her eyes, anger simmering inside her towards her sister's fiancé. 'But that's neither here nor there right now. Robert actually hit you? I can't believe it of him.'

'Neither can I, but I'm not lying, Freda.'

'I know you're not.' She put her arms around Dorothy, pressed a gentle kiss to her hair. 'Where were you when he did this? You couldn't have been at home.'

'I was in town posting a letter for Mum and he came up behind me, all sweetness and light. Oh, Freda.' A sob caught in Dorothy's throat and she pulled back. 'He picked me up, swung me around like he was so pleased to see me and then he took my arm and we walked… and then he…'

Suddenly remembering Kathy was still in the room listening to everything Dorothy was saying, Freda snatched her gaze to her. 'Kathy, you can go.' She forced a half-smile. 'Thank you so much for staying with my sister. It's appreciated. Truly.'

Kathy nodded, her angry gaze flitting from Freda to Dorothy.

'You're welcome. Whoever this Robert is to you, Miss Parkes, you need to get rid of him.'

The frankly terrifying venom in Kathy's eyes reminded Freda once again of the terrible things Kathy must have endured living with her parents. Dorothy wasn't the only one who needed her right now; she suspected Kathy did too. She must speak to Sylvia and Veronica again, but now was not the time.

'Well, as I said, your help's appreciated, Kathy,' she said. 'I'll come and find you later.'

With a final long and pointed look at Dorothy that Freda struggled to determine whether was annoyance with her sister or murderous intent towards Robert, Kathy swept from the room.

'Come here.' Freda took her sister's hands. 'I'm afraid I can't help but agree with what Kathy said about getting rid of Robert, Dorothy. What is wrong with him? How did he manage to hurt you like this without anyone witnessing it? Didn't anyone try to stop him?'

'He walked me into an alleyway and then he just changed.' Dorothy's eyes were wide with confusion and fear. 'I didn't know what to do. He asked me if it was true about the baby, who the father was, but I couldn't speak. When I wouldn't answer him or deny that I was pregnant, he hit me. He asked me again, shouting and spitting, and I still couldn't speak, so he hit me again and I fell to the floor.'

Shock reverberated through Freda, and she tightened her grip on Dorothy's fingers. *My God, Robert has surely lost his mind.* Was his outrage really just about the baby? He had always been a kind and upstanding man – a man her mother wholeheartedly approved of as a suitable husband for her 'good' youngest daughter. Never would her parents or Freda have thought him capable of such fury, such violence. But the war could change a man. She knew that more than most having seen what she had seen at the hospital and investigated at the paper. But still, to hurt her sister this way...

'I'll be tempted to give him the same back myself when I get my hands on him,' Freda muttered, her entire body burning with the force of her anger. 'And if I don't, God only knows what Sylvia will do to him.'

'Sylvia?' Dorothy stepped out of Freda's arms, her eyes wide. 'What about Dad? He'll not only see this as someone beating his daughter, he'll take it as an affront to him as a policeman. Dad will see this as a crime, Freda.'

'Good! It *is* a bloody crime!'

'Don't swear!' Dorothy sobbed. 'You never swear.'

'Sorry. I'm sorry.' Freda led her sister to the settee and they sat side by side, their fingers entwined. 'This war is affecting everything and everybody in so many ways,' she said. 'I don't recognise the Robert you've described to me. The Robert I knew would never have raised his hand to you. Baby or no baby. He's changed. No doubt the war has changed him as it has a million other men. What matters now is that you understand from now on you have your own life to lead and a baby to take care of. And, if you take my advice, that life should be without Robert.'

'But he agreed.'

'What?' Freda stared at her sister in disbelief. 'He beat you and then said he would accept the baby as his?'

'Yes.'

Unease whispered through Freda. 'But that makes no sense, Dot. He can't mean it.'

'He did. He said he will accept the baby as his own and God help me if anyone else finds out that it's a lie, but he'll calm down once the baby is born. I know he will.'

'You don't know that, Dot. No one can know that.' A horrible foreboding tip-tapped along Freda's spine. 'I don't like this at all. Surely you can't trust Robert to stand by you?'

'I love him, Freda.'

Freda stared, disbelief twisting hard inside her. How could Dorothy say that when Robert had beaten her and prior to that she'd been going out with – sleeping with – other men? It was all wrong. She exhaled the breath she was holding and pulled Dorothy into her arms. Now was not the time for her to take the moral high ground. That would not help her beloved – if foolish – sister at all.

'Beating you is not the actions of a man who loves you, whose heart is broken, Dot,' she said quietly. 'Beating you is the action of a man out of control.'

Freda closed her eyes. The good girls her mother wanted so badly for her daughters to be were gone, never to return. Dorothy would be changed forever by the birth of her baby and Freda still wanted to get out into the big wide world and do something more. The Parkes sisters had undoubtedly become entirely different people from who they'd been before September 1939, when Britain had joined the war.

Dorothy began to softly cry, and Freda opened her eyes, pulled her sister more tightly into her arms. The wall opposite blurred through her own tears as she thought of Sylvia and Jesse, Veronica and Officer Matthews, her and Richard. Would there ever be a time when falling in love, marrying and having a family was normal again? She very much doubted it. The war would come to an end eventually, but she had no doubt its damage would remain for a long time afterwards.

36

VERONICA

Veronica walked from the hospital onto the street.

She had barely walked more than a couple of yards when she saw Betty sitting on a bench outside, a cigarette smouldering between her fingers. She suddenly looked up and her gaze met Veronica's, her face lighting with a wide smile before she dropped the cigarette to the floor and ground it out with her heel.

Veronica's footsteps faltered, her heart picking up speed. The more she considered her increasingly concerning reaction to Betty, the more Veronica see-sawed between feeling sick with apprehension or giddy with excitement. What did this attraction to her mean?

Betty came forward, her gaze never leaving Veronica's. 'There you are. Sylvia told me you were finishing at eight, but I was beginning to wonder if she'd got it wrong.'

'I was held up,' Veronica said, looking around her, familiar heat rising in her cheeks. 'Were you waiting for me? Is something wrong?'

'I was waiting for you, but why do you immediately think

something must be wrong?' Betty grinned. 'You, Veronica Campbell, have no idea, do you?'

Feeling more than a little uneasy, Veronica swallowed. 'About what?'

'About...' Betty hesitated before she shook her head. 'Nothing. Look, what are you doing now? We agreed we'd go out for something to eat or a drink once the raids were over and we still haven't. What about now?'

'Now?'

'Yes.' Betty shrugged, still smiling, her hazel eyes shining. 'Unless you have something else on?'

Veronica's heart beat fast, her body treacherously heating under Betty's unwavering gaze and the possible, faint flirtatious lilt to her question. Should she go? What did she have to lose? *Only your career, your self-respect and possibly your friends should things deepen between you and Betty Wilson.* After all, there was little chance of Sister Dyer accepting anything that might come close to resembling a female-female relationship. And what of Freda and Sylvia? She'd be lying if she said she was confident they would be happy about her having romantic feelings for Betty. There was every possibility they'd be equally as shocked and disgusted as Sister Dyer.

'Veronica?' Betty's smile faltered. 'I didn't mean to put you on the spot. If you don't want—'

'All right,' Veronica said quickly, stubbornly burying her fears. 'Why not? Where would you like to go?'

'Oh.' Betty laughed. 'I really thought you'd say no.' A slight colour darkened her cheeks as she looked along the road. 'We could go to a restaurant. Or a tearoom or...' She faced Veronica. 'We could go back to mine, if you like? I make a mean cheese on toast if you fancy something simple?'

Veronica swallowed a second time. 'Back to yours?'

'Why not?' Betty slipped her hand into the crook of Veronica's elbow and the soft scent of soap drifted into her nostrils. 'It's only a short walk and it will save us some money. Don't worry, Mum's at a friend's house tonight.'

Don't worry?

'All right.' Veronica smiled, nerves jumping and swooping in her stomach. 'Why not?'

Betty grinned and they started to walk, Betty happily chatting and leading the way while Veronica did her best to keep up with the conversation and resist having a complete and utter breakdown.

Twenty minutes later, they entered a street not far from the centre of town and Betty stopped in front of a black painted door. 'This is me.'

She put her key in the lock and walked inside, leaving Veronica to follow. The hallway was decorated in beautiful light colours that Veronica had never seen in any other home before. The walls were a pale cream and the lino on the floor a soft beige. There was a side table holding a vase of what looked to be artificial flowers and a row of coat hooks above it on the wall. A light green runner ran up the centre of the stairs, the banister painted a walnut brown, a pretty pink lightshade hanging from the ceiling above her.

'You have a lovely home,' she said.

'Oh, thank you. It's all down to Mum rather than me.' Betty grimaced. 'Home décor is not my thing, I'm more into making my own clothes, cooking, that sort of thing. But, having said that, I will almost certainly be calling on Mum for decorating advice when I get my own place.'

'Your own place?' Veronica followed her into an equally lovely kitchen, decorated in blue and white. 'Do you want to move out, too?'

'Oh, yes. When the time's right. Here.' Betty pulled out a chair at the small kitchen table. 'Take a seat. I have a sneaky bottle of wine in the fridge, let's have a glass, shall we? The one thing this war has taught me is to make hay while the sun shines.' She winked. 'Nothing as classy as a glass of wine with cheese on toast, eh?'

Veronica laughed and a little of the tension left her shoulders. Who knew, maybe coming here and being with Betty for a short while would turn out to be one of her better decisions.

* * *

'My goodness, look at the time!' Veronica laughed and got up from the table, wiping tears from her eyes. 'I can't listen to another one of your hilarious stories, my stomach is aching.'

Betty grinned. 'It's so good to see you smile and hear you laugh. You should do both more often.'

Veronica's heart beat faster from the way Betty's eyes lingered on hers. She stood from the kitchen table. 'I should go. I've been here almost two hours. My mum will be home by now and no doubt worrying.'

Betty immediately got to her feet, tears of laughter still shining in her eyes. 'Of course. I've had such a lovely time, V,' she said. 'Why don't we go out somewhere soon? I'd love to spend some more time with you away from the hospital.'

Veronica knew she was on dangerous ground, but she was unable to resist feeling again as she had felt all evening in Betty's company, laughing and joking... finishing a bottle of wine with their rather delicious cheese on toast.

'I'd like that too,' she said, slipping her cardigan from the back of her chair and putting it on. 'We'll sort something out for when we're both off next at the same time. Or maybe one weekend or something.'

'Sounds good to me. Come on, I'll walk you out.'

They walked to the door and Betty stood there for a moment, her hand on the door but not opening it. She turned. Their eyes locked and Veronica's breathing turned harried as the air around them shifted, her entire body alert and completely aware of the woman standing so close to her.

Betty blinked and abruptly turned, opened the front door. 'I'll see you tomorrow.'

Veronica forced a shaky smile. 'Yes. Right, See you tomorrow.'

She walked out into the street feeling as though she was ten feet tall and walking on a cloud. When she reached her own street, she wasn't even sure how she got there. She couldn't remember seeing a house, another person, a road or even all the chaos, rubble and destruction still scattered everywhere throughout the city. This had to be more than a crush, more than a silly imagining. Everything about her and Betty was wrong. Yet...

'Well, now. Look who we have here.'

Veronica started and turned, trying to orientate herself as though waking from a dream – and then she saw the figure coming towards her across the cobbled street, and the dream became a nightmare. She quickly spun away and carried on walking towards her house.

'Good evening, Mr Riley,' she said over her shoulder.

She rushed forward, her mouth dry and her heart damn near beating out of her chest. Curling her hands into fists, she concentrated on reaching her front door and not the sound of his heavy footsteps behind her.

'Hey, what's the hurry?' He clasped her elbow, drawing her to a firm stop. 'It's been too long, lovely Veronica.'

'Get your hands off me!' She yanked her arm from his grip, anger pumping through her. 'I swear to God if you come one step closer, put your hand on me again or even speak to me, I'll scream and scream until the whole bloody street comes out of their houses.'

'Whoa.' He laughed and held up his hands in mock surrender. 'What's got into you, darlin'? You're usually so personable. Always have the time of day for me.'

'Liar!'

He grinned, showing the gap in the middle of his teeth that haunted her dreams. It had been all she had focused on for the entirety of—

'You're a rapist, Mr Riley,' she hissed from between clenched teeth. 'A rapist and, mark my words, soon you will be in jail and paying for what you did to me and quite possibly other women. You're a father. A father to two young daughters! You make me sick. Now get away from me.'

His dark, almost black eyes blazed with fury as he glared down at her, his vile wet lips shining in the semi-darkness and turning her stomach. His gaze slowly moved to her chest, but she would not give him the satisfaction of pulling her cardigan closed as she itched to do.

He snorted and spat on the pavement. 'Good riddance to bad rubbish. You weren't any good, anyway.'

As he walked away, Veronica's vision blurred and she ferociously blinked back her treacherous tears. 'Keep walking, Mr Riley,' she yelled, her entire body violently shaking. 'The clock has just started ticking for you as a free man.'

'Veronica!'

She spun around to see her mother coming towards her, her

arms crossed and her gaze following Mr Riley for a moment before she looked at her daughter. 'What on earth was all that about? I couldn't believe it when I opened the front door to find you shouting at Mr Riley like that. Not that he doesn't deserve it.' Her mother looked across the road, her face twisting in distaste. 'I've never really been very keen on the man. A little creepy, wouldn't you say? Come on. In the house. I won't have you embarrassing me in front of the neighbours.'

'He's more than that, Mum.'

'What?'

'Mr Riley is far worse than creepy.'

'What does that mean?' Her mother peered at her through narrowed eyes. 'Has he done something to upset you? Something to cause you to speak to him like that?'

Veronica looked into her mother's green eyes so like her own. How could she tell her what happened such a long time ago? How could she break her world apart when so many years had passed? Her mother might be too busy, too wrapped up in her own life since Veronica's father died, but her mother loved her, and Veronica could not – would not – turn her life upside down so cruelly.

'No, he's just a nasty piece of work, that's all.'

'Are you sure he hasn't done anything to upset you?'

'Yes.' Veronica looked along the street at Riley's front door. 'But one day, he'll get what's coming to him. You see if he doesn't.'

37

FREDA

'I don't think I can do this, Freda.'

Freda gently clasped Dorothy's elbow and pulled her to a stop at the end of their street. 'You can,' she said, looking into her eyes and willing her to find her inner strength. 'You have to face Mum and Dad sooner or later and it might as well be now.'

'But look at the state of me. Mum will throw a fit.'

'I cleaned you up, then I took you somewhere quiet to eat. We even managed some window shopping.' Freda arched an eyebrow. 'I've given in to your delaying so far, but enough's enough. You need to tell Mum and Dad what Robert did and what he said, get into bed and start again tomorrow.'

'But Dad will go mad when he sees my face. He'll want to track Robert down and do goodness knows what to him.'

'Maybe, but he either goes mad now or another time. Let's just get it over with, Dot. Please. It will be all right, you'll see.'

Pushing her hand into the crook of her sister's elbow, Freda gently led her to their front door and they entered the house. She did not believe it would be all right at all. How could it be when Robert had shown such violence? Surely the first time a man raises his hand to a woman is the hardest? The second, third, fourth time... must be so much easier.

Their parents' voices drifted into the hallway from the other side of the closed living room door, the wireless playing some show or other. Freda felt sick as she and Dorothy hung their jackets on the hooks by the door and placed their hats on the bottom step to take to their rooms after the dreaded deed had been done.

Inhaling a deep breath, Freda faced Dorothy. The bruising on her face and the cut on her lip suddenly seemed so much more prominent now that standing in front of their mum and dad was imminent.

She forced an encouraging smile, squeezed her sister's fingers. 'Ready?'

Dorothy stared, her eyes glazed with tears before she nodded.

Taking her firmly by the hand, Freda lifted her chin and pushed open the living room door. 'We're home.'

'Your tea is in the oven,' their mother replied without looking up from her knitting, their father still intently listening to the wireless. 'I expected you home hours ago. I cannot imagine what's happened to your sister. After everything she has put us through over the last few weeks... *We're* home? Who...' Her mother looked up, briefly glanced at Freda before turning her attention on Dorothy. 'Where on earth have you... Oh, my goodness!' She tossed her knitting onto the settee beside her and leapt to her feet. 'Clive! Look at Dorothy. Clive!'

Their father jumped from his concentration. 'For the love of God, Mary. Do you have to shout?'

'Look at Dorothy!' their mother cried. 'Look at her face.'

Freda's pulse beat in her ears, her hand clammy around

Dorothy's. She could only imagine how her poor sister was feeling.

Their father seemed to freeze for a moment as he ran his gaze over his younger daughter's face, his brow furrowed. 'Dorothy?' He slowly rose from his armchair and walked closer, gently caught her chin between his strong fingers. 'What happened?'

Freda swallowed. Her father's voice was low, stilted, as though he didn't really trust himself to speak. He had only just accepted Dorothy's pregnancy, and now this. She glanced again at her sister. Dorothy was deathly white, her entire body trembling, tears silently rolling over her cheeks.

'It was Robert, Dad,' Freda said. 'He... found out about the baby.'

'Robert?' Her mother swayed on her feet before she collapsed back onto the settee, holding her hand to her forehead. 'He found out about the baby from someone other than you? Oh, the shame! His mother...'

Anger swept through Freda and she began to shake. 'That's all you can say? Mum, look at your daughter's face.' She faced her father. 'Dad—'

He shot his hand in the air, cutting her off, his cheeks red and his eyes bulging, his entire focus on Dorothy. 'Say something, young lady. You tell me what happened right now!'

Freda clung tightly to Dorothy's hand as she reiterated everything she had told Freda at the hospital. It seemed as though the entire incident had lasted mere minutes with Robert barely asking more than a couple of questions, before finally saying he would marry her and assume fatherhood of the baby, but in his wake, he'd left Dorothy in a worse state, physically and mentally, than she'd been before. How could everything that had happened to her not change Dorothy forever?

'He beat you?' their father roared. 'He *beat* you?'

'Dad, please,' Dorothy whimpered. 'I didn't answer his questions. I couldn't. I couldn't find my voice. I—'

'The man beat you, Dorothy!' her father shouted. 'No man does that to my daughters. Ever!'

Their father glared around the room at his wife, Freda and Dorothy before marching to the living room door.

'Clive! Where are you going?' Their mother scrambled from the settee as the front door being slammed echoed from the hallway. 'Oh no! Clive, no!'

'What will he do?' Dorothy cried. 'Mum!'

'What will he *do*?' Their mother rounded on Dorothy and roughly gripped her elbows, breaking Freda's hold on her. She shook Dorothy, her sister's head flipping back and forth on her slender neck. 'He will find Robert and no doubt knock him sideways, beat him black and blue. This is all your fault, Dorothy Elizabeth. Do you hear me? Your fault!'

'Let go, Mum. You're hurting me!'

Unable to bear her mother's ferocity a moment longer, Freda took Dorothy's hand and whipped her towards the living room door. 'Go to your room and stay there,' she said, tears of anger pricking her eyes. 'I'll talk to Mum and be up in a while.'

'She's going nowhere,' their mother said behind them. 'I haven't finished—'

'Go, Dot. Now.'

As soon as her sister had left the room, Freda swung the door closed, spun around and glared at her mother. 'What is the matter with you?' she demanded. 'Hasn't Dorothy been through enough without her mother – the one person who's supposed to be a source of comfort to her for her entire life – berating her as though she deserves everything that has happened to her?'

'She does! For years I have done my best by my children.

Loved you, raised you to be good wholesome members of the community. Now I have one child dead, another missing, you going off with fanciful ideas of writing for a newspaper and Dorothy...' A sob caught in her mother's throat. 'Pregnant and then beaten by a fiancé so heartbroken by her actions that he—'

'Enough, Mum! I can't listen to you any more. I thought you had changed after finding Dorothy with that knitting needle, but no, all you're thinking about is Robert, his parents, the neighbours. You are not a real mother to any of us! You never listen and you rarely care.'

Freda swept from the room, her mother's wailing echoing in her ears.

The knock on the front door as she made for the stairs lurched her heart into her throat and Freda gripped the banister, closed her eyes. *My God, how much more must I take today?*

She yanked the living room door closed on the over the top racket her mother was making, took a strengthening breath and pulled open the door.

'Richard!'

He flashed one of his smiles that sent her stomach in a loop the loop. 'How are you, Freda?'

She would have laughed if she thought he wouldn't take offence, but that was highly unlikely when she'd steadfastly avoided seeing him since he told her he loved her – and she'd said nothing back to him. Not even in a letter. What could she say when she had no idea if what she felt for him was love?

'Richard, I...' She stepped outside the front door and eased it ajar behind her. 'We're in the middle of a slight family crisis right now. I'm sorry, but I really can't talk—'

'Neither can I, but I had to come here as soon as I heard.'

Freda stilled. 'Heard what?'

He was still smiling, his eyes glittering with happiness. This couldn't be about Dorothy. Surely he wouldn't be smiling if he knew about that.

She crossed her arms. 'Why are you grinning like that?'

'Your brother.' His beautiful blue eyes shone even brighter. 'He's back.'

'What?'

'Your brother, Freda.' He took her hand. 'He's back.'

Freda tightened her fingers on his lest she fell backwards. 'James is back? But how—'

'Two soldiers turned up at the railway station on a cargo train, and one of them is your brother. Seems him and his mate have been on a bit of an adventure to get back to the city, but somehow they managed it.' He laughed. 'The story's yours to tell, Freda.'

'The story?'

'For the paper. William said you have to be the one to write it. If you don't, some other reporter will and that just doesn't feel right to either of us.'

'My brother is here? In Bath?'

He laughed. 'Yes.'

Her mind reeled with a hundred questions and scenarios. Her beloved brother – the one person she tried so hard not to think about since he'd been missing in action – was back. 'My God... Mum will...' She put her hand to the front door. 'I'd better go in. Tell Mum. Thank you, Richard.' She laughed, tears welling in her eyes. 'I'll see you soon.' She leaned forward and kissed him long and hard on the lips. 'I promise.'

She rushed inside and shut the door, tears of joy rolling down her face. 'Mum! Dorothy! You'll never guess what!'

38

SYLVIA

Slightly stumbling on her high-heeled shoes, Sylvia quietly laughed to herself, feeling more than a little happy on this fine, early summer evening. It was the start of her favourite season, the sun was shining, it was her day off, she was young, free and single and Bath was beginning to get back on its feet again in the face of Hitler's attack. Why the hell shouldn't she spend the afternoon in the pub?

Ignoring the niggle of shame that poked at her conscience, she continued on towards the Garrick's Head, her third pub stop of the day. She hadn't dropped in for a visit with her mother since she'd been there with Freda and Veronica, and they were getting along much better these days. So much so, Eileen Roberts – who didn't often admit to having a daughter of twenty-four – didn't seem to mind Sylvia propping up the bar when she found herself at a loose end. And if her notoriously critical mother didn't disapprove of Sylvia's choices about how she spent her days off from the hospital, why should she care about the pesky, judgemental voices in her head?

'What do they know anyway?' Sylvia muttered. 'They've got no idea what I'm dealing with day in, day out.'

'Is this a private conversation or can anyone join in?'

Her heart leapt into her throat and Sylvia ground to a halt a few yards from the pub, the niggle of shame she'd felt before now enveloping her like a damn cape. 'What are you doing here?'

'What do you think?' Jesse said, planting his cane on the pavement and heaving himself up from the wall where he'd been sitting. 'I came to see you.' He grimaced. 'If you know what I mean.'

Just as Jesse had turned up unannounced time and time again at the end of her street or outside the hospital before they started courting, here he was again, looking drop-dead handsome with his brooding thing going on, waiting for her and looking just as sexy, just as strong and true as he always had, his beautiful skin glistening in the sunlight and his dark glasses making him look more shrouded in sensual mystery than ever before.

She swallowed. Hard. 'But how did you—'

'My brother.' He smiled wryly, his jaw tightening. 'He's waiting inside the pub.'

'Oh.' She looked at the taped pub windows, mentally kicking herself for bringing Jesse's lack of independence into their conversation. 'That's good.'

'Is it?'

She faced him, shamefully glad he couldn't see her rare blushing. 'I think so. You're here, aren't you?'

She stepped closer to him, her thoughts running in a million different directions and her heartbeat entirely out of control. She swallowed against her dry throat, confused why she wasn't hankering after a gin and tonic to quench her thirst, but instead all she craved was a good, hard kiss from the man standing almost toe-to-toe with her.

'You really do have a good nose on you, don't you?' she said.

His lips quirked. 'What?'

'Isn't that what you said before? That you'd know the smell of me anywhere? I just hope if you sensed me getting closer, I don't smell like the pub.'

'Maybe the scent of you is diluted with a bit of something less savoury than usual right now, but not enough for me not to recognise you, Sylvia Roberts.'

He smiled softly and hope sparked like a flame inside her heart even if she was more than little embarrassed by his observation. She returned his smile, treacherous tears pricking her eyes. For all she judged herself for spending her afternoon off in the pub, it seemed Jesse held no such qualms about it. Or at least that was what she hoped anyway.

'Does your mum know you're here?' Sylvia tipped her head back and saw herself reflected in his dark glasses. It wasn't a pretty sight, her hair a mess, her make-up smudged. She looked away along the cobbled alleyway. 'I'd bet a pound to a penny she doesn't.'

A muscle flexed and relaxed in his jaw. 'No, and there's no need for her to know. Not yet. This is between you and me.'

'What is?'

'I tried, Sylvia.'

'Tried what?'

'Tried to stay away from you. Tried to set you free. Tried to pretend I could go along well enough without you for the rest of my life.'

Words stuck in her throat, her heart twisting with love, hope, possibility, fear. Everything tumbled and mixed, painful and yet also so very, very beautiful.

But how did he know to come looking for her at her mother's pub?

Her smile dissolved and humiliation twisted inside of her. 'I assume someone told you this was where you might find me? Or was it a lucky guess?'

'One of your neighbours on Castle Street had a whale of a time describing just where I was likely to find you. Unlucky for her, I went to several pubs before this one and you weren't in any of them. So...' He shrugged. 'It seems to me the woman is way off the mark and should stop judging the woman I happen to be in love with.'

Sylvia froze, her abrupt sobriety hitting her square between the eyes. 'What?'

He dipped his head as though looking directly at her, any semblance of a smile gone and the intensity emanating from him making her heart race. His eyebrow quirked above his glasses. 'Which part?'

She smiled. 'The... love part.'

He lifted his hand to her face, gently ran his fingers around her hairline, softly down to her eyebrows. She closed her eyes as his fingers whispered like feathers over her closed lids, lower to her cheek, his thumb moving across her lips.

Her limbs grew soft with desire and Sylvia shivered. 'Jesse—'

'I love you, Sylvia,' he whispered. 'I've loved you since I saw you cleaning your front doorstep on Castle Street, bending over and looking as sweet as a nut.'

She grinned, her stomach knotting. 'I was in an apron and bloody headscarf.'

'What of it? I loved you then and I love you now. The question is...' He drew in a long breath. 'Do you think you could love a blind man when you have the pick of any man in the country?'

Tears burned behind her eyes and Sylvia laughed. Good lord, if he could see the state of her, he wouldn't be saying that... especially when she'd been three sheets to the wind not five minutes before.

A tear slipped over her cheek and she wiped it away. 'Pick of any man in the country, huh?' She slipped her hands onto his waist and he stiffened before relaxing beneath her fingers. 'I'm not so sure about that. Jesse?'

'What, my love?'

She inhaled a deep breath. She needed to see him. All of him. 'Take off your glasses.'

The seconds passed along with her heartbeat, her pulse, thumping in her ears. *Please, trust me, sweetheart. Please.*

He lifted his hand from her face and touched it to the arm of his glasses, hesitated, and then he slowly pulled them off. Her heart swelled with love and admiration for this amazing man standing in front of her, showing her everything he was, everything he'd suffered and how the world would now see him. The world possibly, but not her. The deep lacerations and pitted skin around his left eye were already fading under her gaze, the open, entirely white eye and the other that appeared perfectly normal looking at her intensely... Jesse. *Her* Jesse.

She reached up and cupped his burned, scarred cheek in her hand. 'You're beautiful,' she whispered. 'And I love you so damn much.'

His arms came around her and he covered her mouth with his, his glasses clattering to the floor as she clung to him, tried to crawl inside of him as though it was the only way she could climb out of the abyss that had been building up around her, preparing to take her down. Suddenly, the pressures of being

Sister Dyer's second-in-command at the hospital when all she really wanted was to be at home with Jesse, their children around her legs, melted away – best of all, so did her constant need to have a drink...

They slowly parted and Sylvia matched his smile. 'Welcome home, darling.'

EPILOGUE
FREDA

One Month Later – Mid July 1942

Freda walked into the hospital and smiled as she thought of what having James home again had done to their family. When he'd walked off that cargo train at Bath station just a few short weeks ago, he'd had no idea how fractured his family had been, how close they'd been to their home life falling apart entirely. His arrival had changed their mother from someone who had become completely selfish and sometimes downright spiteful in her pain and grief – which, in truth, broke Freda's heart – to the mother she'd been before the war. The change in her was close to miraculous. Oh, Mary Parkes still had her standards, of course, but having her only surviving son home in one piece – at least physically; it was too soon to be sure of James's mental state – had saved them all.

Even though William, the *Chronicle*'s editor, had been expecting some sort of report about her brother's return, Freda had yet to write a word. Why? Because James had so far refused to explain what he and his friend had been through to get home.

And, as much as Freda feared what he might tell her when he was ready to talk, she had no intention of pressing him. Her beloved, brave brother would tell all soon enough.

Her father had never caught up with Robert because when he stormed to his parents' house, they'd sworn Robert hadn't visited them and weren't even aware that he'd been back to the city on leave. This, of course, had meant their father had left poor unassuming Mrs Grey in a worse distressed state than when she'd thought her only son was serving abroad somewhere. As they had not heard from him at all, they eventually accepted Robert must have abandoned his leave and gone straight back to France or wherever he'd been stationed. At least their father had managed to somehow keep schtum about Dorothy's pregnancy and left Mr and Mrs Grey with no idea about the baby, which was something that had pleased Freda's mother no end. In her infinite wisdom, her mother had decided it was Robert's duty to tell his parents about the baby, but the strain of keeping the pregnancy hidden was taking its toll on Dorothy, and Freda had no doubt Mr and Mrs Grey would soon learn the truth. What would happen then was anyone's guess.

With her mother more than a little perturbed that Robert hadn't immediately married Dorothy, the hope now was that he had gone back to his barracks to arrange a date when he could return home again, get married and spend a little time with his new wife. If that would happen, only time would tell.

Freda walked into the hospital and headed to the staffroom.

Once there, she smiled to see Sylvia and Veronica playfully scuffling over the only full-length mirror in the room. 'What are you two up to?' She laughed.

'She's taking far too much interest in her appearance these days,' Sylvia said, feigning annoyance. 'There was a time she'd barely looked in the mirror even though she always looks so damn beautiful. But these days...' Sylvia wiggled her eyebrows. 'Something – or someone – has made her start taking a bit of notice of what she looks like.'

Freda smiled. 'Leave her alone.'

'Thank you, Freda,' Veronica said, blushing a deep red. 'For your information, Sylvia Roberts, my care in my appearance has nothing to do with anyone else and everything to do with my newfound confidence. This time next year, I'll be a different person. Just you wait.'

Sylvia scooped Veronica into a tight hug, making her squeal. 'Is that right? Well, you'd better not change too much or we'll be heartbroken, won't we, Freda?'

'We absolutely will.' Freda grinned. 'But what we really want is for you to be happy, V, so if that means a bit more preening in front of the mirror, all to the good, I say.'

Leaving her friends ribbing one another, Freda's smile slipped, even if her heart swelled with love for Sylvia and Veronica. On her request, Sylvia had started to warm to Kathy and she was slowly becoming more than a colleague, even if true friendship might take some time... especially with Sylvia. It had come to light that the hostility between her and Kathy had started during their training together. Still, one day at a time. Freda drew in a deep breath. Now that she finally knew what she had to do to make herself happy, worrying about Kathy and where she was living and with whom now that she'd lost her home would have to be taken over by Veronica and Sylvia. Guilt poked and prodded at her as worry her friends would think she was abandoning them threatened to change Freda's mind. But if anything was going to make that happen, it would be Veronica telling her and Sylvia that they had to find a way to deal with Mark Riley once and for all. Freda finished pinning on her hat and blew out a breath. No, she would never abandon either of them and she would do all she could for Veronica *and* Kathy. She just might not be as nearby as they had been used to, that was all.

Freda closed her locker and pulled back her shoulders, her heart thundering as she faced her friends. Now was as good a time as any to tell them her plans – after all, if all went as she hoped, she'd be gone from the hospital – from Bath – within the next couple of months and who knew when she would return? She looked at her watch. They had ten minutes before shift. If she told them now, they wouldn't have a chance to immediately challenge – or as she suspected with Sylvia – attempt to shut down her plans altogether. They'd have to mull it over until lunchtime at least.

She pointedly cleared her throat. 'Right, now you two have finished playing around, I need to talk to you.'

Sylvia and Veronica exchanged a curious look before slowly shutting their lockers and joining Freda in the corner seating area. She sat on one of the two armchairs and looked at her friends in turn as they sat and stared at her expectantly.

'Right, I'm going to say something and then I want you both to get to work,' she said firmly. 'I'll talk more about it later, but for now I just want you to accept what I'm about to say.' She looked at Sylvia. 'Without argument.'

Sylvia narrowed her eyes. 'I don't like the sound of this.'

'Is everything all right?' Veronica asked.

'Everything is more than all right.' Freda smiled. 'Since James has been back, life is different – better – than it's been for a long time at home. My mother is happy, Dorothy is leading more of a life of her own now that my mother has James to fuss over, and my father is working as he was before, safe in the knowledge his home won't be a battleground every time he walks through the door.'

Sylvia pinned her with a stare. 'So, what is it you have to say exactly?'

Freda smoothed her slightly perspiring hands over the skirt of her uniform. 'My home life might be better, but as far as Richard is concerned, I am still uncertain how I feel about him. Especially now he's told me he loves me. So much so, I'm finding it difficult to see how I can work with him at the *Chronicle*. But' – she swallowed – 'the one thing I am certain about is that I still want to be involved in some way with the front lines of this war, just as I always have. Nursing in Bath is still not enough for me.'

'What are you trying to tell us?' Veronica asked, looking from Freda to Sylvia and back again. 'Are you leaving the hospital? Is that it? What about your work with Miss Beckett in Bristol?'

'I still hope Susan will call on me if she thinks I can help, but she has so much more support now, she'll go along well enough without me, I'm sure. So, to that end...' Freda pulled back her shoulders, her back ramrod straight as she braced for the fallout – especially from Sylvia. 'I intend telling Sister I'd like to be considered for a transfer to one of the field hospitals.'

'What?' Sylvia laughed. 'Don't be daft!'

'It's not daft and you know how long I've wanted to do more, Sylv,' said Freda, pleading with her friend. 'Don't make me feel bad about this. It's what I want to do. I've thought about it ever since James came back and the time is now. Who knows? This war might well be over by the end of the year, and I'll be back before you know it.'

'Yeah, in a box!' Sylvia leapt to her feet, tears shining in her eyes. 'Freda, please. Stay here. With us.'

'I'll be all right,' Freda said, swallowing the unwelcome lump that rose in her throat. She looked at Veronica. 'You understand I have to do this, don't you?'

Veronica stood and took Sylvia's hand and gestured for Freda to take her other, her eyes also glinting with tears. 'What I understand is all three of us are trying to find our happiness in the hardest time Europe has suffered since the Great War. We're managing, of course we are,' she said, looking at Sylvia and then Freda. 'But none of us are entirely happy. Not yet, anyway.' She squeezed Freda's fingers. 'Do what you have to do with our blessing. Right, Sylv?'

The silence stretched as Freda prayed Sylvia let her go – let her do what she needed to do – because she loved her friend so very much and just the sight of her upset was already sending a splinter across her heart.

'Oh, bloody hell...' Sylvia pulled her hand from Veronica's and threw her arms around Freda. 'I love you, girl. Do what you have to do, but you'd better come back to us in one piece or there will be hell to pay.'

'Hear, hear,' said Veronica as her arms came around Freda and Sylvia.

Freda laughed through her tears. 'I love you both so much.'

She had no idea how long they stood that way but before she knew it, there were brisk footsteps and then a rather loud 'Ahem' behind them.

All three of them snatched out of their embrace and turned to see Kathy Scott standing there, hands fisted on her hips and her eyebrows raised. 'When you three have quite finished, Sister Dyer is on the ward having a near-seizure wondering where you are. I came to give you fair warning that you'd better move quick smart.'

'Thanks, Kathy,' Veronica said with a smile.

'Yeah, thank you.' Freda winked. 'You're a... real pal.'

'Hmm,' Sylvia murmured and then smiled. 'I wouldn't go that far, but feel free to join us for tea and cake at the tearoom after shift, if you like? There's a seat going spare with your name on it.'

'I'd love to.'

Freda laughed as she and her friends left the staffroom, leaving an ecstatic Kathy to follow, grinning like a loon.

* * *

MORE FROM RACHEL BRIMBLE

Another book from Rachel Brimble, *The Home Front Nurses*, is available to order now here:

https://mybook.to/HomeFrontNursesBackAd

ACKNOWLEDGEMENTS

I want to thank the entire Boldwood team for all their support and encouragement through the months I've been working with them, but a special thank you goes to my wonderful editor, Isobel Akenhead. I absolutely love working with you and long may it continue as we both get to know 'my girls' better and better!

ALSO BY RACHEL BRIMBLE

The Home Front Nurses Series

The Home Front Nurses

Dangerous Days for the Home Front Nurses

ABOUT THE AUTHOR

Rachel Brimble is the bestselling author of over thirty works of historical romance and saga fiction. The first book in her series, The Home Front Nurses, is set in Bath.

Sign up to Rachel Brimble's mailing list for news, competitions and updates on future books.

Visit Rachel's website: www.rachelbrimble.com

Follow Rachel on social media here:

- facebook.com/rachelbrimbleauthor
- x.com/RachelBrimble
- instagram.com/rachelbrimbleauthor
- bookbub.com/profile/rachel-brimble
- tiktok.com/@rachelbrimble

Sixpence Stories

Introducing Sixpence Stories!

Discover page-turning historical novels from your favourite authors, meet new friends and be transported back in time.

Join our book club Facebook group

https://bit.ly/SixpenceGroup

Sign up to our newsletter

https://bit.ly/SixpenceNews

Boldwood

Boldwood Books is an award-winning fiction publishing company seeking out the best stories from around the world.

Find out more at www.boldwoodbooks.com

Join our reader community for brilliant books, competitions and offers!

Follow us

@BoldwoodBooks

@TheBoldBookClub

Sign up to our weekly deals newsletter

https://bit.ly/BoldwoodBNewsletter

Printed in Great Britain
by Amazon